CURSE
OF THE
WEREPOODLE

———†———

PAUL LUBACZEWSKI

D & T
PUBLISHING

ACKNOWLEDGMENTS

(or, ass kissing for dummies)

First off, a thank you to my beta readers, people who knew what I'm like, but still volunteered to read this book before you did, Samantha Hawkins, Doug Grove, Bob Erdman, Paul Synuria, Edward Mignot, Steve Knoll, John Hicks, and Janelle Derstein.

Secondly, as always, thanks to my family. As you read these pages, remember, I am like this all the time, and yet....

Finally, a special thank you. Horror has a lot of fans, certainly more than the mainstream industry realizes, but some are a special breed. To you Superfans, thank you. You know who you are, always leaving recommendations in Books of Horror, reviews on Goodreads, following us on Twitter and Facebook and laughing at our memes, harassing your local library and Barnes and Nobles to carry our books, coming to the cons, all the legwork it takes to get our stuff in front of even more readers. You may not think people on my side of the horror lit equation see you and appreciate you, but trust me when I say it, people like you are the backbone of this whole scene, and authors love you dearly for it.

CURSE OF THE WEREPOODLE

CHAPTER 1

"I really think he's the one" – *Marla Maples 1992*

Suzanne woke with a start. "Oh, crap!" She'd fallen asleep at his place! They'd made love late in the afternoon, she told him she had a flight to make for her trip and that she couldn't stay for much longer than a quicky. So of course, it had been good and she'd fallen asleep. She looked over at him as he snored happily, damn him! Didn't he understand the meaning of the word quicky? He knew she had to leave before now, why didn't he set an alarm? Already the sun was dropping over the horizon through his grimy window. Men, why couldn't they ever manage to clean a damned window? Why did they discover stamina when you didn't want them to? Or set an alarm for that matter? She was being illogical, she could have set an alarm herself, she had her phone, but Suzanne didn't have the time for logic at this point there was only enough time for baseless recriminations.

No time for anything but a mad dash, she'd just have to grab her clothes and hope for the best.

She stumbled out the bedroom door and down the hall, dressing as she went. Not that it would matter soon, but still, she needed to get outside and as far as she had time to go unmolested. Naked as the day you were born would always get you a conversation, and that was if you were lucky. It was a struggle to get into her skirt, it wanted to hang up on everything and she was forced to stop her forward progress and do a mad hop to pull it up and zip it, wondering why she hadn't worn one of those sarong things for nights like this. Well, in this case, because she had been absolutely positive she was going to be out of here at least two hours ago. Also, to be fair, she didn't own a sarong, that was damned well going to change after tonight, that was for absolute sure. Fool me once and all that.

Shoes in hand she finally rushed through the front door pulling it closed behind her and stumbled into her flats out in the yard. Footwear in place she started running as fast as she could.

The door opened minutely behind her, the rush of the screen door closing popping it back open.

———————|———————

Christopher Richter woke up at around nine p.m. with a smile on his face. That smile diminished slightly when he realized Suzanne was no longer in the bed, but as soon as he got enough neurons firing correctly, he remembered she had a business trip she had to take so it was probably a good thing the bed was less full at the moment. She wasn't expecting to be still be here, she'd just let him sleep the sleep of the post-coital when she left, which was nice of her. At least it appeared she must have woken up on her own so she could make her flight. He hadn't meant to fall asleep, he'd been working late last night on a project for work, and in his defense, when he fell asleep, he was feeling *really* relaxed.

He didn't bother to check his phone yet; he knew Suzanne hated texting but still promised to send him one tomorrow when she was all checked in. She said that her focus on anything but the phone came from her time in the military, where it was always the job at hand until you had official downtime. Personally, he thought it was because she didn't like using the little keyboard. For a second, he glanced at the empty hollow where she had been forlornly. The rest of the bed was lit up in the bright moonlight, creating a dark place of shadow where the sheet had been curled around her, a spot in his bed that not only looked empty but positively abandoned. He liked Suzanne quite a bit and he couldn't help but wonder how much at a moment like this. They hadn't been dating long enough for it to be love or anything like that, but it was definitely at the like-quite-abit stage. He had learned early in life to wait to say love, girls got creeped out if you dropped it on the second date. In this day and age, you probably had to be dating longer than they had to say it was love, otherwise, you risked coming off as a weird stalker type.

Chris got up while scratching himself and cast his eyes around the room for something to wear. Deciding that he wasn't going out anymore tonight anyway, he pulled on a pair of boxers. He had no illusions about how sexy he looked right now standing there in a pair of Teen Titans boxers and his black work socks, but the reason to look sexy was on a plane to Minnesota and he lived alone, so he'd dress any damned way he felt like. Up to and including having Raven and Beast Boy covering his naughty bits.

Significant others of the world, know this about your man right here and now, this is what we dress like when you aren't around to give us dirty looks. It is only your scorn at our behavior that prevents us from going outside like this. Even in winter, we'd shovel the sidewalk in boots and Batman shorts if you let us.

It was amazing how empty the rest of the place felt without her. He'd lived here since he was a kid, this was his house and since his parents died, it was almost always empty, but it usually didn't feel that way. Usually, it felt cozy and full of memories. In the throes of young lust leaking over to love though, its emptiness was more than ample to make a formerly comfy home begin to feel like a set of spooky echoing chambers, a situation fit to drive one to a spate of Poe-level madness. Okay, now that *sounds* melodramatic, but that's still how it always feels around that time in one's life when you're mooning for your significant other. His melancholia wouldn't last though, after he'd gotten some food he'd be on his laptop and any existential dread would be quashed in a wave of Twitter posts he'd feel compelled to respond to against his better judgment, which constantly tried to tell him Twitter was a cesspool. With the wave of missing her crashing down on him, he was being full Christopher; a Hot Pocket, and some internet time from now he'd be back to Chris. There were no Snickers in the house.

He walked into the dimly lit kitchen, making a point of aggressively ignoring the dishes in the sink. One more plate wouldn't change anything and doing the dishes before eating made no sense. Since he was still a bachelor, really, doing the dishes when he still had clean dishes available didn't make a ton of sense either but he'd been raised with standards and they said that once you could no longer see either drain you had to do the dishes. A loose pepperoni pasty fell out of the freezer the second he opened the door, leaping free from where it had been precariously balanced on top of a thing of Ben and Jerry's. It landed on his foot. If that wasn't a sign from above that he needed a Hot Pocket, Christopher didn't know what was. Possibly it was assault since that had hurt a bit.

He slipped the violent assault pastry into its little microwave sleeve and popped it into the nuker. While it cooked Chris decided that he might as well see what was on TV, you needed viewing material while you devoured a feast like a pepperoni pizza pocket and he didn't want to get pepperoni grease on his laptop. Without something to distract yourself with you might truly begin to consider what you were putting into your body, and that might make you consider the rest of the chemicals masquerading as food you had in your fridge. No, that way lay madness, and better health, but definitely madness, so it was best to maybe find an episode of South Park instead.

While the microwave did whatever it needed to do to turn a frozen lump into crispy cheesy goodness, Christopher wandered out of the kitchen to head for the living room to channel surf. What was eating a Hot Pocket in your underwear without Adult Swim or South Park on the TV, that was his motto, well if he had a motto that was, which he didn't. Well, maybe not JUST the stuff about Hot Pockets and animated adult TV shows, that really sort of limited your life if that was your only motto. The point being here, that if he had a series of mottos to fit different occasions, that would have been in there somewhere for moments like this.

As he got back into the darkened hallway to head for the living room, he noticed a sliver of moonlight on the floor. It took his conscious mind a moment to understand why his subconscious had immediately seized on it. It shouldn't have been there. His eyes followed it back to its origin. The front door was open just a crack, letting in the moon's stray ray for it to catch his eye. What the hell? He never left the door open. He quickly considered it and decided that Suzanne must not have pulled it shut all the way when she'd left. Seeing as no one had murdered him in his sleep or stolen his precious

Hot Pocket supply, he'd call it no harm, no foul.

Seeing the open door beckoning he figured he'd get his mail while he was at it. He could see the moon was up pretty high so it would be bright enough to get to the mailbox without killing himself. None of the neighbors would be up at this hour, his neighbors were mostly elderly, so who cared how he went out? Yes, technically he should wear more than boxers, but at night the boxers looked like shorts anyway. It had been hot this summer, the neighbors had seen him without his shirt before, and he'd seen more of them than he cared for in broad daylight. Mr. Abernathy half a block away had made a snide remark about it in passing once, but who cared? The guy wore a dress shirt every day, even in his own yard on a day when the temperature hit the nineties. Now that, was weird. So not caring about incurring the wrath of the one neighbor who said anything and who was probably asleep anyway, Chris headed out into the night air to go acquire the missives he had been far too busy to retrieve previously.

He liked when the moon was like this, where you could almost see everything. All the whites seemed brighter, the darks contrasting more strongly and hiding their secrets against the glow of the world. You could actually see where you were going, which was nice, but the whole world seemed ghostly and somehow crisper than on a normal night. Maybe he'd just get his Hot Pocket and eat on the porch. The weather was nice and cool, the day's humidity had finally dissipated, it might be nice.

First things first though, he needed to get the mail. *Need* might be too strong a word, it was probably junk mail, but he'd formulated a plan of action here and wanted to follow through. He covered the distance quickly, making a point of staying on his walk. It might be nice out, but dew was already forming on the grass, one false step would mean soggy socks for the rest of the night. Nothing could be in the mailbox that warranted soggy socks. Opening his box with a creaking noise he instantly couldn't help but feel he shouldn't have bothered; nothing but bills, junk mail, and junk mail about consolidating his bills into one low easy monthly payment. Oh well, at least the air felt nice and he'd achieved something adult, you had to look at the positives.

Chris was making his way back to the house when a noise brought him up short. Coming from the yew bush next to his steps was a low and constant growl. He would have been more concerned if it didn't have the distinctive high pitch of a smaller dog undercutting the implied threat. He couldn't see the thing in the deep shadows of the bush, so he wasn't sure who's small dog had deemed him a mailman-level threat. There were quite a few to choose from, there were still quite a few older people living in this little suburb, people who had bought in when the development had first been built – like his parents had. That being the case, the small dog quotient around here was far above average.

Chris felt a little worried about the little varmint, which was still issuing a non-stop challenge from the depth of the bushes. While this wasn't exactly the wild wilderness out here, he'd seen in the news that coyotes were getting closer all the time. He'd hate to think of Mrs. Dallas' little bichon frisé becoming coyote fecal material, Mrs. Dallas rarely saw her grandchildren and had a lot of love to share, she'd be devastated. He knelt down to peer into the darkness. Yeah, he was sure he saw something undersized and furry hiding in there making all that noise.

"Hey pup," he called out in what he hoped was an encouraging fashion, "why don't you come out, huh? You probably got a collar on; I can see who you belong to and take you back to your Mommy and Daddy. You'd like that, wouldn't you?" Chris started to make that weird, squelching, clicking noise that people for some reason think that dogs are unbelievably attracted to. If anything the growling intensified, probably rightly so.

Well, this wasn't going to work. He tried to think of what he had in the fridge that he could offer the thing to maybe convince it to come out. He realized he had the solution close at hand without ever threatening one scrap of pepperoni from his Hot Pocket. Hot dogs! He had a couple left that frankly were a little past their sell-by anyway. Mutilated, seasoned, unnamed, and unrecognizable beef and pig parts in a tube. That'd bring the little miter running. Once they were friends, hopefully without causing the thing severe gastro distress, he could figure out whose dog he had and get it back to them. After putting on pants of course.

Chris stood back up and brushed his knees off with his hands. He found himself being impressed by the little beast's lung capacity; it had been growling almost non-stop since he'd gotten his mail. "All right, I'm going to get you a treat, and then once I've bought your affection like a good American, we can be friends. All right?"

His foot had just landed on the bottom step when a streak of light brown fur burst from the bushes. A sudden lightning bolt of pain shot up his leg as the thing buried its teeth into his ankle! Chris yelped loudly, it hurt way more than he would have possibly thought from something that size. Not that it made much difference at this point, but he couldn't remember anyone in the neighborhood owning a Lhasa Apso like the one that was now hunching its shoulders and trying to rip a chunk out of him so vigorously. Chris did the only thing that came to mind, he swung his leg in a wide sweep trying to dislodge the vicious mongrel. At first, he considered this a grave mistake, as it caused the teeth to start tearing at his flesh. His mind was almost going blank from the sudden pain he'd just inflicted on himself when at the top of the swing of his leg the beast lost its grip and went hurtling across the lawn in a descending growl, landing some distance away with a yip.

The neighborly thing to do would be to check if it was Okay. But his neighbors weren't the ones whose sock was soaking up blood right now, so his neighbors could go fuck themselves. He darted up the stairs as quickly as his injury would let him and slammed the door behind himself. He leaned against the door for a minute contemplating what had happened. He had just been savaged by a small designer dog to the point where he was going to have to actually have to put a bandage on himself was what had happened. He was currently hiding inside from said purse dog. Dear Lord, what if the thing had been rabid? It wasn't foaming at the mouth, it didn't look sick, but still, it happened, animals got rabies. He'd heard the shots sucked. All of this because he tried to be nice. How could that even happen? Because, life was like that, that's how.

Slowly, Chris made his way to the bathroom trying not to drip too much blood as he went. He lived alone, nobody would complain about the mess, but really, who wants to spend time wiping their own blood off the floor? Not even the gross factor, more the, 'I am stuck doing this because I'm an idiot who got hurt and bled all over the floor like a doofus,' factor. Especially in this situation where he'd just been mauled by a dog known mostly for their long flowing hair and lack of legs. You couldn't even feel like a tough guy about it, it was like breaking a bone at the Build a Bear Workshop. Full weenie was the only thing you achieved if you ever so much as mentioned it.

He tried his hardest not to look at the wound as he propped his foot up on the sink after stripping off the wet sock. Fumbling with his medicine cabinet he brought out some hydrogen peroxide which he dumped over the still oozing wound with a quick glance to make sure he was aiming the bottle in the right location. Wincing, he waited for the hissing and bubbling to settle down some, before smearing some antibiotic ointment on it and slapping a band-aid over the thing.

Chris couldn't believe this. If he didn't find the beast or put it with an owner that could verify the little monster was healthy, he might actually have to get rabies shots over a bite from a mini rodent dog. If it had been a German Sheppard, or a Pitbull, or even a Lab, you could walk into your doctor's with your head held high even if you were limping as you did it, but a dog with long flowing Fabio locks? Not even a little bit.

By the time he had hobbled his way into the kitchen, his Hot Pocket was cold.

It was nights like this that beer was created for, he grabbed one while re-heating his meal.

Chris woke up the next morning on the couch with regrets. First and most pressing regret, was putting whatever he had put in his mouth that had proceeded to die there. He had a beer for the ouchie, then another for the ouchie, and then one because, hey, he was stuck in at home all night anyway, and then there were a couple because he missed Suzanne already and. Of such moments, mornings after are made of, even if at this moment he didn't remember any of the reasons he'd given himself, he only knew the tragic results.

Thank all the gods that had ever been prayed to that he always set up the coffee maker right after he had his last cup the day before. As he sat there on the couch for a moment trying to remember if he had spent much time online last night and if he had done anything particularly embarrassing when he had, the smell of coffee wafted out to him from the kitchen. He could hear it pop and gurgle as it was just finishing up, which put the time at roughly nine a.m. It was a weekend, and if for whatever weird mutant reason he needed coffee sooner than that he could turn it on. But normally, without outside impetus, nine was his expected weekend wake-up. So, as bleary-eyed as he felt, he must not have had too many last night or he'd still be snoring. Good, he was learning, he could be taught. Too much booze and putting your hands on the burner both hurt, try not to do it again little Chrissy.

Cup of coffee in hand, he sat down on the couch to piece together how he'd gotten himself into this sorry state. This was not a usual occurrence, so something needed to be the trigger. Suzanne left without waking him, which only bugged him a little bit, so it wasn't that. Work was fine, he didn't have cancer. That was when the real horror loomed up in his mind. Oh yeah, psychopathic hair model dog ravaging his poor heel. It was no wonder it took him a minute to remember, it wasn't hurting at all now. Chris let out a long sigh propping his foot up on his other leg. The adult in him knew he should probably check the damage and then make an informed decision about a doctor.

He winced when he saw the big piece of gauze he'd taped down on it last night, even more so the large red stain in the middle of it. He'd have to burn those socks, no way would he want to wear them again, even washed he'd always remember them being soaked with blood. Slowly he pulled at the tape, making faces as it ripped out hairs as it came away. Finally, he'd gotten the pad clear so he could see.

What… the literal… actual… really real fuck?

There was no open wound under the bandage at all!

Chris started pawing at his heel, then he poked at it. It wasn't even sore. He got up in a rush and headed for the bathroom forgetting his coffee entirely. Coffee would only be redundant; he was completely awake now. There was his sock, just as he'd left it on the floor. He snatched it up and looked at it, it was a dark sock, but he could see the even darker parts that had been soaked with his now crusty and crunchy blood.

Okay, the key here was to not freak out, there had to be some perfectly logical explanation for this.

So, what in the hell was it?

He was Wolverine.

No, wait, logical explanation, he didn't even have sideburns.

He walked slowly back to the living room and slumped into the couch, bumping the table causing some of the abandoned coffee to slosh onto the coaster. Well, he guessed he didn't have to get rabies shots. A dog bit me! Okay, where did it bite you? Well, you can't see it because it was completely healed by morning. He went in with that kind of song and dance he'd end up getting to talk to a completely different kind of doctor. The kind that asked questions like, 'Do dogs remind you of your father? Do you feel that dogs are always persecuting you? Is the little dog in the room with us now Christopher?'

Chris tried not to think about the bite and its healing on its own after that. He tried not to think about it because it was so weird. He had no idea *what* to think about it. But since he was alone in his house that was almost all he thought about. For every time he said to himself he wasn't thinking about it, was as many times as he went to look up what to do about dog bites, how fast dog bites heal, and of course rabies information on Google. Most of it was very informative but in no way useful for his specific situation since everybody agreed that it shouldn't have healed that fast. Except for WebMD, which didn't say anything about healing per se, but of course, diagnosed it as cancer and decided he had only days left to live, but since it did that for everything including a mild itch on the buttocks, it could be pretty easily dismissed.

But other than tapping on his phone or computer, getting a completely useless answer, swearing he wasn't going to do it again, and then doing it again five minutes later… other than that it was a slow day. He took a walk around the neighborhood to see if he could find the offending brute, but no luck on that front at all. The owners probably saw the blood on the little savage's jaw last night and were helping it lay low until the heat was off. Aiding and abetting was what it was.

He sent Suzanne a couple of text messages as well. He really didn't have any hope of her answering them, she was usually incommunicado for these trips at first. He just thought it was a nice thoughtful way of telling her he missed her. That way, when she finally did get around to checking messages she'd know he was thinking about her. Cutesy little love messages people, it's what separates the brief flings from the marriage material.

Note though, the book said cutesy, there's a fine line between that and crazy stalker shit, so make sure to check yourself before you wreck yourself. If you're not sure, ask your mom to see if she would have found it romantic. If you're afraid to ask your mom, you already know the answer, don't you?

After watching a baseball game and having a dinner of a personal pizza, Chris found himself at loose ends again. He supposed he could watch a movie, but he felt uneasy and ended up pacing the house while he thought about what to do with himself. Finally, running out of patience with his own constant mobility, he decided he'd just get in the car and drive for a bit. Yeah, it was Sunday night, but not everything closed on Sunday. Maybe he'd go see what was playing at the theater or something. There wasn't anything in particular he could remember being enthusiastic about coming out, but you never knew.

The moon was just beginning to show itself on the hood of his car as he pulled away.

The movie had been a mistake. Not the whole idea of going to the movies, that had been fine and dandy, a solid time-killing idea. He'd enjoyed numerous movies in the theater before, he knew the theory was sound. No, this particular one had been a tactical error in judgment. Chris would be the first to admit that he was a weenie about horror films. Well, that wasn't accurate, all of his past girlfriends would have leaped up to admit it way faster than he would, but still. He let himself get too wrapped up in the things; like it didn't matter how bad the plot or the acting, or how low the budget, every jump scare would have him acting like Shag and Scoob in a haunted house.

So of course, knowing he'd be alone tonight in the house, he had to go see something called Blood Droplets about a crazed serial killer who was possessed by an evil ghost. He had practically run from the theater to his car. And since he was one of all of five people who had watched Blood Droplets, the parking lot was especially creepy and empty when he got out there. Full moon, empty parking lot, crazed ghost possessed serial killer out there somewhere since of course, the killer found a way to come back at the end of the movie... nothing to worry about. Chris wasn't risking it, he had a hearty jog going, with his keys in his hand the whole way. Not that mere car keys would have stopped the serial killer, the machine gun at the end of the film had only slowed it down, but keys would have to do, Chris didn't have a machine gun handy. He might have to rectify that and being an American meant it wouldn't be a problem to acquire.

So, the perfect mindset to go home to a dark and empty house. At least he'd left the porch light on before he left. Like every other time he had done this to himself, he spent the trip home chiding himself for being a ninny. At least it wasn't hyper dark, the moon made sure of that as he drove back from the mall where the theater was. He tried listening to some music to soothe his nerves, only to discover that he had left the Misfits hooked up on the mp3. There was no hope, he'd just have to run for the house after he parked and pray that any serial killers out there had already met their quota for the night and were now tired and going home to rest and wind down by making stupid comments about things on Twitter and Yahoo news stories. He'd feel bad if said serial killer had gotten to Mrs. Abernathy down the street, but this was clearly a her or him situation and she'd lived a long life.

Parking the car, he took a deep breath. There was no one there, nobody cared enough about him to kill him. Not even as a random victim of a serial killer, he wasn't their normal type. Twenty-something guys who worked in resources were just not your normal serial killer victim. Anyway, what on earth would a serial killer be doing out here? This was more or less suburbia, there had to be better spots to find victims than in Chris's yew bushes. He was positive that further out in the country there were some summer camps, for instance, just packed full of teenagers contemplating sex and drugs.

He had taken three steps towards the house when suddenly he sensed he was not alone. Later he would puzzle at that. Common sense would say that if you were afraid of becoming a notch on a serial killer's knife blade, at that moment you think you're not alone you run like hell. Instead, Chris froze where he stood like a prime victim ninny. He turned and looked towards the bushes slowly. There it was.

It was the damned psycho dog.

Except this time it wasn't growling at all, it just stared up at him with those weird velvet Elvis painting eyes the things have. Emboldened by the thought that maybe it wasn't rabid, and more importantly, he'd have a dog to present to a doctor if he still wanted to get checked out, he took a step forward and knelt down with his hand out.

"Come here you little varmint. Guess we got off on the wrong foot, huh? I'm not going to hurt you, I'll leave that to a vet if it turns out you're rabid," he said in a sing-song voice that people use on animals and small children. He didn't bother to change what he actually said since the dog couldn't understand him anyway – and he was still annoyed at being attacked by the thing.

Chris shuffled forward a little more, leaning his hand out so the thing could sniff him. For a moment it leaned out of the shadows where it was hiding. It sniffed the air cautiously. This was actually going to work, he'd get the dog, find its owner, find out from them that, 'Precious was a little nippy sometimes,' and this whole thing would be over.

The dog's eyes somehow contrived to get even wider at that instant.

It bolted.

Well, on the plus side, he could probably stop worrying about rabies. Any animal that could manage a turn of speed like that wasn't sickly in any way, it was just an asshole.

Suzanne was packing. Thankfully she hadn't been here long enough to accumulate the amount of stuff that meant it would take her all day. She was still pretty pissed off about it anyway. Especially since she knew it was her own fault. Nobody likes to move, moving as the ultimate act of ghosting a guy was ridiculous. Ridiculous and yet still necessary. She should have never let him come over to her place after the movie, how stupid could she be? At least due to growing up an army brat, she was an expert at packing quickly. Her time following her father's footsteps had made her even more efficient.

There was going to be trouble, no ifs, no ands, and no buts about it. But when someone came looking for Suzanne to complain about it, all they'd be finding was a bunch of disconnected numbers and the glitter she couldn't seem to get to come out of her rug no matter what she tried. One stupid 'girls' night' with some of the girls from the office and the stuff wouldn't go away. Well, hopefully, she was leaving that behind too, but probably not, there was probably some of it in all her clothes. She wished the new renter of this efficiency all the luck on earth with getting it to come out as she loaded her last suitcase into her Rav4.

It was a shame, she'd liked Chris. A lot. Obviously.

CHAPTER 2

"I never did get my snow cone" – *Ethel Stephens*

It had been a week now and still no word from Suzanne. Chris had tried calling an all too large number of times that was just shy of creeper, at least he hoped it was shy of it. It's hard to tell sometimes, especially when you're a bit worried. This sudden disappearing act wasn't like her, so of course, he was worried. He felt within his rights here as her boyfriend. It was one thing to go radio silent on a business trip, it was another to just vanish all together. She was supposed to have been back home two days ago, and she was still incommunicado, this was almost call the cops territory.

This is why Chris was driving over to her apartment to check on her. Maybe she had caught something on her trip, in which case the decent thing to do would be to babysit her until she got better, take her to doctor's appointments, that sort of thing. If she wasn't there, he didn't know what to do next. But at least it was a start, at least he wasn't just sitting there staring at his phone hoping it would ping with a reply. Her place was a basement efficiency nearby, he had joked with her that if she wanted he could rent her two rooms of his house and it would still be bigger than this place. She had not found that comment particularly amusing. The idea of her just sitting there in that tiny little place, possibly ill, made him drive just that much faster.

The nice part of the place was that it had its own door, so at least he didn't need to be buzzed into a building. The same door he was standing in front of now. He took a deep breath and knocked solidly. Nothing happened.

This is a moment that makes all of us become awkward. Now we are standing there in broad daylight randomly attracting attention to ourselves, but not the attention we want, i.e., the door to open. We start looking around nervously at this point, waiting for somebody to demand we tell them what we're doing, and why we're there. It is, in fact, as close to being a burglar as most of us achieve in life. Even more so if whoever's door it is has suspicious neighbors and we get to talk to the cops who just happened to be in the area when the 9-1-1 call went in.

He knocked again. This caused him to look around slightly more frantically to see if anyone was looking at him. The reason for this, as every door knocker knows, is that the next step after knocking twice is to look in the window to see if anyone is home, which looks creepy no matter how you do it, but curiosity and impatience are harsh mistresses. If no one looks home, it's your cue to leave. If someone is, it's your cue to think of clever ways of getting their attention in case they're listening to earbuds or something. If someone is and they are sitting right there in the living room, looking right at the door with a disgusted expression, you should definitely leave, probably in shame.

Chris leaned over towards the window next to the door, putting his hand over his eyes to peer inside. He just stayed there for a long moment after that, not believing what he saw.

A voice of an older woman broke his reverie, "You lookin' for Suzanne?"

His head jerked away from the window guiltily like he had been caught cutting the glass. He stared up at the stairs going into the upstairs apartments, and the woman standing there looking down at him. She was a solid-looking woman. Very good... European folk stock in appearance. While she was dressed in modern clothes, everything else about the woman looked like she should be in one of those films from the Soviet era starring as one of the women in the bread line, wearing a babushka and possibly pulling a cart usually reserved for horses.

Chris smiled anyway, "Yes, umm, have you seen her?"

"Naw, she moved out a few days ago. Shame, she seemed nice," the woman replied, more or less confirming what the empty room Chris had been peering into meant.

"Oh," Chris said quietly

Chris did the only thing you can do in a situation like that. He climbed up the steps without saying another word, not even a sheepish, "Thanks," because that would invite more conversation than he could handle at the moment, and started trudging back to his car. He certainly did not want to discuss with this stranger right now the most pertinent subject of the moment; how he had just gotten spectacularly dumped. He was so stunned by everything that he couldn't figure out which part felt the worst, her dumping him, her not telling him she was dumping him, the complete lack of any indication it was coming the last time he'd see her, or the fact that right now it looked like she had left town all together rather than date him. There were a lot of options on his table.

All things said and done, this could be counted as a major blow to the ego, no mistake about that at all.

What could you do at that point? Chris didn't know where she worked, her phone wasn't picking up – hell she'd probably blocked his number. Moving out entirely without telling you was the ultimate breakup move, it was ghosting times infinity. He went to check her Facebook and Twitter and found she had blocked him from both of those. He'd only been dating her for a month. So he certainly wasn't going to mention it at work past, "Things didn't work out." No male in his right mind wants word getting around that he had failed so catastrophically in his last relationship that the girl had gone into witness protection to get away from him.

If only he knew why. Sure, he'd still be bummed, he thought they had a good thing going which he would be sad to lose, but at least he'd have closure. At least he might potentially learn something from this that might ensure that nothing like this ever happened to him again. Had he been too clingy, not clingy enough, toxically masculine, a wimp, what had caused this? The last time he had seen her, he had been falling asleep next to her after making love, he wanted to know how it had gone from there to her hiding out from him. But that understanding was not to be. Maybe it was something with her, maybe she had sprouted a tail while on the business trip and didn't want to risk his rejection. He wished he'd at least given her the opportunity to say something reassuring like, "Come on, demon girls with tails are hot, ask any tattoo artist!" He was sure he could have worked around whatever it was, but it appeared he wasn't even given a chance to find out if he could.

He had nothing to do but sit around and wonder where it had all gone south, at least until Friday. Friday he was over at his best friend Jake's apartment because it was healthier, which was not something he normally thought about being at Jake's. Ostensibly the reason he was at Jake's was to have a few beers, order a pizza, and play video games and maybe watch a movie. When they had made plans after Chris had told him he was suddenly single again, this was the stated mission of the evening. And it was indeed what they were going to do... as soon as Chris stopped crying.

Most guys would probably not go in for or accept this sort of behavior from another guy. But this was Jake, they had been friends since they were five. His parents still lived a mile up the road from Chris. They had seen each other cry from boo-boos playing in the playground, when Chris's parents had died, and in this case, because of the most brutal dumping in either of their life histories. Jake was totally understanding on this one, even about the snot that was running down Chris's nose. Chris had returned the favor before, and even Jake was willing to admit that this particular instance was kind of brutal.

"Well, look at it this way," Jake finally said when it looked like Chris was running out of steam, "better to find out now, right?"

"Find out what?" Chris asked as he snatched a paper towel to use as a tissue.

"Dude, the chick clearly had some deep-seated, undiscovered, massive level crazy. I mean who the fuck does that? Leaves you sleeping after having sex and then moves the fuck out of her apartment? That is some serious hidden emotional issues buddy boy."

"I guess," Chris replied looking down at the location of the coffee table where it hid under all of the magazines, discs and other junk Jake had let accumulate. His beer was sitting on a copy of Game Informer from last year.

"Dude, can you fucking imagine if she broke out that shit later?

You're on vacation together, and you come back to the room from, I don't know, doing vacation stuff alone for some reason, and boom all her shit's gone? Who knows what other fucked up psychosis she could have? Maybe she had her mummified Mom in the closet of her place, you don't fucking know. Come home one day and your pet rabbit is in a pot being boiled," Jake laid out his case, waving his arm expansively and not noticing that his Flyers jersey had just dipped into the pizza that was sitting next to him on the couch.

"Dude, those were two thoroughly ancient movie references there," Chris smiled a little.

"Movies?"

"Regardless, I don't even have a rabbit."

"You could get one at some point in your life, they're cute if you don't mind pellets everywhere. You never know when crazy like that might surface. A month of your life, which involved getting sex I might add, is totally worth it to dodge a bullet like that," Jake laid out his conclusive argument as to why this was a good thing.

"Well, we're back to hanging out on Fridays I suppose," Chris replied.

"See, I knew talking it out would cheer you up," Jake smiled broadly.

It was all Chris could do not to start crying again.

Much to his surprise, it did get better. He even went out on a date. It wasn't a good date, but the fact that he was willing to try it should show he was almost ready to stop sniffling at random moments. Jake did help as well, at least in the only ways he was able. Jake's emotional immaturity made it hard to wallow in misery when you were around him. When your best friend views being out of beer with the same emotional gravity that some people view a stock market crash, it's hard to continue to take things that seriously if only so you aren't talking over his emotional head. He also told Chris a lot of fart jokes and sent him roughly a thousand memes every day, which also helped distract him, even if it was only to make him say "Ewww" at some of the more objectionable memes involving orifices.

Chris wasn't sure why he was that much more mature than his best friend, who he loved like the brother he was in all but biology. Maybe it was the house. When you had a house, you had things you *had* to do. Like when Chris's parents died, Oit automatically thrust him into the role of being a real adult with real responsibilities. It's hard to view everything still in terms of who from college is throwing a killer party when you pay property taxes. You especially never want to throw a party anymore yourself, even if you finally had the room, because you knew all the shit you've done to other people's houses while drunk over the years and no way in hell do you want someone doing that to your fish bowl. Chris didn't even have a fish bowl, but it didn't mean he feared it happening in his home any less. Someone could easily bring a fish bowl.

They were both approaching their late twenties completely differently, even though they both made about the same amount of money. Maybe Jake made more, he had a more distinct set of skills in computers. Chris had a small portfolio invested for his retirement, Jake had really killer bass amps in his car. That wasn't to say Chris was incapable of fun, it was just that Jake always seemed to be having more of it, and at a much louder volume. Still, when they got together, they might as well still be in college, which they went to together, even renting a small apartment off-campus that Chris probably remembered more fondly than Jake. For Chris, it was the good old days, for Jake little had changed but the address. Chris vacuumed on a regular basis, and Jake still lived the way he had back then mostly. If vacuuming occurred at Jake's, it was because he spilled his stash and wanted to get all of it back.

Chris wasn't with Jake tonight, or worse, trying another Tinder date, he was home. Jake had convinced his on-again-off-again girlfriend to go up to New Hampshire and rent a cabin to go hiking. This seemed like a completely ridiculous action by Jake, since Jake had never taken much of an interest in hiking before. The only thing that he could figure was that Jake was trying to convince Hannah that he had changed somehow, and that being rugged and outdoorsy was a sign of this change. She had accused Jake of being a slug repeatedly, and Chris supposed, hiking in New Hampshire was indeed non-slug behavior and was useful for proving his non-oozing slug existence. It was an interesting gambit because if Hannah bought it, Jake would be stuck trying to actually be outdoorsy, instead of pretending to be so for one weekend to get his girlfriend back. Assuming of course he did not collapse in an exhausted heap on some New Hampshire mountainside, moaning, "Cheetos… stat…"

Chris wished him luck, but tonight with no date and no best friend available, Chris would be watching something on Netflix and eating some Chinese from a local place he liked. Otherwise known as the 'Sad single guy's special.' Tonight the movie was something called *Last Phases*, which was some kind of horror movie, and General Tso's as the accompanying meal. A horror movie because you never got to watch them when you first started dating someone unless you struck gold, and she liked horror too and said it up front. And General Tso's because it was yummy and hard to screw up. Also, a horror movie because Chris had a bad learning curve when it came to his own behavior as it related to irrational fears.

As the moon started rising, Chris couldn't help but notice that he was inexplicably sleepy. No real point in fighting it, if he was tired, he was tired. Hell, he was at his own house, right? And it wasn't like he had anything he really needed to stay up for. That particular anything he'd had before had left suddenly without leaving him a forwarding address.

Something was poking Chris in the thigh. It was clearly way too early, he was barely able to sense any sunlight at all, but somehow he was lying somewhere being poked and whatever it was, was definitely sharp. He opened his eyes. Okay, dirt is not a good thing to see in front of you when you wake up. Chris went to jerk upright and immediately crashed into the shrubbery above. He was outside? WTF? This was especially not good since his nerve endings had just reported in that there was cool morning air everywhere, definitely every square inch, which meant he wasn't wearing any clothes at this moment.

Chris looked around as wildly as the bushes he was in allowed for. Okay, he was under a shrub, and that was his car out there. He was nude, under a shrub, in front of his house. So, not Okay then at all really. This seemed like a good time for "WTF?" to put in another appearance. He tried to remind himself that it could be worse before he started hyperventilating, he could be in Mrs. Abernathy's hydrangea bushes, which would definitely count as worse. Thinking quickly, which since he hadn't had any coffee should indicate the urgency he was giving this, he put together a plan. It wasn't a good plan, but it was frankly the only one he had.

He slid out from under the bush and ran like hell for his backyard.

His back door was still open, thank God. He made a brief mental note of the hole in the screen door before he rushed inside. Shutting the actual door, and now safely ensconced away from prying eyes, he started immediately looking out the windows to see if anyone was stirring out there. From what he could see in the dim light of early morning he'd made it back in unnoticed. Which left him back at "WTF?"

Chris thought this had the possibility of being the theme for the day, maybe multiple days. Nothing usually happened that left him nude in his front yard, at least not since college. It earned the title of "WTF?" here, an even bigger one than that time in college had earned.

Once he got his thoughts under control a little, he turned on the coffee maker and went to hunt down his clothes. Those were in a pile in a living room. He put them on not caring that they hadn't been washed, he just didn't want to be standing around naked anymore. Fully clothed, Chris was proud of himself as he walked back to the kitchen to get coffee. Despite having every reason to he was not freaking out. At least not yet, it was clearly still a viable option to be explored later once the morning had time to get underway.

He tried to look at it rationally and calm down a bit. Okay, so he had sleepwalked, it happened, it is not the end of the world here. Waking up under the bushes nude was not ideal, that was undoubtedly a fact, but thank God this was a quiet, mostly elderly neighborhood when his unconscious mind had decided to go walkies. At least everyone had probably, hopefully, been asleep for his sonambu streaking. He was probably just still upset about a bunch of stuff, his now ex-girlfriend, not having a new girlfriend and his best friend being hundreds of miles away and his subconscious had reacted poorly. Why this had translated into, "take off your clothes and take a walk" was beyond him, but who knew how your subconscious worked anyway?

No, it was a one-time deal, it had to be nothing to be worried about. He was going to have a nice normal day, maybe go to a park, and forget this ever happened.

———————｜———————

The next morning, he woke up on the hallway floor, nude again.

Chris snapped his head up immediately and got to his feet. Okay, once he could just blow it off as a fluke, this wasn't once. It happening more than once was sort of the definition of not once. He had to do something about this, something that didn't involve telling Jake about it ever happening for preference. Not that Jake wouldn't try to be helpful, more that he would never, ever let it go. As he quickly threw clothing on in case a neighbor came by to complain about seeing him last night, he desperately tried to think of a way to keep himself from doing this again,

Handcuffs, he'd handcuff himself to his bed! Even if he had the key there was no way he'd be able to unlock them while asleep. He looked down the hall at the open back door and had a moment of doubt, but he quickly dispelled it. Opening a door was one thing, you did it all the time, it was second nature to open a door. He distinctly remembered from when someone in Junior High School had a pair that the key to handcuffs was kind of fiddly, no way he'd be able to manage that while asleep. Especially if he hid the key somewhere from himself that was still in reach. Foolproof! Rope he might be able to wiggle out of, or just untie himself, no way he'd get out of handcuffs. He was making decisions before coffee, which wasn't normally recommended, but sometimes you have to take the... you know what, let's wait until he has clothes on to finish that thought.

Now the next question was, who in the hell sold handcuffs? And for the reader, was Chris a bit of a prude for not knowing the obvious place immediately?

As he set the coffee pot brewing, got dressed, and considered getting breakfast together, it dawned on him who was sure to have handcuffs for sale. Today's outing did not promise to be his proudest or finest moment, no doubt about that. There was one place he was sure would have handcuffs, he distinctly remembered from the time he'd gone in there on a dare in high school. Adult bookstores always had handcuffs for sale...

On a plus note, the lining they put on the kind they sold meant he wouldn't chafe his wrists.

The trip to Boobie World had been one of the more mortifying experiences of his adult life. First off, there were other people in there, all desperately trying not to look at each other, probably hoping to avoid being forced to testify later. Except for like two guys, and you *really* didn't want to look at them but you could *feel* them looking at you. Then there were the noises he could hear coming from the video rooms. He knew logically it was just movies being run, but then the thought of what guys did watching those types of movies came into his mind and he was even more mortified. So, there Chris was searching desperately for what he wanted among a plethora of toys and things he could only guess the use for while porn moans thumped away from the back rooms all while trying not to look at anyone and also avoiding any images presented by his own imagination like the plague.

Finally, the one object he needed appeared before him hanging from the walls next to lots and lots of stuff in black leather and latex. Chris quickly snatched them off the hook where they were displayed and made his way towards the cashier as quickly as he could while still trying to avoid the spinning racks of merchandise between him and home free. As he went, he remembered that he had seen handcuffs in the local party store the one time he'd been asked to pick up stuff for a cousin's birthday. He had no idea why they were there for, but he'd seen them. Probably a magic trick or something. Of course, if you were into that kind of thing, the ones here were for a different sort of magic trick.

Oh well, he was here, and at least these had fuzzy stuff on them so they wouldn't chafe.

Chris couldn't make himself make eye contact with the clerk as the guy scooped up the cuffs and put them into a bag. The kid, who looked like he was college age, said, "You know, the party supply place sells these, right? I mean you don't look too comfortable in here."

Chris looked up and grinned sheepishly, "I wish I'd thought of that twenty minutes ago."

"What we go through to make 'em happy, huh? Twenty bucks my good man, on the dot."

Chris glanced up at the kid before digging out his wallet, the guy was at most twenty-two, except for his eyes. After working here his eyes looked like the soul behind them had aged one-hundred years from what he'd seen, or worse, had to clean up in here.

Chris handed over a twenty, "Thanks."

Chris went outside followed more closely than he would have cared for by one of the perverts who must have been in the back room. Kink shaming might be wrong, but no way in hell was he going to want to shake hands with the guy.

Just as Chris reached for his keys a younger female voice screamed out from a passing car, "HI DAD!"

Chris figured it was just someone being funny, but he couldn't help but notice that the perv guy had ducked behind a car.

Back home he fiddled with the handcuffs over and over again. Making sure he could get them on, making sure he could get them the hell off in the morning, going around to various spots in the house trying to decide on the best thing to handcuff himself to. There were a lot of things to consider there, comfort being one of the main ones. Sure, he could cuff himself to the banister, but who in the hell wanted to sleep on the steps? Unfortunately, the cuff really didn't fit right on the post to the headboard of his bed, bondage had not really played much of a role in Chris' sex life before this so he'd never had to consider these things before.

Eventually, after scouring the house for the best location, he decided that around the leg of his dad's old pool table in the basement was his only really viable spot here. That meant bringing out a sleeping roll he'd used for camping once, and grabbing as many blankets as possible. He needed to get this wrapped up soon, for whatever reason he'd been drowsing off early the last two nights. That was something else that was worrying him, he had never been the easiest sleeper on earth before but the last couple of days it seemed just as the moon was rising, he was falling.

He brought down a few beers, an early dinner, his laptop, and proceeded to handcuff himself in place. He'd like to see himself get out of this one to go streak the neighborhood, He was also proud of himself for making sure it was his left hand he'd cuffed so he could still type.

He yawned hugely and figured it must be getting late out there already. Oh well, he had a movie running, he'd just lie back and enjoy it.

CHAPTER 3

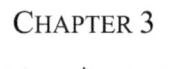

"Pull this dream over to the curb right now buddy."- **Rick Nielsen,
polka dot enthusiast**

Chris knew he was no longer in the basement instantly; his only consolation was that he was on the rug so at least he had to be inside. Right after that thought came the thought that just because it was a rug was no guarantee that it was *his* rug in *his* house, causing his eyes to snap open. Thankfully, it *was* his rug, he recognized the pattern that had caused him to think a dozen times that he should replace it with something that was less, "something my mom bought." While that was one problem sorted, him being in his own house, not the rug's overall "mom-ishness" there was still the problem as to why in the hell he was upstairs to contend with. Also, the nudity thing was once again an issue.

For a moment he was torn between starting the coffee and going down to the basement and seeing what had gone wrong with what should have been a fool-proof plan. That train of thought lasted only a moment though, he decided that whatever the basement showed him, he could at least have fresh brewed coffee waiting for him when he came back upstairs. Even though he was pretty awake from the surprise of once again waking up on the floor in spite of his preparations, he knew that adrenaline was bound to fade, and when it did he would be even more grateful for the magic of caffeine.

Back downstairs in the basement, there were his clothes in a heap. To make matters more confusing there was a set of handcuffs hooked to the pool table… unopened.

Well, now what?

The only thing he could think of was another set of handcuffs for his ankle and maybe calling a shrink tomorrow. He didn't have a lot of hopes the next set of cuffs would do any better than the first ones, but at least this time he knew that he didn't have to buy them in a porn shop. Chris was thrilled by that, he figured he had already risked catching something nasty just by buying the ones he had from that nasty place the last time.

As we go through life we have no idea what is going to be the thing that gives us immense joy sometime in the future. Mainly because we don't imagine ourselves in those situations where it's applicable, it's outside of our life expectations so we never consider it. It could be finding twenty dollars, meeting that special someone at a baby shower, doing some remodeling on your house, and finding fifty grand stuffed in a wall, you never know the whats or whens of when it will happen. Still, it would be reasonable to assume that if someone had told Chris a couple of weeks ago that he would almost weep with joy at waking up to find himself handcuffed to a pool table, not only would he have not believed them, he might very well have gotten away from that person as fast as possible for being a creep.

Yet here he was.

He let the immense relief wash over him for a long moment before it dawned on him that despite his joy at waking up on the floor, in the real world which resided upstairs, naked or not, he still had to get ready for work. It took him a few heart-racing moments to remember where he had hidden the keys. Not being able to remember and being stuck here had a level of suck he didn't even want to contemplate.

After you call 9-1-1 and they come down and get you out of it, how exactly are you supposed to explain that to the firefighters? The non-dying of shame version that was, that was the goal. Exactly, there isn't any explanation that would be believable and not end up with your face flushed red.

Freed from his bonds and with a spring in his step, even despite sleeping on a nest on the basement floor, Chris made his way upstairs to get the coffee going and to get showered and ready for work. Maybe even his subconscious recognized that he needed to work on Mondays and it could only be doing that weird streaker crap on weekends. Maybe, he might actually trust himself enough to sleep in his own bed again! Without handcuffs! Begrudgingly he also admitted that even if this did settle down some he might need to consider going to a shrink over this. He loved his parents and had stopped wetting the bed at a very young age, Chris had no idea what in the hell the psychiatrist could possibly discuss that might help him, but he was willing to try for no other reason than he didn't want to have a talk with his elderly neighbors about the time and place for nudity.

Work was work. It was unexciting and vaguely unfulfilling as always; he never once used his degree in economics during the day making him zero for forever on using it. Not that economics and having degrees in them were excitement city, so it was probably a good thing. It had helped him land this job, but it was a rare day on the floor of the call center when even the best human resources manager was called upon to explain the differences between Keynes and Hayek. It had been so long since he had to do it in fact, he probably would have just summarized it by saying something nasty about Hayek and Pinochet. (See? this book can do smart jokes, it won't all be sex shop jokes, only mostly jokes like that).

Today he was more than happy to be at his dull boring old cubicle. It took his mind off his bizarre weekend. Resources gets called constantly and it's almost impossible to spend too much time dwelling on your mildly weird home life when people are routinely calling in with some absolutely psychotic reasons for why they wouldn't be into work today. He had spent most of the day wanting to respond, "Yes, your wife falling through the porch this morning is unfortunate and unusual, but I woke up today handcuffed to a pool table and I still made it in, buddy!"

The nicest part was he still felt that joyous lifting of the weirdness that had happened all weekend when he got home. He stayed up to a normal time, watched horror movies because of his continued lack of a learning curve, and when he woke up the next morning he was still exactly where he had gone to sleep the night before.

Within a few days of no nudity and weird places to enjoy that nudity he decided to try using his actual bed. After that worked fine, any well-meaning promises of going to see a psychiatrist were rationalized away. He felt fine mentally, no deep-seated issues seemed to be bothering him in any way. Suzanne leaving didn't count as deep-seated. There were some other surface ones; since he was spending a lot of time over at Jake's and the worm had turned and it was his best friend that was the one feeling mopey. Jake and Hannah had reverted to off again after the New Hampshire trip. It had turned out that Hannah had not been so overawed by the scenic beauty of the state and the effort Jake had put in setting the trip up that she couldn't help herself and just spent the entire time in bed with him overcome with animal lust. Within a day, she had exposed the fatal flaw the plan had always had, the possibility of having to go hiking. So now his time with Jake was often punctuated by moments of intense whining, either about missing Hannah, or exactly how far it was to hike up Mount Washington and how much Jake thought parts of him still ached from the experience.

At least there had been a couple of more dates in there since Suzanne had left, so Chris told himself he wasn't moping, and if he was actually moping a bit, it was certainly not with the intensity Jake was managing. He wasn't finding true love either, but he was giving it the old college try. He loved Jake, he really did, Jake was his best friend. That being said, he didn't want to grow old all alone with just Jake. He could see them now, eventually surrendering to perpetual bachelorhood, Jake moving into Chris's house, the pair of them puttering around the place in their underwear trying to figure out what was edible in the refrigerator, or in Jake's case possibly the floor. No, he loved Jake like a brother, but Chris still liked women. He wanted to be with a woman in a way that Jake just didn't do it for him. Like picking up after herself, reading a book, important things. He was honest enough with himself that he was willing to admit boobs were also a plus in the equation.

Since he had been suddenly thrust into being single again, he had also formed the opinion that dating apps should all have their corporate headquarters burned to the ground so that cleansing fire would ensure they never were able to sprout back from the ashes. Of course, he didn't delete those apps, because as bad as they were, they were still infinitely better than bars. Chris couldn't help but wonder what people did to meet each other before dating apps. Maybe old-timers had stronger pheromones or something. Maybe that was why they needed the roll-on deodorant and that really strong perfume his grandmother used to wear. They needed to cover up the smell to keep from humping each other in the streets. It would explain that WW2 photo of the sailor and that woman.

He settled in to watch TV for a night at home. Chris could see the full moon starting to work its way over the horizon. Man, he felt sleepy all of a sudden, good thing he'd already eaten.

Chris dreamed that he was running. Not only that he was running, but that he was moving more gracefully over the ground than he ever had before. He imagined that the ground flowed under him as his limbs bunched and extended for every mile devouring stride. He had never been much of a runner, being the first to groan when it was announced that they'd be running a mile in gym class, but this... this was simply exhilarating. He could feel the wind he created as he moved, rushing over him, flowing over his fur…

His what?

Suddenly Chris realized something that seemed pretty important. Despite the fur issue, this w'sn't a dream, he really was running.

This was quickly followed by the realization that he was doing it with more legs than he was used to having.

He was lucky he didn't fall directly into the street he had been running down.

Chris' mind was awash with confusion as he stumbled to a halt and stood there panting. When he looked down, he didn't see his feet, he saw paws. This couldn't be right! He didn't have paws at all, he had feet, he was a man, he had a job and a 401K and everything, dogs didn't have retirement plans! He blinked repeatedly hoping it was something left over from some especially weird dream, he even shook his head a bit before looking back down. Nope, still paws. Confused and bewildered, he sat back on his haunches and was even more confused when he realized he had haunches to sit back on.

This had to be a dream, he was a man, he distinctly remembered going to high school and college, and dogs definitely don't do that except in really bad comedies from the 80s. He was not a dog with lots and lots of curly fur. Somebody would have noted it during gym class for starters. Or maybe the available evidence was correct and he *was* a dog, and he had just been dreaming he was a man. No, that didn't wash, he didn't have any doggy memories, he had man memories. You start accepting you're a dog just because you happened to currently be in a dog's body, well, next thing you know you're playing fetch and someone's saying how good you are with the kids.

He began to walk, trying desperately not to think about the two extra legs involved in the process or that his eyesight had gone all weird, or that he seemed to be able to smell things that he hadn't even known existed before this. If he didn't think about it, it seemed to come easy and naturally, but as soon as he thought too hard about it, it was all he could do not to stumble and land flat on his… face? Snout? Right now he wasn't even considering his direction, he'd work that out in a minute, he just felt that if he kept moving, a solution might suddenly come to him by some miracle. That, and at the moment he didn't recognize where he was, and a strange neighborhood is no place to sit around after you've suddenly discovered that you're a dog.

As he was passing a bush in a darkened part of the sidewalk between street lights, he heard an urgent whisper. "Psst!" hissed a voice from somewhere inside the bush.

Chris stopped, "Who? Me?"

There was a pause, before a vaguely annoyed male voice said, "Is there anybody else on the fucking street at this moment?"

"Umm, no, I mean you are, but other than that."

"Well then, of course, I'm fucking talking to you," said the voice from the darkness of the bush.

"Hey, I'm having a weird day, be nice. Anyway, who are you?" Chris demanded in a terse voice. Talking was weird because he could hear two voices when he talked. He heard his voice talking like normal but overlaying it was a series of growls and he could feel his body making little shifts in posture. As soon as he realized that, he also realized that the other voice talking to him had been nothing but growls as well, but he'd understood it perfectly.

"You just realized you're a dog, and I'm the fucker who is nice enough that I'm going to explain why," said the voice coming toward him. There was a rustle of leaves and a moment later a small figure emerged from the shadows.

"You're a pug!" Chris exclaimed.

"And you're a fucking poodle, no need to get racist about things," the pug snarled.

"I am? I mean a poodle, I'm definitely not racist."

"Yep, nothing has that much stupid curly fur as a full-sized poodle does. Hey, could be worse, you could be a toy poodle, right?" the pug said.

"I'm… a poodle." Chris sat back down with a defeated flump.

"Yep. By the way, my name's Sal, nice to meet you and all that. We can sniff butts if you want," said the pug.

"Why in the hell would I want to do that?" Chris demanded, standing up and backing away from the little pug a bit.

"I don't know, we're dogs, it's shit dogs do," Sal sniffed.

"I do not want to do dog shit."

"Didn't seem to stop you last month," Sal snorted under his breath, which isn't particularly easy to do for a pug.

"What does that mean?"

"Listen never mind, we won't sniff each other's butts if it will make you feel better. I don't know if I could get my nose that high anyway, too much chance of a disaster jumping up to try. Let's talk instead. I'm guessing you got questions, huh?"

That froze Chris for a second. Yes, he had quite a few questions, endless questions, but which one to ask first? Before he could think of how to say it his voice overrode his brain and said, "What, the actual fuck?"

"Quick, concise, and to the point, I like that," the little pug grinned. "Well to answer your question, we, are werewolves. There you go, simple as that. Bet you got bit one night recently, and don't tell me, it healed right up, right? Kept waking up naked?"

His brain still in shock, Chris responded automatically, "We are not werewolves." He held up a fur-covered paw, "Does this, in any way shape or form look like a wolf to you? No, it doesn't, it looks like a fuzzy designer mutt to me."

Sal was quiet for just a second before he said, "Yeah, not wolves per se, not wolves exactly. More like what happens after you cross-breed and domesticate wolves for thousands of years and then get weird about which traits you actually want to keep. I'll grant you that. More, were-dogs, but definitely were something or others."

"But... how?"

"Fucked if I know, they don't give out pamphlets, 'Hey you turned into a dog!' I mean, I normally weigh 250 pounds, but three nights a month this is what I'm stuck with. Where does the rest of me go? That would be the thing I'm fucked if I know about. I go with magic, because what in the hell else can you go for, right?" Somehow the pug managed to shrug. He looked around and then added, "Come on, let's walk some, just sitting out in the open is just asking for trouble, we're listening in human, but all other humans are hearing is a couple of mutts growling and barking outside their window. While we walk I'll see if I can't give you some practical pointers on dealing with your new lifestyle choices."

They started walking without talking for a while down the sidewalk in what looked to be a suburban neighborhood, which meant Chris was probably not too far from home. Chris thought of something else that was bugging him eventually, "How can I still think like a human? I thought werewolves became, well, wolves."

The pug nodded a little, "I got theories on that. For the first month, maybe as much as three or four depending, you got no idea at all what's going on. It's too much for your mind and you act like a dog that's having an adventure. But the thing is, a dog, well men have put a lot of mankind into a wolf to get a dog, haven't they? We teach dogs commands, they learn words, all kinds of things. So the mind isn't that far off from a human anyway. At some point, your human mind just accepts it and wakes up. Either that or some people are just vicious bastards and enjoy being vicious wolves and let the wolf brain run things when they're changed and maybe some of the dogs you used to run into are just us, other were-dogs who never woke up. I've known some of us who were going through some emotional stuff where the dog just takes over for a while, even after they realize what they are. It's like their repressed human mind needs the break from it all, anyway. I figure overall you must have your shit together."

"Except for the fact that I am now a were-poodle," Chris said bitterly.

"Well, yeah, except for that of course."

———————

Suzanne felt like shit, and not just because she was learning her way around a new neighborhood, and let's face it, that puts everyone off their game. No, it wasn't learning which deli was best, Suzanne felt like shit about herself in particular. She shouldn't have just up and ran this time, it was the wrong thing to do. But once she had, she didn't know how to put it all back. It was instinct, you had a problem like that you left it in the rear-view mirror. She really did like Chris, quite a bit, and just pulling up stakes and booking was cowardly on her part, but she'd panicked and let her instincts run things. It was especially cowardly considering the other part of what was nagging her.

She couldn't remember it, but the more she thought about it, the more she was pretty sure she'd bitten him.

The end result was that she'd more or less left someone she was also pretty sure she cared about more than a lot to figure out how to be a werewolf all on his own. Lord only knew what kind of dog he'd been changing into if she had bitten him. Oh no! What if he had turned into a Boston Terrier? That would be ADORABLE! But the point was that even in his safe little neighborhood, he wouldn't stand a chance of survival on his own. Heck, stray cats might eat him. She knew for a fact that there were worse things out there than just cats. Which was why tonight she was carefully making her way around her new neighborhood to find out who lived here. This was not her first move that she'd had to make in a hurry.

But what if she had bit him, she should be checking back there to see how he was getting on…

First things were first, she lived here now. If she wanted to keep living anywhere, that meant knowing the lay of the land. Chris would have to wait.

———————|———————

"So what do I have to watch out for in this new, exciting, and exceedingly curly-haired life of mine?" Chris asked as they trotted down a gravel road between two rows of houses.

"Well, you almost never really see animal control, it ain't like the comics where there are dog catchers everywhere. I mean, especially not at night, people expect dogs to slip out at night, right? And nobody wants to have to rush to the pound to save their dear Fluffy so they don't get euthanized. But, I'd still probably avoid official-looking vans, cops especially, for that matter. You don't want to be changing back in a kennel now do ya?" Sal replied before snuffling at a telephone pole.

Chris couldn't help it, he chuckled at the thought.

Sal interjected quickly, "Look, humans, in general, should be avoided. Like, let's say you see a guy you hate, just loathe him, remember what I said about us losing control when strong emotions were involved? Now you're stuck with that asshole for the rest of your unnatural life in an even smaller community. But most importantly, avoid the big dogs."

Chris actually slowed his pace in confusion, "The… big dogs?"

Sal snorted, "You know, Shepherds, Pinschers, that kind of thing. Most of them look at smaller dogs as dinner. Say they're the only real werewolves and us smaller breeds are an abomination that should be annihilated. Pleasant crap like that."

"But they're dogs, too!" Chris barked.

"And everyone being human has stopped a racist when? Look, to get back to your survival guide, the only things that can kill you are silver and other werewolves, so even though with your size you might be all right, who knows what those assholes think of poodles, even full-sized ones."

They trotted on in silence for a while, it seemed they were just moving aimlessly. Finally, Sal said, "Hey but it's not all hardship, there's a lot of shit only dogs can get away with you can't do wearing dockers. Tearing up somebody's garden, chasing raccoons, we could find a bitch in heat, we could..."

"Wait, what was that last one? You don't actually do that do you? That's fucked up!" Chris gasped.

"That's not what you thought last month when you were all dog," Sal sniggered, which a pug is uniquely equipped for.

"What!" Chris yelped.

"Keep your fucking voice down will ya? Someone might hear ya! Anyway, it'll be at least another month before we find out for sure if there are any mixed breed poodles around here," Sal replied as he started trotting off.

"Dear God help me," Chris whined as he followed behind him. He was pretty sure the pug was just screwing with him, but that was the problem with memory gaps featuring so heavily into last month, try proving it.

Chris woke up on the floor the next morning. At this point he wasn't exactly shocked, a bit bummed it had happened again, but at least he was inside. Man, he felt beat. Sitting there blinking his eyes for a moment, he decided that the reason for that had to be the insane dreams he'd had last night. No doubt about it, those had to be dreams. Like he was running around all night last night with a talking pug, sure he was. He was also the queen of England if his dreams were to be believed. He had always wondered about that particular dream. Still, you always feel like you barely got any sleep at all when your dreams were particularly vivid, so him being a little under the weather made sense in that context. Dreams were one thing, reality was another, and reality said it was a work day.

Work was more or less boring. It had that working for the weekend

Friday feel, sure, but it was still pretty boring. Maybe even worse because the boring was between everyone and the weekend. Since the call center he worked in was open on the weekends, not everyone thought of Friday as a proper Friday, anyway. So those folks put an automatic damper on any premature celebrations on the part of those who were getting off. Chris didn't even know how long he'd still have a Monday through Friday shift either, it was only a matter of time until somebody realized he didn't have kids and suggested that they needed another guy from resources working weekends. Until somebody brought it up, he wasn't going to say anything, that was for sure.

He toddled back home once the day was done; his initial plan had been to go over to Jake's, but with his dreams and everything, Chris was feeling more than a bit wiped out. Jake had suggested they go do something cool tomorrow maybe get some mountain biking in. He wondered about that, maybe Jake was trying to build up his outdoor stamina for another run at Hannah. Chris had agreed but had caveated it by saying unless his being tired today meant he was coming down with something. Jake had responded, well of course we won't go mountain biking if you're coming down with something, what the hell, are you stupid? Chris had responded with, that's no reason to be a bitch about it.

This went on for quite some time, because now two male best friends had reached the insult portion of the conversation, and look, while some authors might be looking to pad their word counts, we aren't that desperate. Yet. If it gets that bad and our publisher leans on us we'll do two paragraphs describing some hedges or something later, overall it would probably be more interesting and not involve the words "booger face."

Back home Chris decided to take a nap, he figured an hour or so on the couch watching TV, well, in reality, dozing off in front of the TV and he'd be right as rain. Which was a weird phrase in and of itself, 'right as rain.' If rain is right, what's wrong? Snow? Sun? Digressions by the author right in the middle of the story like this? He clicked on a movie on Netflix he'd already seen twice, and just like clockwork, within moments he was snoring.

He didn't know how much later it was when he woke up. All he knew was that he was burning up from heat and that he suddenly itched like crazy. When he was finally, fully awake he noticed first that he had kicked off his socks and his shirt in his sleep already, and even with that he still felt like he was in a sauna. Chris was confused and groggy, but in that mindset, he wondered if he had gotten something on himself somehow and that the best solution would be to wash it off in the shower.

Shucking his pants off he finally noticed his skin. More importantly, he noticed how much less of it he could see. Hair had been sprouting out like mad all over his arms and chest, and...

Oh no.

Nononononononono! This couldn't be...

He felt something crack in his leg, causing him to drop to the floor with his pants and underwear down around his ankles. Something in his face decided to join the hideous cracking noise festival. It hurt, or more, it felt and sounded like it should hurt, sort of like when you bang your elbow on something, and you say, "Ow" only to realize that it didn't actually hurt, it just made a loud noise. Exactly like that, but *way* more intense, like intensely more intense. Chris could feel hairs sprouting everywhere, which itched like crazy. He could feel bones rearranging themselves which felt weird, and cracking and snapping as they did which was even weirder, but it wasn't actually painful. It sounded like it should be, when he thought about what was happening he was positive it was, to the point where he let out a low moan even. But when he stopped panicking for just a second he realized it really wasn't painful at all. Not even the part where the tail started coming out of his ass, which even describing it here sounds painful. Looking back to see it happening on your own tailbone? Major shudder.

When it was over, Chris said the only thing that sums up finding out that it wasn't a dream last night at all and you really are a were-poodle.

"Fuck," he said.

Well, now what? He was, in point of fact a were-poodle, unless this was another dream. If it was, that didn't really matter since he was currently starring as a were-poodle in it. He almost howled his frustration at the concept, but then he remembered he had neighbors. Old neighbors on top of that, ones who would definitely notice a dog howling in his house, assuming he hadn't howled in the house the other times he'd turned into a… turned into… turned… turned into… a… poodle. The other times he had turned into a god damned poodle.

God this was embarrassing.

Dickheads from corporate probably got to be huskies if they got bit.

CHAPTER 4

————|————

"He's not going to make another 70's music reference, is he?"–
everyone reading this book under the age of 40

Having decided that he wasn't going to just sit inside all night feeling furry and sorry for himself, and frankly looking forward to peeing wherever he pleased, Chris made his way for the back door. This led to another problem, every time he'd opened the door previously he'd been operating on animal instincts, and frankly, he had no damned idea how he'd managed it. Clearly, it was doable, he'd done it, now if only he could figure out how that had worked.

First Chris tried the most obvious solution, clamping his jaws on the doorknob. Which caused his teeth to immediately slide around the brass doorknob in a way that felt decidedly uncomfortable, like icky uncomfortable, not painfully so. Not only had it not been the solution he had been hoping for, even if it had seemed obvious at the time, he'd also left the doorknob all covered in dog spit to boot. He had obviously had no problem opening it when he'd been a dog, so he wasn't going to let this setback daunt him, but he was going to try and remember to hit the doorknob with some cleaner tomorrow.

Unfortunately, the next obvious solution was his paws. He still wasn't fully comfortable with what he'd have to do to make that work. First thing he'd have to do was 'sit.' It felt humiliating on some deep-seated level, 'sit' was a command we gave dogs we were training. He wasn't a dog, Chris kept trying to remind himself of that, he was just a person wearing a poodle's gangling, fuzzy body. Nothing unusual about that at all, so he needed to stop thinking about that too hard in case he started screaming. Which would come out as howling which would only make things worse. The other part that bothered him about sitting, he didn't like the idea of his bare anus being planted on his hall carpet.

As much as he tried, Chris just couldn't see a non-sitting option available. He planted his rump in front of the door before rising up on his haunches putting himself in a position he tried not to think of as "beg." It took a bit of scrabbling, but at last, he was able to get one paw under and one paw over the doorknob itself. Pressing his pads down as hard as he was able, he pulled with the lower paw, and pushed with the upper, straining to keep pressure in this awkward position.

The door popped open smoothly.

You would have thought that Sal would have been decent enough to mention wanting to get a doggy door last night. Of course, Chris didn't think this was really happening to him when he woke up this morning. So, in Sal's defense, it wouldn't have made any difference if the pug had said anything. Speaking of Sal, it was time to see if he could find him to see what other wisdom the pint-sized pontificator might deliver. Chris carefully pulled the door closed behind him with his teeth stopping just before it clicked fully shut. Noting that now he had to clean the outside knob as well, Chris sighed and jogged off into the night.

Outside presented him with an all-new question, how to find Sal. The little pug might be rude and crude, but he was also the only one Chris had met so far who had any idea what he was going through. Sal had no problem finding him last night, he had practically told him point blank that he'd been keeping an eye on him even last month. So, the question was, how had he done it? Also, speaking of questions, who was barbecuing this late at night? The smell was driving Chris's stomach mad with desire, he could practically taste the burning meat where he stood.

Oh yeah, smell. He had a vastly superior nose now.

He put his nose to the wind and inhaled deeply, which started him sneezing and walking in circles. It was all too damned much; he'd have to learn to separate out all the various scents and what they meant or he'd never be able to do much with the one major upgrade this shape came with. Until he'd figured it out, for the moment, trying to track by scent was out. Not knowing what else to do, he moved out onto the sidewalk and got trotting in the direction he remembered coming home from last night. He'd just concentrate on working his sense of smell out along the way or cause himself severe doggie sneezing fits the entire time.

As he got further away from his own house, he began to increasingly get whiffs of other dogs, especially near open lots and fire hydrants. Other dogs, sure, but so far, nothing that smelled like pug. He might be new to this whole dog thing, but pugs had lot of rolls and weird breathing problems and... nothing else quite smelled like pug. Even if the pug in question had been human-shaped only an hour before, pug smell worked that fast. Even humans could smell pug, Chris had to believe that for him, with his new nose, it would be a neon beacon.

Chris kept trotting in that general direction until he had started to move out of the suburbs where he lived. Office buildings were beginning to stick up here or there changing the view. Not only that, the smells were getting more overwhelming by the moment. He was considering turning around when he heard, "PSST!" coming urgently from a strip mall to his left. Chris froze dead and considered his situation here. There was no traffic and there were houses across the street from the strip mall itself. Ahead was another strip mall, this one larger with a huge Wal-Mart as its main store. He considered which way would be best to run if that wasn't a friendly "psst," Sal had warned him about other dogs.

"Over here dumb ass, I was just heading your way to get you!" said Sal's obviously annoyed growl.

Chris practically trembled with relief as he headed toward the dark corner at the back of the line of shops. Sal stood there practically bouncing with tension. "We gotta go," the pug growled, "unless you want to find out on your second conscious night if the big dogs are willing to give you a pass because of your size. Cause if they ain't, you're gonna be fighting for your life in a couple of minutes. So maybe we gotta go now, huh? They raid the dumpster of the Mexican place for food, and I sure as hell don't want to be here when they show up."

A short distance away, behind the row of shops, they heard a loud bang. Such as might be made by a dumpster lid being lifted open and released.

"RUN!" wheezed Sal before darting toward Chris' neighborhood as fast as his pudgy legs would carry him.

For all that Sal had been running as fast as he could, Chris had barely had to trot to keep up with his smaller friend. They needed to take a break after a while just for Sal's sake. Which meant that now that they were a few blocks away, hiding in the bushes of a ranch house with the porch lights off, Chris was waiting patiently to see if Sal would have a heart attack right there and then.

Eventually, the pug got enough breath to say, "Why in the hell didn't you stay in your own neighborhood ya' dumb mutt!"

"I was looking for you!" Chris protested. "I looked over my neighborhood, and there was no sign of you!"

The pug snorted, "Look at my legs, how fucking fast do you think I could have even made it there? Anyway, I had to avoid the pedigree pups if I didn't want to end up Rottweiler poop."

"You didn't say how far away you lived. How was I supposed to know?" Chris' tail drooped between his legs as they started walking again.

"Well, you meant well, that's the important part I guess. Good thing I found you when I did though, God knows what would have happened if you ran into them. Avoid them at all costs until you get your paws under you, that's my advice."

"So, what are we doing tonight?" Chris allowed his ears and his tail to perk back up a bit.

"Tonight... tonight you get to meet the pack," Sal snorted.

Chris followed Sal further into his own part of town. Now that he had time to appreciate things, he was trailing behind the little dog looking and sniffing in wonder. The implications of what he had heard were of this vast were-dog of various breeds world and society that had been existing without anyone knowing it. A monochrome world of heat and smell that Chris had never even considered as a possibility. Even if you had a dog you didn't spend a whole lot of time thinking deeply on dog social structure. Even more surprising was the idea of that exact world existing in his own neighborhood without him having a clue. It was like finding a lost Amazonian tribe hiding out in the local Whole Foods. It was a good thing that were-Lhasa Apso bites were rare, because as many nights as Jake had been over at Chris's and they'd had too many and decided to go walkies... Frankly, it was a surprise that neither of them had been bitten years before this.

Sal walked up to a chain-link fence around a local park and without saying a word started squirming under it in a spot that had been broken at some point in the past. A moment later he was standing on the other side shaking himself vigorously. Turning back to Chris he said, "Okay, you nex... oh, that's gonna be a problem, ain't it?"

Chris took one look at the tiny hole Sal had been able to wriggle through and could only agree. "Yeah, no way I'm getting through that."

Sal thought about it for just a moment, "Hold on, there's a gate a little way down from here, you can nose it open, easy!"

"How easy?"

"Look, I ain't asking you to use that great big body to leap the fucking fence, just nose a gate open. Now come on already, the night's wasting."

Chris snorted with disgust, causing him to make a mental note to control his emotions better. It was a lot harder to hide a thing like that when you were a dog, every little movement had intent, and that snort had a lot of it. Sal had to notice it and was just making allowances. Annoyance aside, Chris wanted to show willing, he needed friends, so he trotted along as Sal ran at a breakneck pug speed down the fence line. He didn't want to seem ungrateful. Sal had been his guide through all of this so far, he'd be losing his mind completely without him. But still, they were going to have to start making adjustments for each other's size differentials if this was going to work out long-term.

Chris saw the gate that loomed up a short distance away from them. Sal was right, it was one of those easy to open park gates and it wasn't locked. So, despite any annoyance on Chris's part, it was easy enough to nose open so Sal had been the one in the right there. If anything, Chris was surprised it was even closed, half the time you saw them left open. Out of some weird sense of propriety, he nosed it back closed once he was through.

Turning he found Sal waiting for him, "See? Hell, if you can open a house door, something like that's a piece of cake. I had faith in you."

Before Chris could answer, Sal had turned and was heading deeper into the dark of the park itself. Chris did the dog equivalent of a shrug and followed. Now that they were inside the fence with the smells of other dogs wafting over him, Chris wanted to chuckle. Even though they were mystical creatures — humans turned into legendary monsters by the light of the moon — it would seem that enough human instinct prevailed. They had located themselves inside the local dog park because that was where dogs belonged. Chris thought he could see a discarded tennis ball with chew marks on it protruding through the grass and couldn't help but notice the instinct that told him to grab it and chew it more. It warred with the other part of his mind that told him to pick it up and throw it.

Sal let out a tentative woof. A moment later, it was answered from ahead of them. Four small pieces of the darkness detached themselves from the shadows resolving into four equally small dogs.

"Meet the pack," Sal said pride infusing his growls and yips.

A Scottish Terrier, a Dachshund, Miniature Pinscher, and a Miniature Pomeranian that was so small Chris didn't notice it at first when it came slinking from the shadows. Sal continued in his spokesman role to make the introductions, "Hey guys, this is Chris. Chris is new to all this, and even though he looks like a full-sized dog, he is still a poodle with no intentions of eating anybody. Right, Chris?"

Chris, who had been having a hard time fully accepting and believing he was really seeing the group of small dogs in front of him in relationship to the word 'pack,' jumped a bit. "What? Oh yeah, no eating anybody. Hi!" he tried to put some enthusiasm into that last bit, but it sounded lame and forced even to him.

Sal ignored him and introduced the others, "This is Trish, Gavin, Todd, and Vince, collectively we are the Pack. It's a good idea to be a pack and stick together, look out for one another these days. Only way to keep yourself from ending up like poor Tony."

The other dogs whined a bit at the mention of the absent dog's name. This was not a good sign, but at that point, you just can't stop yourself from asking the question, "What happened to Tony?"

This brought more whines from the pack before Sal cut in and said, "He decided to have a night out by himself a couple of months ago. Torn to pieces by a German Shepherd."

Chris, yet again, couldn't stop the question from falling out of his muzzle, "But what happened when the sun came up? Were there like pieces..."

Even Sal whined a bit at that before answering, "Uhhh... yeah... no. Despite what you see in old movies, you stay whatever shape you died in. God, can you only imagine. I mean it was bad enough as is, Tony being a Shih Tzu... fucking fur everywhere..."

This time Chris caught himself before he made any of the Shih Tzu jokes that leapt like graceful dolphins to the front of his mind. Everyone else was in a moment of sadly quiet contemplation on the scene of poor Tony's demise, so he took advantage of the moment to take the pack in. He was thrilled that the only girl was a miniature Pomeranian. Sal had been hinting darkly at dog sexual escapades since he'd met the pug and he had been avoiding that train of thought completely. At least with the only female of the group being that small, it would most likely be physically impossible to even consider. So, that was one less awkward thing to worry about.

"Hey new pup, what's your story?" said a feminine-sounding voice causing him to come out of his thoughts to look back where the other four were. It had to have been Trish. There was a problem there...

"You're Trish?" he said with far more surprise than he really wanted to.

If a dog could be considered to chuckle Trish managed it, "I know, it's the Scottish Terrier thing. It makes me look like I have a beard."

"Trust me she looks completely different as a human," the Pomeranian piped up.

"I should think that's fucking obvious Gavin," the Dachshund growled.

"And that makes him my husband Gavin, since he knows what I look like when I'm not so furry," Trish added quickly, ignoring the Dachshund.

"So that leaves Todd and Vince," Chris said.

"Yo bro, I'm Todd, and I sure as hell wouldn't want to be Vince bro. Bro doesn't take care of himself, he even gets drunk before the change," the Pinscher interjected, practically vibrating with energy as it talked.

The Dachshund gave the other dog a withering look before turning to Chris, "And obviously I'm Vince, and you'd get drunk too if the rest of your night was going to involve your dick constantly catching on gravel."

Chris blinked; he couldn't help it. Finally, he managed to stammer out, "You know, I've never even considered that."

"I wish I'd gotten this far in life not having to," Vince replied morosely.

Wishing to change the subject immediately Chris said brightly, "So what does the pack do for a few nights a month?"

"Come out here to the suburbs, run around, chase a few cats. You know, dog stuff," Sal said. Chris couldn't help but notice that at the very mention of the word run, Todd was practically shaking even more violently with pent-up energy.

"Why not stay in the city, why come out here?"

"Big dogs, they run the city with an iron paw. Parts of the real serious country too, I guess. Haven't checked myself. This is about the only part of the area that's safe for us. I keep telling my wife we should get a place out here, but she wants to be close to my sister," Sal replied.

"Does she know…"

"Come on, enough of this yammering bros. We got the park, let's get our run on. Come on big fluffy bro, show me what you got!" Todd interrupted as he started bouncing in anticipation. Before Chris could even respond to the miniature Pinscher the dog took off into the night leaving a scent trail behind him that was so vivid to Chris' new senses he could practically see it.

Chris hadn't even decided if he wanted to run before the smaller dog took off. So it came as a total surprise to him when his body ignored his brain entirely and acted on instinct to go scrambling off after the little bolt of black fur. The other dogs couldn't help themselves either, he could hear them behind him tearing up the grass to keep up. His human brain wanted to be annoyed, Todd hadn't asked if it was time to run, he had just decided for everyone. The problem with that was the rest of him was overjoyed to let his new muscles really cut loose and just run freely. No restrictions, no anything, just the joy of feeling a body designed by nature to run being able to do it to the best of its ability.

He was so lost in the moment that he ignored Todd's yips at first as he closed the distance between them. He still ignored them as the group fell behind him. They were falling further behind when Chris realized those weren't just excited little dog yips and that Todd had been saying something. What he had been saying had been, "Bro!" But he had also been throwing in "Bro?" which is completely different. It dawned on Chris that maybe he should see what in the hell the mini-Pinscher wanted.

As he slowed down, he noticed that he had been circling the park and that the other dogs had stopped in various places. Including Todd, who just stood there wheezing out, "Bro" over and over. Chris was surprised when he felt his tail tuck between his legs as he trotted over to the other dogs.

"Your first real group run, huh?" Trish said from where she sat grinning as he came up.

"And that's fine," Gavin added as he caught up to Trish, "but you really shouldn't get too far out into the dark parts of the park by yourself."

"That's what I was trying to tell you, bro," Todd snorted.

"Yeah, he might be Okay though, look at the size of the fucker. I mean ain't it funny Todd, you're the little version of a big dog, and he's the big version of a little dog," Vince said from where he had rolled onto his back on the grass.

"What's that supposed to mean, bro? You wanna go?" Todd growled.

Sal quickly interjected, "But that's what I was trying to tell you guys. Chris is actually big enough to be safe without us. If he only runs into one of those assholes, you know they're pussies on their own. Hell, remember that husky that ran off from us when we all went after him? No way one of them would go after this big guy on their own."

"Sal does have a point," Gavin agreed.

"What I wouldn't give to have those legs," Vince said before he started snoring where he lay.

Some time later, it was just Sal and Chris ambling down a lonely street. The other dogs had trotted off to where they lived, or in the case of Gavin, been picked up by Trish and carried at a trot. Not too long from now the two of them would split up as well. Chris was already worrying a bit about Sal getting home, but the pug assured him that it wasn't too far and he'd be fine. It had to be true what he'd said about having a route that was completely safe. Chris couldn't imagine for the life of him a pug being able to flee; or worse, fight off anything that was more mobile than a turtle.

"So, your wife knows about this?"

"Yeah, she deals with it pretty well, all things considered. She even makes sure I can get in all right, I ain't got your height advantages to let myself back in," his companion replied.

"And you haven't bitten her yet?"

"Kid, you ever been married?"

"No, of course not. I haven't even had many serious relationships," Chris was taken aback by the suggestion.

"Trust me, you try being married for thirty years and then tell me you feel like biting anyone. I fuckin' dare you."

"Ahhh…"

"I mean, I love her with all my heart, don't get me wrong. I mean if someone ever threatened to hurt her, you know I'd bark and growl and all that shit, but, biting? Those days are behind us, hell, after the third kid was born, if I even gave her a kiss that went on too long our brats would give us a dirty look. You just get used to living without the passion. Or, you get really good locks on all your doors, those are your choices," Sal expounded.

"Good locks?"

"Kids never fucking knock. It was a miracle we found time to make three of them. You'll find out one day."

"Not likely, I mean considering my recent handicap," Chris sighed.

"You'd be surprised kid. I mean look at that whole Twilight crap, chicks find that werewolf aura sexy," Sal chuckled.

"If only I was a werewolf. A great big, powerful sleek timber wolf. Instead, I'm more of a werepet, which can't be sexy to anyone."

Sal was quiet for a while before saying, "Well, yeah. Okay, I'll give you that. But hey, chicks love poodles right? There's a girl out there for everyone. I mean Trish ain't left Gavin yet, and he's what? Basically, a powder puff with eyes, right?"

"God I hope you're right. It'll be hard to build a relationship on, '… and I can never see you three nights out of the month, and I really like you, so stay inside, Okay?' I mean, what girl would go for that?"

"You'd be surprised kid, you'd be surprised."

Day three started like any other, which means he was naked and had somehow curled up on the floor again. Which was stupid, there was a perfectly good bed, a perfectly good couch, and here he was naked curled up on the floor. Was this some kind of bred into dogs' behavior? They knew they didn't belong on the couch at some deep instinctual level? He would have to find a way to get it through to himself that the bed was fine. Or at least the couch, maybe he could leave dog treats up there or something, and lure himself in.

One unfortunate part to waking up and knowing immediately what his being on the floor and nude meant, it meant those weren't dreams. They were fuzzy memories, like somehow not everything translated from canine back to human. So they could only be dream-like in his memory. Just not dream-like enough to still believe they were dreams. So much of the information must be brought in by smell and hearing and nuance and all kinds of doggy shit like that. When looked over the next morning by his human mind, there was just no way to make sense of it all. He had been able to piece together enough at this point though that he couldn't deny it happened anymore. His mind still tried hard to make it make sense; like he was pretty sure that he and his other sufferers of lycanthropy hadn't been talking using English words, or Spanish for that matter. Things were just translated using scent and posture and small noises that he thought he remembered everything he could still recall as if they were words.

Fellow sufferers of Lycanthropy. He could see the ads now, 'Friends, is this you? (shows footage of person turning into a Shar Pei) You are not alone, there are hundreds of your fellow sufferers of lycanthropy out there! Are you tired of waking up on your floor nude? Try our new always-fit pantsuits, guaranteed to shrink down to dog size and expand right back the next morning! No more running for your house with your hands over your privates because the dog door jammed!'

To be completely honest, Chris was pretty sure he'd be first in line to buy something like that.

Speaking of dog doors, his jaw ached from trying to open and close the door with his teeth. He had a project for the day. He needed a damned dog door. He'd worry about how he'd explain it to Jake later.

CHAPTER 5

———————|———————

"It's a dog eat dog world out there"– *George Donner amateur meteorologist*

The shiny new dog door had been installed, which meant sweat along with cursing had been achieved. Chris did not consider himself especially handy around the house, so this had been an adventure for him. He had been forced by the necessity of owning the place and not wanting to go broke to get much better at it over the years than he had ever thought possible. Better than he had ever thought possible still left a LOT to be desired. His dad had left a lot of tools, but even with the power to do things, Chris would have never listed home repair as a strong suit. It hadn't been for Dad either, but the man had tried; the consequences of many of those projects still afflicted Chris to this day. This little project had pushed what little handyman abilities he possessed to their outer limits. It had even involved power tools, most of which quite frankly frightened him. His shop teacher back in school, Mr. Wilmore, only had three fingers on one hand and loved to inform students what a power saw had done to their missing mates. That kind of thing leaves an indelible mark on the mind of an eighth-grader.

But there it was a shiny new dog door. His damp shirt and potty language had yielded results. And if he ever found an actual cure for this he would be better suited for dog ownership. He'd certainly be able to empathize with the thing far more than a normal pet owner could, Chris'd seen the world from the other end of the opposable thumb crowd. Thanks to his labors, in a couple of hours when the moon came up he'd no longer be at risk of chipping a tooth or hurting his paws. He wanted to be proud of himself. Instead, he sighed inwardly. He had managed to do only one positive thing to deal with his new reality and it involved putting a fucking dog door in.

That led to another series of questions. Was he just going to accept this? There had to be some cure for it, some way to control it, otherwise, the entire world would be crawling with weredogs. Of course, who was he to say it wasn't? He didn't know everyone's personal lives. He barely understood his own anymore. But that was something he could do with his remaining time fur-free today he supposed, he had the internet, he could research werewolves. How hard could that be?

Fifteen minutes later, he came to the conclusion that there was a ton of bullshit on the internet. You would have thought he'd have already known that considering he was an adult, but some people need to be reminded the hard way. Also, a lot of really weird porn, which he couldn't help but linger over for the same reason you slowed down at car accidents. He found some stuff on a psychological condition of lycanthropy, and that would have made his day if he believed it was all in his head and that was what was happening. That would have been a great conclusion to this, it's all in your head, go see a shrink you loon. Problem with that was unless there happened to be all those other people who had the same psychological issue that met at the dog park, odds were it wasn't all in his head. Not totally impossible, but not likely. Hey, what was a cult but a shared delusion? Of course, those usually took charismatic leaders, and that left Sal right out. What he didn't see a lot of was cures. There was wolfsbane mentioned a few times, and good ol' wolfsbane combined the handy features of being both rare and incredibly poisonous if misused, so not a lot of help from that sector as far as finding something he could get done by tonight.

Speaking of which, he couldn't help but notice that the sun was setting.

Turning into a dog wasn't as uncomfortable tonight, thank God. He knew to expect it, and knowing is half the battle GI Furry Joe! It still wasn't a happy, joyous occasion, but it seemed that the mental jump from seeing colors to smells was less abrupt, his mind made the transition more smoothly tonight. He also decided that he needed to take cleaning more seriously. This place smelled like an armpit being wedged against a crotch in August. It may not smell like that in the daytime, but it did now. No wonder he had been so desperate to get out of here when in poodle form that he could figure out the door.

Speaking of leaving, the way to solve that problem lay in his newly installed doggy door which was begging for its maiden voyage. It was a bit snugger than expected, but he guessed that the idea was that dogs are better squirmers than burglars were. Fido can leave, but your TV won't. Or, maybe he should have also gotten an alarm system while he was at it. Still, for one more night it should be fine, he couldn't remember the last time a house was burglarized on this block. Anyway, he figured the doggie door should lower the attraction of the place since dogs make noise and bite. Well, other dogs did, he had yet to bite anything and hoped to keep it that way. If he infected some other poor soul, lord only knew what they'd be showing up at the park as next month. You couldn't help but wonder if you had civil liability for something like that.

Now that he knew to head for the dog park he bypassed looking for Sal or anything that could lead to adventures. He didn't go straight there; he did make some stops around the neighborhood to tell the other dogs he lived there. Chris didn't see much point in roaming around aimlessly too much, what was he even going to do? Other than pee and sniff a lot, which could be done on his way after making a few specific deposits to claim his territory. There was too much chance of chaos at this point in his doggy life. At least at the park, he had a support group, his personal "Werewolves Anonymous." He wasn't really a dog, and he certainly didn't know how to act like one. Trying to get to know real dogs might be something for later, but he'd probably make a hash of it if he tried now. For all that matter, his experience with k-9s told him that a lot of the stuff they really enjoyed doing was kind of gross, like rolling around in deceased raccoon bits. So, all things considered, maybe staying with his own was for the best.

He ran into Sal as he was reaching the gate to get inside. "Good thing you got here when you did. Damned gate's closed again and someone fixed the fucking fence. I don't know how in the hell the rest of them are getting inside, but I didn't feel like sitting here crying until somebody lets me in."

Chris dutifully went over and nosed the gate open for them. "So what's on tonight's agenda, more running?"

"Naw, not tonight. Tonight we're gonna go out on the town some," Sal replied, trotting through the open gate into the park.

"Oh?"

"Hold up, this is my bright idea, but instead of explaining twice, why don't I tell everyone, huh?"

Just like last night, the other dogs trotted out to greet them, except for Vince who more weaved out.

"Hey guys, wanna do sumthin' fun tonight?" Sal said to the group after greetings were out of the way, which was met with various degrees of, "Yeah, sure."

"Cool, there's a pizza joint not far from here that I like. The little woman called in a bogus order just a little while ago, and guess what? They toss that dead order stuff in the dumpster behind the place. Think about it people, pizza with a dog's taste buds," Sal beamed at them.

"Cool idea, but how in the hell are we gonna get it out of the dumpster?" Trish demanded. "Dumpster lids are high up, and we aren't."

Sal looked meaningfully at Chris.

"Yeah, how are we gonna pull it off?" asked Chris like an idiot. Right after he said it he realized all the other dogs were staring at him. "Wait a second… I don't even know if I could successfully get into a dumpster when I'm human, let alone…"

"That's your problem buddy, that's what we need to cure. You need to start thinking like a dog while keeping that wonderful human intelligence," Sal replied.

"I know how we do it," Trish said.

"Do what?" Vince said, he hadn't been paying attention and had been drunkenly trying to clean his privates with his tongue, which had mainly resulted in him falling over a lot.

"Never mind Vince, you'll like it," Sal said.

"All we probably have to do is have one of us jump on Chris to get the lid open," Gavin mused.

"Bro! Let me do it, bro! I can totally do it! I mean look at these pecs!"

Chris couldn't help but stare at the Pinscher in amazement. How often did you really get to see a dog flex?

"Are you sure we have to do this?" Chris asked.

"Yes, we do. We're dogs, dogs steal crap from the trash, and you need to act more doggy. Also, pizza is probably fucking delicious with this nose," Sal said with finality.

The rest of the dogs moved after Sal as he trotted into the night, leaving Chris to mutter, "But using a complex plan doesn't sound very fucking doggy to me…"

"What was that buddy?" Sal called back.

"Nothing."

The pizza joint was a few blocks away, but they were able to get there without incident by staying to the shadows and diving into people's yards whenever a car came. They also managed to set a couple of pet dogs to barking with their presence. Chris thought it was pure jealousy on the part of the other dogs, any one of them would give one of their paws to be trotting along behind the pack right now instead of indoors or tied up outside. On the other paw, Chris would be thrilled to change places with their owners who were probably watching Netflix and having an adult beverage of their choice. Who was living their best life was clearly all in your perspective.

The place Sal had told them about was closed when they got there, which was probably for the best. Chris didn't think most Italian restaurants did that Lady and the Tramp crap. Thinking about it, it was kind of a weird stereotype, saying Italians just naturally gave spaghetti to stray dogs. Walt Disney was weird enough to think it was realistic, even as a kid Chris wondered about ol' Walt.

It was nothing short of humiliating to stand there like a statue while Todd scrambled onto his back using him as a step stool to get up to the dumpster. All he could do was just try and stay still while the miniature heaved himself up repeatedly. He let out a minor yelp when Todd finally got some purchase by grabbing some of Chris' fur with his teeth and then scrabbling up the rest of the way by kicking his legs around wildly digging into Chris' sides.

After what felt like an eternity, though he felt him hop off, meaning Todd was on top of the dumpster. "Oh, no shit bros. The back lid was already opened!" The small dog clacked across the plastic and peered inside. "Score! There's a couple of boxes in here, let me drag them out."

The pack sat and listened to Todd grunt and growl as he got a hold of a box that was within his reach and worked it onto the dumpster lid. At last, they could hear him panting but only Chris could see him. "All right, that's one, I'm going back in."

Sal called up, "I don't think we need more than one, so...."

He was interrupted by a yelp and a soft-sounding thump from inside the dumpster.

Echoing from inside, they heard, "Lil' help?"

Chris groaned before heading to the back of the dumpster. Hopping up to put his front paws on the lid, he could just look over to see Todd standing there on a pile of boxes out of his reach. He hopped back down and looked to the others, "We could do a chain I guess; I could lower someone in and Todd could grab on."

Vince shook his head and moaned, "Fuuuucckkk, I'm the long one. Todd, you owe me so much for this you shithead."

"I ain't no shithead, take that back man!" Todd growled from inside the dumpster.

"You want to grab onto me to get out?"

"Yeah, of course," Todd replied.

"Then I'm not taking it back," Vince said. To Chris, he said, "Just dangle me over the edge, I'm the longest he'll be able to grab my hind leg. If he grabs my dick by accident, drop us and leave for a while, because I intend to bite the hell out of him."

Chris looked for a second and had to consider where in the hell he was even going to grab the wiener dog. Dogs in his experience had collars, if you had some sudden need to direct the dog to some other location you used the collar.

"Grab him by the scruff of the neck, it's how mamma dogs move their puppies, it's how I carry Gavin," Trish supplied guessing correctly at Chris's confusion.

"I knew that," he said, secretly thankful because he absolutely did NOT know that. He should have since he'd actually seen Trish carry Gavin that way, which made it even more of an embarrassment for her to remind him.

He reached down and tried to gently pick the other dog up, only to have him slip right out.

"You really got to use your teeth dude, don't sweat it because for one thing I'm still drunk, and for another, mother dogs do this all the time, like Trish said," Vince said helpfully.

With no choice open, he gripped the scruff of the other dog's neck tightly and lifted. Nobody could have been as shocked as he was when a second, later he was able to lift Vince off the ground.

"Good deal, now just put your paws up on the edge of the dumpster."

Still shocked that Vince wasn't screaming to high heaven about this Chris did as he was told. The other dog was heavy, but he was surprised at how well his neck muscles and front flanks responded to the extra weight, it just took another bunch of muscles to hop up and he was able to bring Vince up with him as he put his paws on the lip.

"Flop me over the side," Vince told him.

"Yeah hurry the fuck up already," Todd called from nearby.

"Fuck him, take all the time you need," Vince interjected.

It took a couple of tries to finally get the wiener dog flopped over the side of the lid since Chris was doing this on a feel more than sight. Chris winced every time the other dog's hips banged into the side of the dumpster. But finally, when he heard yet another thump it was on the other side of the metal. It was followed by, "Not so hard, asshole!"

"I gotta get a grip, bro!"

"Yes you do, but you don't have to bite my fucking leg off!"

A few moments later he heard Vince, "All right new guy, pull us up."

It took Chris a long moment to figure out how to even do that. He couldn't just lift his head up and bring them up, they weighed too much combined. Eventually, he had to settle on taking his paws off the lid of the dumpster and doing a combination of oozing down and occasionally hunching his shoulders. His only evidence of progress was when a cheer went up from the other dogs.

A moment after that Vince said, "Okay, you can let go of me now new kid."

Chris looked up to see Todd standing precariously on top of the dumpster, with Vince still dangling from Chris' teeth.

"Stay still and I'll hop down bro, and then let's eat!" Todd enthused

In defense of the whole fiasco, pizza did taste a lot better as a dog. He hoped he remembered to have some delivered to the house half an hour before the change one day. Also to not tell Sal that he had, since this would probably constitute some grave crime against doggyhood, using his human daylight powers to acquire pizza. Then again, Sal had his wife call in the fake order, so maybe not. Maybe he should leave it on the table so he'd have to reach up to steal it later like a proper dog or something.

After that, it was more or less back to the dog park for a normal romp. Later still the gang began to go their separate ways leaving Chris with Sal trotting alongside going towards Chris' place. "Well, I guess that's it until next month, huh?"

"Yeah, I mean, when you get older, my age, you get used to having friends you don't see except for once a month at most. You being younger, it probably seems a bit weird and all. But, look at it this way, you're with us for three whole nights, you'll get to know everyone a lot better soon enough."

"Let me ask you something."

"Shoot kid."

"Does Todd ever stop acting like a bro douche?"

Sal thought for a second and said, "Naw, not that I've ever noticed. I mean, deep down he's a good guy, but up top at the surface, a total douche. Alright, kid, this is my stop, I'll see you next month." With that, Sal crossed the street and headed off into the night.

They had called it a night kind of early tonight, so Chris was on his own. He still had more than enough time to goof off a bit if he wanted. Give the dog door a spin, chase a squirrel, go by Mr. Barry's house and howl for an hour to make up for the time the old grump called the cops on one of the rare parties Chris threw. He had possibilities and was considering exploring them some. He was just about to trot in the direction of a certain easily irritated pensioner when he heard a yelp coming from the way Sal had gone.

His first instinct was to ignore it, it could be any dog, hell it could be Sal and he just stepped on something gross or pointy. Streets usually had plenty of both available so it would be a good guess. When Chris kept thinking about it, Sal did not strike him as the type of dog who would yelp at just about anything. He definitely had an aura of "been there, seen that, rose my leg and peed on it" about things. It might not even be Sal, but Sal had been vital to Chris trying to figure out his new life. He'd befriended Chris and made everything so much easier for him. If the little pug was in trouble and he ignored it he'd never forgive himself.

Chris found that even though he hadn't heard another noise, he had no trouble figuring out which way the pug had gone. His nose did a magnificent job of pointing him to the trail. This was the first time he really had to depend on it for something so that he wanted to concentrate on just one scent, and he was amazed. It was like there was practically a line drawn on the sidewalk telling him every single step the smaller dog had taken. It wasn't seeing, yet it still felt like he could practically visualize the trail floating hazily in front of him.

Chris followed the scent into an alley where he froze at what he saw. A much larger dog of some kind, possibly some kind of husky shepherd mix, had Sal frozen in place against a wall. Every time the little pug would try to dart one way or the other the bigger dog would take a step or two to cut him off. Even from where he was he could see Sal was shaking, he could also smell urine from where the poor guy's bladder had cut loose.

Unbidden a growl rose in Chris' throat.

The other dog quickly shot him a glance. If anything the dog seemed to smile, well, at least his teeth were showing and his tongue was lolling out. He barked back at Chris, "You want to share? Don't look to me there's enough of this little freak to go around. We'll be doing our kind a favor getting rid of him, but you might have to just get your own."

That's when it dawned on Chris, this must be one of the big dog werewolves Sal had told him about. He didn't want to fight the other dog, he wasn't sure what the results would be, but if he engaged him at least a bit it would give Sal a chance to run like hell.

"I want you to leave my friend alone," he growled.

The bigger dog seemed to chortle at this, his tongue hung even longer in amusement, "Your friend? Dude, I got news, except for the stupid fur you were blessed with when you got bit, you ain't got nothing in common with a rat like this. I'm putting this one out of his misery, consider it me doing him a favor. I mean look at him, he can barely jog without panting."

"I said back the fuck off," Chris barked. After he did, he froze for a minute, he was shocked to find that his fangs were bared.

The other dog was still chuckling as he turned away from Sal and towards Chris. Sal took advantage of the respite and darted away, down the street. The husky called after the fleeing pug, "Run all you want snorty, I got yer' scent now. After I'm done with him, I'm coming for you." Then back to Chris, he said, "Fluffball wants to be a badass? Well, let's see what ya' got buttercup. After I take you down, I'm grabbing your pal anyway."

Chris froze at the change in the situation. He wasn't a fighter as a person, let alone in a canine form that he was still coming to grips with. He had been strictly middle of the road in school, not a target or the targeter, he'd gone along to get along most of his life. Now, it looked like he would actually have to get into a fight for his friend's life, in a form that he wasn't 100 percent sure he knew how to operate. His only operating manual for it was currently running like hell to get away from here.

Then he thought of the alternative, him getting savaged by this brute, and Sal getting worse. Just for doing what they were built to do, be dogs out on the town doing the kinds of things like dogs love to do. That was bullshit! They hadn't done anything to this asshole, but he was going to treat them like this? Chris felt his fur stiffen along his spine, well, as much as his curly hair could stiffen, maybe visually nobody could see, but he could feel it rise.

"Looks like you have some fight in you, after all, I was sure you were gonna bolt the second you had a chance," the husky continued to grin, his tongue continued lolling out dripping saliva as he came closer.

Chris barely had time to notice the gums pull back from the other dog's teeth before the brute launched himself at him. Chris did the only thing he could think of, he ducked. He could feel the other dog's claws clip his ears as he went over, feel the heavy fury body that would at any moment come crashing down on him and give the other dog the advantage. He did the only thing he could do, not having any other ideas he closed his eyes instinctively, reached out with his teeth, and bit the first thing that his jaw came into contact with hard.

Panicked, squalling yelps erupted from the other dog almost immediately, claws started scrabbling at his back.

Chris opened his eyes in shock at the noise. It took him a moment to realize what he'd bitten, but it certainly explained the yips and yowls and yelps above him as the other dog's paws flailed to try and get off and away from him. Disgusted Chris let go of the husky's balls.

A moment later the pressure on his back was gone and the other dog took off running, yowling as he went, until his cries diminished into the night.

Chris was still trying to get over the shock at what he'd done when Sal came out of the shadows to sit down next to him.

"Bit him right in the family jewels."

"Gross."

"Right in twig and berries."

"Shut up about it."

"Took a chunk out of his golden nuggets."

"SAL!" Chris cried out.

"All right, all right, but that was fucking brilliant. I wish I had my phone to film it. If he ever recovers he is going to be *pissed* at you, but so fuckin' worth it!" Sal chortled. "I really didn't think you had that shit in you. Good time to find out you did, wouldn't you say?"

They sat there for a moment while Chris recovered a bit from the first serious fight of his life. He spent that time trying to wipe his tongue with his paw and making gagging noises."

"And kid?"

"Yeth Thal?"

"Thanks a fuckin' million, that bastard would have torn me right the fuck apart. You saved my ass kid."

"Ooo wan me to walk oo ome?"

"You know something? Just this once, my ticker can't take too many scares like that. If I keel the fuck over from a heart attack, at least someone will be around to keep me from getting thrown in the trash.

And just like that, it was over and Chris didn't have to worry about becoming a poodle again for twenty-eight days. It was like he had taken a three-day weekend from his own species. Which reminded him to look up when full moons were happening and to start scheduling his paid time offs around them. He almost never took an actual vacation, so they'd piled up on him, leading to numerous hints from management about spending a few PTOs anyway. Since normally he took paid time off because he had to when too many piled up which was a stupid reason, having a day to mentally recuperate or prepare for being a poodle all damned night did not seem stupid to him at all.

It also meant that he could do something on weekends again for a little bit. He knew that something was going to be hanging out with Jake, providing of course Hannah didn't take him back, but it would be nice to do something. Maybe they could go to a bar or a club or something and he could fail miserably at meeting new women. Chris knew that was what would happen, he had long since given up on the optimistic, "Maybe I'll meet someone." bit. He was shy, and that was the way of it. Meeting Suzanne had been a fluke where they had been the only two people in a Chinese restaurant for lunch, she had gotten bored sitting by herself, and decided that Chris looked lonely. By which she meant, she wanted someone to talk to and he was there. It was only dumb luck that they'd hit it off as well as they had.

At least he had his Sunday free this weekend. Of course, he had no idea what in the hell to do with it, but it was free. Maybe he'd give it an hour or two and see what Jake was up to. He scratched that thought, Jake would have been drinking last night, better give it until noon at the earliest.

Suzanne was sitting in her apartment looking at her phone. She was looking at her phone because she was debating calling someone. She was debating calling someone because there was a new dog in the city. Word travels fast in the werewolf community, and even though he lived in the burbs, and she was a sizable distance from there, whispers had reached her.

A new dog that had first been spotted soon after she had left.

Out near the burbs.

Not that she was sure...

But maybe she had suspicions that were getting to be more than suspicions now.

CHAPTER 6

———————|———————

"Team building is the key to a happy workplace, also Kevlar helps a lot."- *The US Postal Service, unpublished training manual (1989)*

Jake and Chris were in the park throwing the baseball around. It wasn't because of any deep-seated love of the game or anything, it was just something they did when they were kids when they couldn't think of anything else to do and adulthood had not given them a reason to change this particular habit any. In Jake's case, adulthood hadn't managed to change most of his habits, it had only added beer and weed to them. Chris tried very hard to not resent his friend for being overall happier and enjoying life more than he was, but when Jake was going through a story about throwing up on a famous person's shoes and still getting a selfie out of the deal, it was hard.

There had been a brief pang of guilt when they had walked past the dog park attached to the park they were using. It felt like an accusing finger pointing directly at him. Chris felt stupid about that, what in the hell did he have to feel guilty about anyway? It wasn't like he exactly *wanted* to become a fucking poodle three nights out of the month, did he? And if he was going to be a poodle, well, of all the things he could be doing, running around a dog park with some mutual sufferers was probably the least offensive. At least, that was the logical train of thought he tried selling himself. But he still knew why it made him feel guilty deep down, even if he didn't fully form the idea in his head yet. He was keeping secrets from Jake. They had been friends ever since they were little snot-nosed boys, all the way to them being here as big snot-nosed men. Before now the idea of not telling Jake everything that was happening in his life would have been the dumbest idea Chris had ever heard. Of course, before now he hadn't been a cartoon parody of some terrifying beast of myth, legend, and lots and lots of horror films, most of which he'd watched with Jake. He had no idea what in the hell to do about it, how do you even begin that conversation anyway? "You know those three nights I said I had plans? What if I told you those plans involved raising my leg to pee?"

"So, when you going to get back up on the relationship horse?" Jake demanded as he whipped the ball towards Chris.

Chris knocked it down instead of catching it. Years of doing this and it was always up in the air if either of them would actually catch the ball instead of just knocking it to the ground in a last-minute act of desperation. They had spent a lot of their time in little league sitting next to each other on the bench. Neither of them was dishonest enough to tell potential girlfriends about how they could have made it in the big leagues if only a nagging injury hadn't slowed them down. Both of them were content with the knowledge that a nagging injury could have only improved their quality of play.

"Jesus Jake, are you gonna ask me when I'm going to give you grandkids next? If my mom was alive you'd sound just like her, but you know, more bass to your voice," Chris replied as he sent the ball hurtling back the way it came and discharging his responsibilities to it.

"You gotta' do it sooner or later. Otherwise, your right arm is going to get overdeveloped man, and people notice that shit. Not to mention, I can't wait to hold the little miters in my arms and spoil them rotten on their day with Granny Jake," the ball came flying back. "You even met a filly you want to cut out of the herd?"

"That sounded gross and sexist," Chris replied as he went looking for where the ball had gone.

"So sorry woke-meister general. A she/her person of the female persuasion willing to overlook your multitude of shortcomings long enough to make the monkey with two backs more than once. Happy now?"

"That was only marginally better," Chris replied throwing the ball back.

"It shows personal growth on my part. Maybe one day I'll be fit for human company," the ball came flying back in Chris's general direction.

Chris paused for a second in shock to see the ball actually in his mitt this time before replying, "Not likely, not in this lifetime. Hannah forgiven you yet?"

"The ice is thawing. That's it, you and me are going out tonight." Jake replied as he caught the ball, two catches in a row was probably a sign of the apocalypse.

"God help us," Chris replied making a stab at the flying orb that was returning, saving life as we know it by missing and letting the ball fly by.

"Not tonight buddy, I don't think this is his department."

Chris did not want to be at a bar. He wasn't even sure if it was a bar, it had a DJ, people were dancing. The only reason to think of it as a bar was that it just didn't seem large enough to be a club. You couldn't smoosh the words bar and club together to describe it with either, car was taken, so was bub, clar just sounded stupid. He had already told Jake that hell or high water, he was calling them a cab at 11, so Jake absolutely shouldn't vanish. Jake agreed, told him no problem, and almost as soon as the words exited his best friend's mouth Chris could no longer see him anywhere.

Chris was hanging out at the bar proper since he really didn't dance but he did drink. He'd been goaded into attempting to dance at various times by various women, and it was universally agreed that it was not a good look for him, usually by those same women. The time that he and Jake were double dating at a club years ago, and the girls had called over a very flamboyant gay guy who had danced by just to help them critique Chris' dancing had felt entirely uncalled for. Accurate, sure, but uncalled for.

He was sipping a beer and trying to catch fleeting glimpses of Jake when he realized he wasn't alone. Like, he already knew he wasn't alone, there was a bar full of people here, more that he wasn't alone in that there was someone sitting next to him who had not been there before and they didn't seem to be leaving, like, that not alone. He turned to a very pretty blond woman who was a little older than him who had sat down and was sipping on some kind of flavored seltzer looking at him.

Chris felt her scrutiny boring into him so he said as sheepishly as he could and still be heard over the music that throbbed away through the building, "Hi!"

"Hello," she replied, her facial expression not changing.

Now Chris felt at a loss, which is why he always tried to keep a hold of girlfriends, and preferred meeting girls in less meat market settings. Opening gambits was where he tended to be the worst at these things. "Hi" was the beginning and end of his repertoire. Maybe he could say his name or ask hers, but he was running out of ideas already. If the well on his public conversational skills wasn't dry, he could definitely see dry stone down there. He absolutely refused, under threat of death to say, "Come here often?"

Finally, she broke the stalemate, "I haven't seen you in here before."

"Huh? I don't think I've ever been in here before. My friend Jake dragged me in here, 'to help me out' and then he vanished," Chris said with a shrug.

"I'm Trish," the girl said holding out her hand.

Chris took it politely and said, "Chris."

She smiled, "I thought so, I'm here with my husband, Gavin, he's in the little puppy's room."

Chris took a moment to get over the realization that he had been barking up a taken tree when a furthermore important realization dawned on him. "Oh," he said by way of reply.

Just then a hand dropped on his shoulder. "Let's go, you said you wanted to leave by 11, I called us a cab, they're outside," Jake said tugging him towards the door.

"But..."

"Next time don't give us a curfew," Jake said tugging harder. Trish disappeared from view within moments.

They were crashing at his place tonight. If they were going to do an all-nighter together Chris preferred his place which had a spare bed. Jake preferred his place because…something about preferring his game controllers to Chris's. Chris rarely viewed Jake's controller preferences as a sufficient reason to give Chris back issues by making him sleep on a shitty couch. Jake had tried to argue his case, but Chris was not having it. Anyway, he pointed out, his fridge was stocked with beer and he had multiple bags of Cheetos which more or less crumbled Jake's already weak defense.

When they walked in the door and Chris hit the lights he noticed something he'd forgotten about before he'd gone out tonight.

Unfortunately, Jake, did not, "Dude, what's with all the dog hair?"

Chris just stared at it in horror for a moment before quickly blurting out, "Shit, I completely forgot, I was watching my neighbor's dog for an afternoon a while back."

"And you didn't vacuum?"

"Wait, are you questioning my housecleaning? So, I forgot some dog hair because I didn't feel like vacuuming! I have found a bowl of macaroni and cheese under your couch that had a live mold colony on it before I threw it out, so I don't think I need the tips, Martha Stewart," Chris fumed happy to be back in more familiar territory, namely Jake's pigsty of an apartment.

"I'm still pissed about that macaroni you know, " Jake replied solemnly.

"You're what?"

"I had named that mold Larry, I was gonna teach it to do tricks."

Chris sighed, "Turn on the game system, I'm gonna go grab us a couple of beers."

Chris had just gotten home from work when he was surprised to hear his doorbell ring. It wasn't quite Girl scout cookie season, and Jehovah's Witnesses didn't come to this neighborhood after what the

Andrews' metal head son did to them that one time. It was only lucky all around that the cop who came after the Witnesses called 911 had a good sense of humor about everything.

Chris couldn't help but approach the door with trepidation. This was a digital world; human interaction had been reduced to something you could control. People talked online; they didn't show up unannounced like this. Well, except for Jake, but he would already be in the house and on his way to the fridge to get a beer if it was him. The world had been getting like that before, but covid had just enforced the behavior in everyone's head. God, he hoped it wasn't the police. He couldn't think of anything illegal he'd done lately, or much of ever, at least not while in human form, but still. Okay, he'd been outside naked a few times, but with the dog door, that wasn't exactly lately.

Chris carefully looked out the peephole after remembering he even had one. Standing on his step was a short, slightly overweight man. He was bald, but since it was a nice day, he wasn't bothering with a hat. The most dominant feature of his face with his rather large dark mustache. Chris had no idea who he was, but he was so relieved that it wasn't the police he was pulling the door open before he could stop himself.

"Hello? Can I help you?" Chris demanded, staying slightly inside the doorway.

"Hey Chris," the shorter man said.

Chris was just about to demand how this person knew his name when it came to him, he knew exactly who it was. It could really only be one person, he was perfectly how Chris had always pictured him, except for maybe the mustache.

"Sal?"

"Good guess kid. I know we try to keep our little three-day weekends separate from the rest of our lives, but I figured we should talk. Can I come in?"

"Umm yeah, sure I guess," Chris replied stepping away from the door.

Sal stepped inside and automatically looked around, "Nice place you have here, clearly you ain't ever had kids."

"Ohhhh kayy…"

"No weird stains, mine are all grown up now, but there's still spots on the rug where I don't know what in the hell happened. I still find Legos, too," he smiled.

"So what…" Chris waved his hand.

"Do you owe this amazing pleasure? Simple, with me almost getting jumped last full moon, we were thinking of renting a place on this side of town. Not a house or nothing, like maybe a garage. The walk from where it's safe to where it ain't but we live there…well it ain't safe. So, since we got to all go in on this together to make it work, we figured, well…we should all officially meet. I mean, I know you now that we're meeting and all, and I know Gavin and Todd. Todd knows Vince. Gavin obviously knows Trish. Maybe we should socialize with less fur on. I bet those big mutts do it, and we kind of need to stick together more than they do," Sal explained.

Chris nodded, that made sense to him. "It's not a bad idea, all of it makes sense. I think I've met Trish already."

"No kidding? You do her?"

"What? No! She's married for the love of God!" Chris protested.

"Like that stops people," Sal harumphed.

"You are being a pig," Chris chided.

"A dog for three days and a pig for the other twenty-eight, ain't that the life? Well, before I go, I figure we could exchange numbers, play some phone tag, and set a date," Sal said with another smile. Chris strongly suspected he was saying stuff like that specifically to get his goat, Chris only hoped that one day he wouldn't rise to the bait so readily.

"Ummm yeah sure, but do me a favor, keep a lid on the doing Trish comments when she's actually in the room, huh?"

"For you kid, anything!"

After considerable phone tag, they had finally all agreed on a local chain restaurant to meet for the first time on two legs. One of those places that show their food a lot in the commercials, but really, their main selling point was that they had a bar to go along with those overpriced burgers. These kinds of places specialized in after work or lunch meals for young workers who were stressed to the gills but not paid enough to go to an actual nice restaurant. The kind of people that still really wanted a beer to unwind, but considered themselves far too professional to go to a bar.

Chris recognized the waitress when he walked in the door. He wasn't proud of that fact, it made him think that maybe he needed to expand his horizons a bit. Unfortunately, he could only think of places that were for all intents and purposes exactly like this one to host this many people, and at least they knew what he liked here. Technically, he was a millennial, or maybe Gen Z, he was borderline, and the press swore that his generation was destroying these places, but the reality was he hated cooking and it was on his way home from work. Sometimes generational solidarity had to bow to simple expediency.

Chris stood there for a moment, looking around when he saw Sal waving from a table across the room. He had just started forward when the hostess saw him and asked, "And how many for you tonight?"

He came up short and then said, "Oh, I'm with a group, I guess they didn't feel like waiting, they're already in there."

Whatever she said next, or if she said anything he didn't hear. He was already moving in the direction where the group was seated. Chris felt like he was sneaking in at moments like this. Like he had gotten around the invisible line that separated respectable diners and the outside world without paying the fare of waiting to be called. He had to move past people who were sitting on benches waiting to be seated holding the little buzzer things, Chris imagined he could feel their envious glares at the back of his neck as he vanished into the restaurant's dim lighting. He felt no pity here, who actually waits for a table at one of these places? If this one was busy, there were twelve identical ones within a twenty-mile radius.

When he got a little closer, he finally got to see the whole group. Sal he knew, Trish he'd met, Todd was obvious by his large beard and muscular physique, which left him to guess at Vince and Gavin. This was not made easy by the fact that there was a similar-looking professional-looking man in his thirties on either side of Trish. This meant that any assumptions he had made as to what Vince and Gavin were like based on how they were as dogs were dead wrong.

Sal saved him, "Everybody, this is Chris, say hi!"

It turned out that Gavin was the one with piercing blue eyes, while Vince's eyes were a brown that went with his light brown hair. Gavin was not small in any way, and Vince was drinking water tonight. At least Todd was exactly what Chris had pictured Todd being, in fact, there was no other way Chris could have possibly pictured Todd as looking. He was a bro as a dog, and in human form, he was still a bro.

"Alright, we know why we're here and all, to pool resources and look over some garages in the area.," Vince said in a businesslike manner. Everything about his entire manner was like that, which made it hard to square with the sloppy drunk dachshund they normally dealt with.

"Do people really rent out their garage?" Chris asked.

"You would be fucking shocked kid. A lot of people have dream cars, even in a city. You don't want to park that in front of your house, the animals would key it in a week. So people in the burbs who have the space, they rent it out, we actually got a few we need to go through," Sal said sagely.

"A garage is a garage, isn't it?" Gavin asked.

"You would think, but we have special circumstances to consider," Vince replied. "Ease of access in and out, considering we won't always have thumbs to work with. Isolated enough that we won't have neighbors calling animal control. Clean enough that we won't mind waking up naked on the floor. In our case, a garage needs some special amenities."

Trish nodded, "It'll be cold concrete if we don't bring some cushions. So how gross the floor is could be the difference between keeping those cushions or not."

"And I need transit in the morning, gotta hit the gym bro. I don't skip because of werewolf reasons," Todd added happy to be making a contribution.

"Of course Todd. We might want to also consider just parking our cars nearby. We'll be able to drive in the morning," Vince said patiently.

Todd looked dumbfounded for a moment, "Yeah, I suppose we could do that too."

"Do you have any especially likely prospects lined up? Or was the plan to check everything close by?" Chris asked.

"Ah, that's where I come in. I'm a whiz at real estate," Trish perked up. "I brought my tablet so we could all look."

Since Trish claimed to be a whiz at it, once a decision had been reached on a place, they had sent her to rent it out and see if she couldn't chisel a bit off the price while she was at it. Chris was beyond relieved that they'd all agreed on something, especially since he had a garage which Sal had been nice enough not to mention to everyone. He was still desperately trying to keep the werepoodle aspect of his life separated from the rest of his life, especially from his home located in a neighborhood of nosy, bored old people. He was still trying to maintain a world where the elderly people who lived in his neighborhood continued to think of him as 'that nice Richtor boy' and not 'that curly-haired bastard who keeps pissing on my begonias.' If we wanted to maintain this delicate balance, housing a convention of toy breeds in his garage was not the way to go about it.

He had visited the garage with them to see it before they rented. It wasn't as far from his house as he would have hoped, less than a mile, but at least they weren't using his actual garage. Chris had the decency to feel like he wasn't being a great friend here, but he reminded himself that none of them were putting up anybody at their house. This was the one solution that minimized all of their personal risks but kept them from having to walk through the parts of town that the big dogs had claimed as their territory. Territory they threatened to protect with bloodshed.

The month had gone and the change was coming any day now. He had stashed a spare set of clothes in the garage just in case. He wasn't paying for the place, but nobody seemed to mind, and having an emergency port in the storm couldn't hurt. They were all going to change there tonight, which would be an amazing spectacle, but one Chris would be forgoing from the comfort of his home. He was still self-conscious enough about changing to want to do it without an audience. Even if he was there he wouldn't be able to fully appreciate seeing the others change anyway because of all the fur and teeth he'd be sprouting all on his own, so he wouldn't be missing much.

Which was what he was doing at that exact moment. It seemed like the length of time between full moons was exactly perfect to make you forget that you had this to look forward to, making it all that much worse. By week two, you were almost able to convince yourself that this was all a weird recurring nightmare you were having. People didn't turn into werewolves, let alone were-domestic dogs. But in the week leading up to the full moon, you started getting tense, looking at your calendar, dodging personal messages already shutting yourself off. Your sleep suffered. You tried and failed, to put it out of your mind, you couldn't ignore it, you knew it was coming.

And then one night you were traipsing through a dog door into the cool summer air.

As Chris expected, the gang was all there at the park when he got there. The place they'd rented was closer than his place, but even before they'd always seemed to manage to get there sooner. As much as he tried to tamp down the call of the wild and everything, it was still his own neighborhood that he had to pass through. He needed to make sure that all other dogs knew about that fact and respected his territory, and he had made sure to drink plenty of water in the day leading up He couldn't help but wonder what would happen if he bit another dog, would it become a different dog every full moon? A person? Best to never find out.

Everybody had more energy tonight; they hadn't had to walk here from their various homes in town. Skulk and sneak might be a better description of their previous journeys, but regardless they hadn't had to do that either. Consequentially they also looked more relaxed, but it would be hard not to be all things considered. They hadn't had to hide the entire time in terror they might be found out by one of the big dogs for once. They had started coming to this neighborhood in the first place because there weren't any big werewolves in this part of town, and now they were starting their night here never having to so much as consider them. In reality, there was technically a big dog here, but he was one of theirs and therefore didn't really count. Vince even looked halfway sober.

The best part of the night was the fact that nobody looked apprehensive or worried when it was time to leave to go to the garage to change back. There weren't huskies waiting for them in every alley for a change.

By night three, Chris was willing to admit that maybe he had been mentally overreacting about his worries over his were-life and his life-life getting too close. In fact, he hadn't even realized how bad it had been bugging him until he also realized it shouldn't be. The reality was, the last few days were the most fun they'd had as a group. The other dogs were freer and more cheerful now that they had the threat of being turned into a ball of fur and blood on their way home removed from their general mental makeup. They'd even gone into some of the small areas of woods that could be found nearby, which was something they'd never felt like they'd had time for before.

They were rolling around in one of the safer parts of the dog park, at least in terms of dog logs to avoid, getting ready to call it a night. It was actually a shame; this had been a great weekend. Chris had gotten to know his companions in the curse a bit better. Vince, now that he was relatively sober, turned out to be very smart and almost urbane. Gavin had a great sense of humor which is what made him such a great match for Trish, who loved a good laugh. Sal, it turned out had been behind the whole idea of getting the garage, when Chris had prodded him on it, he admitted it was because he worried about Gavin being so small and Vince being drunk going home. Even Todd had some good points. Yes, he lived in the gym, but he actually took it seriously, he even had a degree in sports medicine and some serious personal training certifications. And his fitness freak thing was not even just because he wanted to look buff, he said the actual chemistry of how the body did all this stuff it did was cool. Of course, with his totally one-track use of his intellect, he still said bro a lot, so Todd hadn't totally changed. There was just a topic you could direct him toward where he didn't sound like a total idiot.

It was a shame to let this go.

It was at this peaceful moment when their sensitive ears picked up the quiet growls on the other side of the fence. Big dog growls, and more than a couple. All of the smaller dogs along with Chris were on their paws in an instant.

"Oh, shit," growled Sal.

"Succinct, and to the point as always," Vince replied.

"What do we do bro?" Todd asked.

Chris thought fast, "Sniff hard, see if you can pick up their scent, and where. The garage isn't far from here, and I know the streets. Once we're inside and the doors closed we should be able to hold them off."

"Here's hoping none of them know about gates," Gavin replied.

A voice came out of the darkness in almost a snigger, a canine snigger, "So here they are! We got worried about you. We ain't smelled our little pound puppies all through the moon. Thought you might have gotten picked up by the dog catchers or something."

The voice materialized into a Rottweiler, dark and sleek and powerful. This monster looked like he not only could beat up the junkyard dog, he could also give the junkyard car crusher a run for its money. He was followed by a Doberman pinscher and a husky who seemed to be walking with a bit of a limp.

CHAPTER 7

————|————

"Feels good to have a few dogs 'round the place"– *Ma and Pa Kettle Go To Transylvania*

"Oh shit," Sal whimpered.

Chris didn't even bother to think about what he did, he just bolted for the other gate that was situated behind them, leaving his friends to gape at him in shock at his abandonment of them. He didn't look back at them as he ran, there was no time to explain. When he got to where he needed to be he quickly nudged the gate latch open before running back, completing his goal before they even had time to ask why he'd done it or even to chase after him.

"Man, I thought you'd left us to rot," Todd said as soon as he got back.

"Yeah, that's what I thought too," an unfamiliar voice barked. "You must be the bitch that made Jerry walk funny. Jerry wants a word or two with you about that," the lead dog of the trio added as they reached the other gate. He appeared to be laughing as he reached up with his snout and began to prod at the latch, trying to figure out how to open it.

Chris turned to the others and said in a low growl, "Will you run like hell already?" There was a clank as the latch fell open. Chris added, "I'll catch up if I can, but just go! Get!"

His friends couldn't help themselves, the word 'Get!' reached something deep in their doggy brains and automatically kicked their paws into gear.

Chris turned back to the other dogs who were just making their way into the park. He was glad at least that he could hear his friends running away behind them. Which just left him with all new things to worry about, like hoping to not get torn limb from limb here for starters. Now that he got a good look at the non-injured members of this pack it seemed a distinct possibility. He let out a low growl and began to back up towards where he knew the other entrance to the park was, hoping he could get close enough to be out and gone before these three crossed the oh-too short distance between them.

The Rottie let out what sounded like a chuckle, "Looks like your buddies ditched you there fluffball. That's Okay, don't think any of them would have been good for more than a snack anyway."

"What the fuck is your problem?" Chris barked loudly as he continued to back away from them.

This elicited another chuffing noise of amusement from the Rottie. "Look, we're supposed to be werewolves. I mean, am I right? I mean at least you're an actual dog unlike the rest of them freaks. I mean, if a dog catcher shows up, can they run? Fuck no they can't, at least not fast enough. Someone figures out we exist, can they fight them off, tear 'em apart so nobody ever knows about us? What are they gonna' do? Gum somebody's toe? They aren't real dogs, and they are a fucking liability to all of us. Bet you know where they're running, don't ya'? Tell you what, you save us having to sniff them out and lead us to them, we ain't got no reason to fight."

Jerry the limping Husky had something to say about that, "Hey fuck that Koy! That fucker almost bit my nuts off! I want his ass!"

The rottweiler turned and barked loudly in the injured dog's face, "What I'm asking for is more fucking important than you losing a fucking fight you started Jerry! Get with the fucking program!"

A light suddenly turned on in one of the nearby houses, followed by a porch light. A human voice yelled out into the night that hid them from view, "Get out of here you dogs! My wife's calling the damned pound, and I got a gun!" It was clear from his silhouette that he was indeed holding up a rifle of some kind.

"Shit!" barked the Pinscher who had been quiet up to now.

The three of them didn't turn back towards Chris until they heard the gate bang shut behind him.

Chris was running as fast as his paws would take him the second he got the latch to fall shut on the gate. It was only a delaying action at best, but at least it gave him a small head start. The next part of the equation was; where in the hell was he going to run to? All things considered, this could be a majorly important piece of information his brain had not supplied him with yet. His damned brain had just yelled, "Run like hell!" and had washed its hands of the rest of the situation. He couldn't run home, there was no way he could keep the pack out of the house with that dog door. Well, maybe, if he just bit every snout that poked through the dog flap, he could possibly keep that up for the rest of the night. The downside there, and it was a very, very big one, was that they'd know where he lived. He'd have to operate like a prisoner every full moon, trapped inside for fear of who was waiting for him.

On the other paw, they wanted him to lead them to the smaller dogs. If he ran directly for the garage he'd be leading them there just like they'd asked. They had rented the place for it to be their sanctuary for this time of the month and he'd be fucking it up during the first moon using it. On the other, other paw, the garage had a pull-down strap, and would the big dogs even be able to get the door back open? There'd be just a metal handle on the outside, it'd be rough on the teeth to try and lift it.

He heard barking behind him coming in his direction.

Oh well, hopefully, they'd forgive him for having to rent another garage.

He put on as much speed as he could to try and keep those barks as far back as they were now, or even better, stretch that distance a little. Huskies ran fast, but theirs had a limp at the moment. Thankfully Chris was the one who knew the neighborhood, so he was the one who knew when he was turning. Every corner he took on two paws put a little more distance between the bigger dogs and himself. Shortly he could see the open garage door in front of him with his friends standing there looking worried. They looked more worried a moment later when a new round of barking behind him let them know he wasn't coming alone.

"GET BACK!" Chris barked as loudly as he could. At the last possible moment, he slowed down exactly enough to jump up and grab the dangling strap of the garage door. His body twisted in the air as the forward momentum of his torso kept wanting to keep going, his teeth held and then he swung back and dangled from the strap.

The door only moved a bit, and the barking was coming closer!

"Grab onto him!" Sal barked.

Chris yelped through his clenched teeth as he felt the other dogs gab onto his hind paws and his tail. He could also see the shape of the big dogs rounding a corner up ahead and putting on speed to trap them all.

Thankfully, he enjoyed that horrific view only for a moment when the door finally got moving and slammed shut.

Chris lay on the floor of the garage panting around the strap in his mouth.

"Christ almighty that was close!" Sal gasped.

The barking was near now. All of them jumped when there was a loud thump on the garage door.

They whimpered when they heard the voice of the Rottweiler bark, "Why are you making it so hard on yourselves? We're gonna' get you oversized rats eventually!" It was quiet for just a second before they heard the low growl through the door, "You ever see what a cat does to a mouse? Make it easy, or we're gonna' do that to you. Come out now, you get just a quick snap of the neck, I promise."

Chris heard teeth click. He immediately pulled back on the strap and a second later he felt the tension as one of the dogs was trying to pull the door up. Chris dug in his haunches and tried to hold firm, but because of the angle, the door slid up just a little. The snout of the Pinscher popped under the door a moment later. If the big dogs shoved themselves under just a little and pushed up, no way would Chris be able to hold them.

Trish came up with a temporary solution at least. She snapped out of her frozen fear and pounced on the dog's snout, sinking her own teeth deep into his flesh. The dog let out a howl of anguish as her fangs worried at him. The Pinscher was starting to buck to pull back when she let him go. The snout vanished leaving a trail of blood behind it. The yowls of pain could be heard retreating in the distance.

His snout was replaced instantly with a foaming snapping Husky one. It would have been a great plan to keep snapping like that to keep the smaller dogs away if it wasn't for one thing. Dachshunds are bred to go into a weasel's hole and to flush him out. Vince instinctively leaped onto the snout, mouth wide, fangs bared, and began snapping down quickly and powerfully. In only a few moments there was another retreating set of yowls, and another streak of red they'd have to clean up if they didn't want the police to come around with questions.

It was quiet for a second before suddenly the pressure was gone on the door and it banged shut. They could all hear the growl of the rottweiler outside, "Alright, my buddies pussied out, and I can't get the door open without them. I guess you win this round. But mark my words you little abominations, one of these nights I am gonna catch you without your big fluffball buddy. And then it *is* gonna be like a cat with a mouse when I do. Sooner or later, I'm gonna be there when you least expect me."

They all listened intently to the sound of his claws clicking away from the door. As a group, they lay down and panted for a while once the noise was gone.

Eventually, Todd yipped, "Bros did you see that? We totally kicked their asses!"

Trish groaned, "They found our space, and almost had us cornered in it. This was only a victory in the strictest moral sense, in that I always wanted to bite one of those assholes."

Todd would not be deterred, "Bro, that's the only victory that matters. Anyway, it'll be better next month."

"Why? How in the hell is next month going to be any better?" Vince said, taking a break from trying to get husky fur out of his mouth.

"Oh dude, we can just do the three nights out at my folk's farm.

They've been begging me forever to spend more time out there," Todd said happily.

Gavin groaned, "Why didn't you mention this before we rented the garage, Todd?"

"Well, I didn't want to seem stupid. You guys really liked the garage idea and all. I figured you'd all say, 'There's dumb old muscle head Todd making things complicated,' and I don't like being made fun of."

The next morning was awkward for Chris. That is actually an understatement, it was well beyond awkward into damn nigh uncomfortable. They were friends as weredogs, they were at least used to the idea that each of them would be human for some amount of time the rest of the month, but all of that did not encompass waking up nude in a room full of people. Especially if one of them was Sal. It would be the equivalent of walking into work one day and everyone was butt assed naked. Well maybe not that bad, there wouldn't be that creep from accounting who hit on everyone who was now at this moment living his life's dream. There was Sal again, but weirdly, when they all began to wake up Sal snapped to first and was making a point of handing everyone their clothes while averting his eyes. Of course, to get your clothes you found yourself looking at Sal, and there was only so much bleach you could pour into your own eyes.

"Well, I suppose we'll need to keep getting used to nudist camp mornings," Gavin said over his shoulder as he hopped up and down getting his pants on.

"Naw man, not if we're going to my folk's place. We can each have our own spots," Todd reminded them.

"Speaking of which, where in the hell is this place? I mean how far away we talkin'?" Sal demanded as he handed Trish her bra with his head turned away to not look, the result of which was he was just frantically waving this lacy black thing around until she finally snatched it.

"It ain't far from here at all. We're already in the burbs here, another fifteen minutes, twenty by car tops," Todd shrugged.

"But what about your parents? Won't they think it's a bit weird, you and some friends they've never met being out in the barn like that?" Trish asked as she reached for the shirt Sal had thrust in her general direction after she'd gotten the bra on.

Todd chuckled, "Why would they? I mean they know about me turning into a dog every month. They'll just be happy I've made friends like me."

The garage got very quiet.

"I mean, they'll insist on feeding us. My mom loves to cook, and... what?" it finally got through to Todd that everyone was gawking at him.

It was Vince who eventually said very quietly enunciating each word, "Your folks know?"

Todd gaped at him for a second, "Of course, my folks know! What are you, stupid? I had to tell my mom and dad; I love them. I wanted to make sure they wouldn't get bit!"

Everybody else still looked stunned, but Chris was nodding his head, "Actually, that makes sense. I mean that's how the legend goes; we'll try to bite whoever we love except for maybe Sal."

The others joined Chris in nodding. Finally, Sal said, "So we gonna' get to visit before we commit?"

"Oh yeah sure, but expect to get fed. You come out to visit and don't eat, my mom will think you're weird."

One specific part of the discussion stuck with Chris even after he'd gone home. Letting people know about your situation who you loved. His parents were long dead, he wasn't dating anyone, so neither of those were problems. That didn't mean there wasn't one. He had Jake. Jake was his absolute best friend, he loved him like the brother he'd never had. Jake also had no idea that his best friend spent three nights a month longing for the delicious taste of milk bones.

Chris did not want to tell Jake. Hell, he didn't want to tell anyone. This was beyond an embarrassing growth you should get a doctor to look at. If he told anyone it would make it more real than it already was. This was way worse than having an addiction to German porn, or secretly liking Nickelback… well it was at least somewhat worse… almost worse. He turned into a fluffy dog once a month. How do you even bring that up casually? "I saw you looking at that Irish Wolfhound at the park. You know, I too am a dog every full moon!"

At best Jake would laugh if Chris told him, more likely he'd see about an involuntary commitment just to protect his clearly insane friend from himself. And the thing about it was it still didn't matter how Jake reacted to the news. Chris still had to tell him. He couldn't live with himself if a month later there was a new Maltese in town named Jake because Jake had decided to run out for some pizza and Chris was there with the other dogs when it happened. Yeah, staying out at Todd's parents lessened the chances, but it didn't eliminate them. In Chris's mind, he'd been playing with fire with this too long.

He really didn't want to do this thing, but he'd feel devastated if he did the other later.

Chris managed to put it off for an entire week before his conscience got the better of him and he found himself heading over to Jake's to hang out and do some heavy-duty confessing. Chris was not a huge fan of his conscience at the moment. He was still trying to figure out how to phrase this as he got closer. "How do you feel about pets," had been scratched out quickly. Same with, "Have you ever wanted to pee on a telephone pole." That one had to be scratched because of that one night in college that made the question superfluous. He was still trying to figure out what he'd say when Jake buzzed him in.

As he was coming up the stairs to the door, Jake was already standing there in a t-shirt and jeans holding a beer, "We going out, or is this a video game and takeout night?"

"Takeout, definitely takeout," Chris replied, going into the apartment.

"Cool, I got an expansion pack for Zombie Toe Nibblers, we can beat it tonight, easy," Jake replied as he followed Chris. "Beer is plentiful and in the fridge, what do you want food-wise?"

"Chinese, maybe some sweet and sour pork from that place that delivers," Chris replied heading for the kitchen.

"Everyone delivers these days you fool. Still, man after my own heart, it was that or Mexican, and Chinese means leftovers for tomorrow in case beating the game takes us all night," Jake replied.

Chris went over to the fridge and pulled out a beer before going back to the living room and hopping down on the couch. Just like he had so many times before that there was a Chris's butt shaped divot in the cushions. He found it homey, but he realized that other people would see it as a sign that Jake needed a new couch. That was the glorious thing with best friends, you could go in their refrigerator, you could sit in a seat made for you on their couch. They were so much a part of you you couldn't imagine life without them.

Jake came into the living room staring at his phone as he looked up the Chinese place.

Oh hell. Like a band-aid.

"Look, before you call in the order, we gotta talk," Chris said quickly.

Jake looked thoughtful for a moment before replying, "All right, I'll bite, what did I do this time."

"It is definitely not you this time."

Jake smiled and slumped into his easy chair, "Well, this ought to be good, if for nothing else the novelty of it being you for a change. Shoot!"

"Maybe not the best of words. Ummm, hey, you remember American Werewolf in London?"

"Yeah, and what are you a werewolf now being haunted by people?" Jake laughed.

Chris sighed, "Close."

"Wait, are you haunting a werewolf, how do you even do that when you're still alive?"

"Getting colder."

"You are fucking with me here man. No way you're a werewolf. What in the hell possessed you to say any of this? Do I need to call a doctor for your head?"

Chris sighed again, "Remember all the dog hair in my house?"

"Yeah, you said it was a stray dog or something," Jake's face was looking concerned now. Chris could tell he'd thought Chris had lost it.

"There was no stray dog Jake. It was me. I'm not exactly a werewolf though, not nearly as cool as that. Not even remotely as cool as all that. Just my luck I turn into more of a werepoodle."

Jake guffawed, "Now I know you're fucking with me. Good one, weird, but good." He looked at Chris' still solemn face, "You are fucking with me, right?"

Chris shook his head, "A few months back, some little stray dog bit me one night. It was outside, and it was so small. I figured it was lost and I should bring it in to find its owner or something. It took a vicious chomp out of me. Next thing I know, the moon is full one night, and I realize I'm running through the neighborhood as a full-sized poodle."

The room was quiet after that. Chris didn't want to say anything, he'd laid it all out there, what more could he even say at this point? Jake on the other hand was looking carefully at his friend expecting him at any second to go, "Psyche! Got you!" That moment kept passing, leaving Jake to hope that the next moment would be the one where they could both start laughing.

Chris couldn't leave it, now the silence was getting to him, "You know it seems every month around the same time I'm busy for three days…"

"You're serious aren't you? You actually think you're turning into a dog!" Jake looked concerned.

"You honestly didn't wonder about the dog flap in the back door?"

"I thought you had made a friend in the neighborhood, or were thinking of getting a dog."

"Too late, I have one three nights a month, and I don't think I'm turning into a dog, I know I am. I'm not alone, there's quite a few of us in the city," Chris said evenly.

"Couldn't you have just, I don't know, joined Scientology or something? I could have just gotten you one of those guys who un-brainwashes cult members for that," Jake almost pleaded.

They sat there silently for a while. Neither one knowing exactly where to go from here, which was understandable. It's not like there's any background where you would have learned to deal with a scenario that included, "best friend becomes a werepoodle." They don't make books, there aren't any seminars for it. No Ted Talks of, "Your New Lycanthropic Life!"

It was Jake who broke the silence this time, "So, why tell me now? I mean if you aren't just losing your mind and this is true, I had no fucking clue about it."

Chris nodded, this was progress, "Jake, you're my best friend on the whole planet. All the lore says werewolves bite the ones they love eventually."

Jake suddenly reared back like he'd been attacked already, "Dude, if you are thinking about biting me right now, you can fuck right off and come back when you're not nuts!"

"Not as a person fuck face! I'm fine as a person. I wanted you to know for the three nights when I'm not, so you'd be safe. Trust me, it's a total pain in the ass, you do not want this in your life."

"I don't know man, pissing wherever you want…"

"Not worth it."

"You have no idea how much I value that concept, especially if I've been drinking," Jake replied sternly.

"Just trust me, changing alone negates the worthiness," Chris insisted.

"I don't know man; this is a lot to take in."

They both sat in silence for a while. Once again, Chris was the one to break first, "I know it's asking a lot to still be friends with me after—"

"Oh shut the fuck up, you're my best friend even if you look funny on some nights, or you've lost your shit. No, I was just trying to figure out the way this could be cool," Jake sneered at Chris before throwing a t-shirt that was hanging off the lazy boy at him.

"When was that shirt last washed?"

"I stopped wearing it, if that gives you any idea," Jake replied as he ducked to avoid the shirt flying back in his direction.

"Dude, there's no call for that, God knows what I could catch."

"Oh like you haven't caught worse already, you say you're a werepoodle, my cooties have nothing on that."

They were both silent for a moment while they considered that.

Jake clapped his hands together, "I know how you can make it up to me!"

"How?" Chris asked with reasonable trepidation.

"I want to see it; I want to see you change."

Chris shook his head, "No way, it wouldn't be safe."

Jake laughed, "I'm not stupid. I don't want to be in the room, I'll set up a camera. I'd be the only guy on earth with footage of a real-life werewolf transformation."

"You know nobody would believe you if you showed anyone, right?"

"What the fuck do I care, I just want to have it for me. Also, I want to make fun of the look on your face when you're transforming. I bet it's hilarious. Now shut up and let me order food already."

And just like that, Jake was fine with the whole thing. His happy-go-lucky didn't give a damn attitude was no affectation to try and act above the world when other people were looking, he was just like that. At the end of the day, there wasn't much that really made him give a damn. One of the things he had decided when they were both kids was that he cared about Chris. Chris being a were-anything didn't change a thing as far as Jake was concerned other than presenting opportunities to own a once-in-a-lifetime video file. Having gone through it with his best friend, Chris could easily understand why Todd's parents had had no problem dealing with his affliction. Love may not conquer all, but it definitely creates some leeway for weird.

Speaking of Todd's parents, they were next on the list of things that had to be done. It might have to happen, but what Chris didn't actually want to do was go out to this farm and meet them. Nobody really likes meeting a friend's parents for the first time, it's awkward. There's always that tension while you can tell the parents are trying to figure out if their child gets all their bad habits from you. Chris couldn't imagine it would be any easier when you added the whole werewolf thing into it. "Oh, Todd was such a nice, relatively hairless boy, before he started running around in the streets with the likes of you! We had hopes of him meeting a nice Christian girl, now we're wondering what breed she'll be, let alone her denomination!"

It wasn't that long of a drive for Chris. He was in the suburbs anyway, and it was amazing how quickly suburbs became dairy farmland. The rapid change made some sort of sense, city folk drank milk too, and historically they'd wanted it close at hand so there was only so far out that you could put the cows. They were all meeting at an actual diner near Todd's parents. Diners were a dying breed in most places, out here it was almost nice in a retro way to see one flourishing. He could see the others standing around as he pulled into the lot.

"Finally, the last of us shows up. And you had the least distance to drive," Vince noted as he continued to tap his foot.

Chris looked at his watch, "Ummm, I'm ten minutes early."

Gavin nodded looking at his phone, "So he is. I told you you were being impatient. Should we double up our rides and go from here?"

Todd was sitting on the step of his pickup truck, because of course he drove a pickup that needed a step to get into it, "Naw, my folks know we're coming, there's plenty of room in the drive. Just keep up and don't lose me."

No chance of that, Chris thought as he got back into his own ride. Google Earth probably showed images of the truck when you looked at this area from space.

What they eventually pulled up to was indeed a quaint little farm a few minutes from the diner. It had all the prerequisite farm things, cows behind a fence, a few barns, and a large white farmhouse with a prerequisite large shady tree next to it, probably an oak that had been shipped there from central casting for the role. Everything except a big dog running off the porch to greet the vehicles as they pulled in, a dog was probably superfluous all things considered.

What had come off the porch to greet them could only be Todd's parents. While Todd looked like he had been squirted out of a bro mold they keep at gyms for when they need new personal trainers, his parents looked completely different. More of a "Ma and Pa Kettle Save the Day" sort of a vibe. His mom was short and amply round while his father was muscular like Todd, but less of a lifter's build, and more the lanky build of a man who moves grain and hay all day.

After exchanging hugs with Todd, his mom immediately turned her attention to the rest of the group who were milling about outside of their cars unsure what to do. "So you must be our Todd's friends, nice to meet you, I'm Meg, or you can call me Mom if it suits you, all of Todd's friends did growing up."

This was followed by the same half-hearted greetings they had made to the parents of their friends all through their teenage years, even Sal gave an embarrassed sounding "Hello."

"Don't worry about being shy. Seeing how you'll be part of the family for a few nights a month we'll have plenty of time to get to know each other. But to speed this all up, why don't we go inside and sit a bit and I'll get some food. Maybe, Bill, the silent one standing there to who I'm married might say a few words. Say, hello Bill."

"Hello Bill," Todd's father said with a sheepish, what are you gonna do grin on his face.

Chris was shocked. Between meeting and liking Todd's parents quite a bit, and telling Jake, he actually felt better about himself than he had since he'd realized what was happening. He was certain this couldn't last, and he told himself exactly that when he went to bed that night. But since he was so sure of that, he figured he should at least get some good night's sleep until the next calamity happened.

CHAPTER 8

———————⁝———————

"Not all big dogs are created equal." – *Emily Elizabeth*

The days of normality flew by in a blur like they, unfortunately, tended to do. It had become Chris's new normal; everything had begun to revolve around three days. Twenty-eight days with no real problems except for maybe his lack of a romantic life, followed by three days of worry. The thing about that was, even with all the worries that lycanthropy presented, an unexpected consequence was it made his normal life seem so damned dull. A new place opening near the office that did a good wrap didn't compare. In not nearly enough time or not soon enough, they were all at the farm being greeted again by Todd's parents. This time though they'd be staying the night.

"Well come on then, let's get you settled. The chickens are all locked away for the night, so we won't have to worry about you getting at them. The cows kick, so I doubt you'd try that twice. We know the drill from when our Toddy was still at home," his mother bustled at them. "Come on out to the barn and I can show you the beds I made for you for when you come in, in the morning."

The barn was a huge spacious place, filled with dust and hay along with some farm equipment, most of which Chris would have referred to as a "tractor" no matter what it did. It was on a farm, the machine in question had an engine, therefore it was a tractor, past that he had never needed to know. There were more than a few of them parked inside in all different tractor shapes and sizes. Todd's mom had laid out various dog beds around the barn itself, each some distance from the other, and with a small bag next to it. Knowing that this was home sweet home for the night, each of them made their way to pick out a bed. Chris opened the bag to find a robe inside.

As he gaped at it and tried to figure out what it was for, Todd's mother appeared at his side, "For when you wake up in the morning dear, that way you have a little privacy. It'll also be easier to get out of if you want to change into it before… well, you know."

"Umm, thanks, that's very thoughtful of you," Chris managed a weak smile.

"Todd got bit pretty young. Try dealing with puberty and lycanthropy, you learn all the tricks to make the medicine go down a little easier," she smiled and patted him on the arm. To everyone else, she said, "Okay, folks, I do truly understand that none of you want to be here. Todd told us what's happening in the city and that's just not fair at all. I figure sooner or later the big dogs will get bored looking for you and all and find some other mischief to get into, but in the meantime, nobody else needs to get hurt. You'll find you each have a robe, I know when you're changed modesty goes out the window, but I thought you'd feel better for the before and after part if you had the option to cover up. We've got a good forty acres to run around on, even some woods, so you can have all the fun any puppy could want. Only thing we ask is that you be back on your beds by morning, and don't try to come in the house. We'll help you all any way we can, but no offense dears, Bill and I aren't keen to join you out here next month. Any questions?"

Nobody had anything to say. They were being nicer about this than any of them could have expected and nobody wanted to exasperate the nice lady with stupid questions.

"Good, there's some raw meat behind the barn, and when you wake up in the morning, you come join us for a nice hearty breakfast. Have a good night all," she said before turning and heading back for the house.

None of which was weird in any way at all, nope, just good country hospitality. Okay, well… so maybe Chris thought it was a little weird.

Each of them tried to find shadows to slide into to change into their robes. They'd all seen each other naked before, but modesty was still holding some sway, it was a hard habit to break. Thankfully, with only a couple of dim bulbs overhead, shadows were plentiful to hide in. The sun had already dropped far enough to be useless for anything but pretty pictures outside, and a complete non-factor inside.

"I wish you had told us about this earlier Todd," Gavin said as he undid his tie.

"Seriously there buddy, I been running from pit bulls all this time for nothing," Sal laughed.

Todd looked a little sheepish, "Look, I don't like bringing my folks into this at all. I mean seriously Bro, I put all that effort into going to college, get myself a job at a good gym, get myself my own place, and now what? I run back to Mommy and Daddy when I'm in trouble."

Everyone was quiet for a moment. This was an emotional depth that no one was prepared to deal with from Todd. They could all see his point, but it was just surprising to get it from that source.

Trish finally broke the silence, "Everybody needs somebody Todd, there's no shame in it. Heck, we all needed you for this. Otherwise, we'd be out there right now trying to figure out how to not become Rottweiler poop, you know?"

"Thanks for this Todd," Vince added, "I think I speak for everyone when I say that."

That was followed by a bunch of dutiful thank yous from everyone else. Todd shrugged, "It ain't me, it's my folks."

"But you were willing to come to your folks for all of us, even though you didn't want to," Gavin said.

Todd shrugged again. A moment later his face brightened, "But you are going to love tonight. We got a pond we can jump in. There's the woods to run through, it's like you're a real wolf out here!"

Todd hadn't lied about the size of the farm. Though, to be honest, despite the recent revelations about Todd's surprising intelligence Chris still had doubts about him being clever enough to lie anyway. It just didn't seem his m.o., intelligence doesn't always mean cunning. But to the point, the farm was a doggy paradise. There was a pond, that as a human Chris would have been leery of, but after hours of letting his dog run free like he'd been able to tonight, he dove right into paddle across and loved it. The raw meat that had been left out for them, again, as a human it would have been gross, but to his doggy senses, it was manna from heaven. This was a spot that seemed built to let a dog do what it wants to, within reason, of course, they still weren't allowed on the couch, or inside for that matter.

They had shaken off the water from the pond out of their fur and had been rolling around in the long grass in the one field. Chris had to remember to check himself thoroughly for ticks tomorrow. He couldn't help but wonder what would happen to a tick that latched on to a piece of flesh that stopped existing tomorrow morning. Would they just drop off of him, or would they vanish to wherever his long floppy ears went when he became human again?

It was Gavin who broke the silence, "Thanks again for this Todd, this is marvelous."

Todd's head perked up, not unlike a dog who had heard a strange noise to bark at, "Huh? Thank me for what?"

"I think I can say," Vince chimed in. "This has been the first time since I got bit seven years ago that I have really, actually enjoyed lycanthropy much. I mean, you try to make due and find the fun parts, otherwise, you go nuts. But, being a dog in the country, more importantly, being one among friends is actually where the joy of it is. I've done country before, but never with friends to enjoy it with, and it doesn't happen without you."

"I still wish we were safe in the city," Todd responded, probably as a way of brushing off a perceived compliment.

Sal snorted in an approximation of laughter, "We all do buddy. But hey, even if the big dogs weren't psychos, there'd still be all the other bullshit. Cars..."

"Dogcatchers," added Trish.

"Nosy neighbors," Chris chimed in.

Sal picked it back up at that point, "Here if you want to howl, howl. Ain't nobody gonna throw a shoe at you for it."

Todd rolled back onto his back and stared up at the moon, "Well, thanks, I guess. This is just home; you never think of home as being special until somebody tells you it is or you're gone for so long you don't really remember it right. Probably would have been better if I'd thought of it sooner."

"Better late than never," Gavin replied.

Todd suddenly snapped to his feet, "Hey! Who wants to fuck with the cows a bit. Mom's full of it, they don't kick if you do it right! C'mon bros, it's fun."

Sal groaned.

Koy was pissed. Simple as that, no other emotion would do as a description of his mood. Where were the little fucking bastards? He had come so damned close last month; he was sure that this month he'd finally get at least another one of them. It had been a clever idea on their part, he had to give them that, getting a garage so they would be out in the burbs and not have to be on the streets at all. But, there were only so many burbs, and he had dogs checking everywhere for them. Just a scent, just a whiff would be all they needed to track them down again. But despite his best efforts, here it was night three, and not a word from anyone. If he didn't give the other dogs blood, they might start looking for a new leader of the pack. He'd worked so hard to sell them on this superiority thing, no way he'd let himself get relegated now.

He prowled the night determined to find them for himself, just like he had every night of the change. It was important to him, he wanted to be the one to find them, that would really drive it home who ran things. Werewolves were supposed to be above humans, more than humans could ever be. He believed it deep down inside. He had seen the truth of that not long after he had gotten bitten two years ago. Werewolves were the superior race; he knew it the first time he felt himself running through the street. And he had decreed that he alone was entrusted to protect the race. And with his size, even among his own they believed Koy was superior, it was fitting he brought this fight with the rat dogs to a conclusion.

How much of a superior being could they be if they allowed themselves to have pathetic little Corgis romping around and capering like imbeciles sharing space with them? Was that the image a master race wants to portray? Like they were something that might look perfectly at home on the Queen's lap as some kind of pet? Bow to us and see how well we fit into your purse? Koy sure as hell didn't think so. There was an obvious solution, a final one. And he'd carry it out himself, he just had to find his intended victims and act it out. They were out there; he just needed this wonderful nose to tell him where. They could run but they couldn't hide forever. And when they ran out of places to hide, he'd be there to end their suffering. Once he'd shown the pack their power over those pathetic runts... after that they could move on to doing something about humans.

Koy had just jumped the fence to check a cemetery when he thought he heard a scrabble of claws behind him. He whipped around from his perch on top of the stone wall and glowered at the empty street, hoping for just a moment to see a small puff of hair trying to vanish into the shadows. Silence and an empty slab of asphalt greeted him. Not even a parked car one of the little rodents could be hiding under was back there. To make sure he took a large sniff of the night air. It carried nothing his way except a reminder that some humans were gross enough to piss right in the streets. For a dog that was a right, for a human, it was a sign of sloppy inebriation.

Koy snuffed in annoyance and finished hopping into the graveyard. He doubted they'd be in here, the walls were pretty high, he'd had to scrabble a bit himself to get onto one before he could hop inside. But, you never knew, these places weren't meant to be rabbit-proof, and what the hell were those things, but rabbits with delusions of grandeur anyway? They could have slipped in through a hole in the fence or something or through the metal gates people came through. That idiot, perm having poodle could have boosted them up too. It wasn't a bad idea for a place to hide, Koy had been looking for them for three straight nights and he had only just now considered coming in here himself. You just didn't think of graveyards as being occupied by anything, even though life flourished happily among the monuments to death.

He stalked through the graves with his nose close to the ground just hoping for a whiff of them. Even an old scent that showed they had been there... anything to tell him he was on the right track. Occasionally he'd stop and put his nose to the air hoping for something he wished was there that remained absent. Just one little tingle to tell him where the little bastards had been hiding, any kind of clue, that was all Koy needed. Even if they'd already left, if he got their scent here at least he'd know to be waiting for them when the moon rose again next month. It would be something at least, and boy wouldn't they be in for a hell of a final surprise when the moon rose again?

He heard something scratch on stone behind him. He whirled quickly and froze. Standing silhouetted with the light behind it on top of the wall to the cemetery was the biggest damned dog he'd ever seen in his life. It took a moment for his mind to fully register what he was seeing. It couldn't be a dog. No simple dog looked like that, not as big, with flowing hair, so like a... wolf.

A growl carried across the still night air, "Mutt! Half-bred vermin! Dog!"

Maybe it was looking for the toy breeds as well.

"I see you there, I smell you, thing they call Rottweiler, you MONGREL!" it growled.

Oh, shit.

Koy didn't even consider trying to talk it out of its opinion, he turned and bolted immediately. He didn't look behind him to see if the wolf was following, he knew damned well that it was. He recognized that tone of voice, it was his tone of voice when he was seeing one of the toy breeds that called themselves werewolves...Werewolves... He had never put as much thought into it before, but his panicked mind was doing a sudden flurry of thinking at this exact moment. If there were werepekineses out there, and he was a wererottweiler, then maybe, just maybe, there would be the real deal out there somewhere. And worse, maybe it felt about him the way he felt about it... he would have been a lot happier on the whole if the werewolf had stayed out there, instead of hopping in this graveyard with him. Koy had a rough idea as to what was on its mind... he'd seen those thoughts from the inside.

Koy tried to put on more speed. The loose grass of the graveyard flew behind him as he fled. A new scent came wafting towards him as he ran, something primeval that spoke of ancient woodlands, and most importantly it was something that smelled of pitiless murder. He knew the wolf was gaining on him. His muscles found new strength when hope sprang up and gave them reason, up ahead he could see another wall. Maybe he could get out of there, he could get onto the streets. The monster wouldn't dare show itself out in the open like that. In the middle of the street was even a risky proposition for Koy, for the wolf, he'd be totally exposed. It would be worth whatever scrapes he got getting over the wall. Even being caught by animal control at this point would be better than what the wolf intended to do to him.

As soon as Koy gauged that he was close enough he leaped for the wall. His front paws found purchase and he started to scramble to get up on top, his claws scratching at the stone desperate to propel him onto the wall. Just as he went to lift his rear paw up to the top, pain shot through it hard enough to make him yowl. A moment later when the wolf pulled him back he crashed to the turf hard enough to expel the air from his lungs.

He scrambled to get his paws back under himself, causing a jolt as pain to shoot up from his now useless hind paw. His mind was racing to find a direction to keep fleeing until he was violently butted back to the ground by the bigger animal's head. Even in the shadows by the wall, he could see the wolf as it loomed over him. Its lips were back in a snarl, drool dripped from the muzzle down onto Koy's own fur. He couldn't help but be fixated on those teeth! Those sharp, white teeth.

Koy whimpered and began to piss.

The wolf snarled, "Pathetic weakling!"

Instinct took over, he rolled onto his back to show submission. There hadn't even been a fight, but he had surely lost anyway. No one could see, he didn't need to look tough now, he just needed to live, to survive this. He remembered you needed to show that you had really submitted to the alpha male to get it to stop. Hopefully, it would be enough to please the wolf. He turned his head and closed his eyes exposing his throat.

It wasn't enough.

Koy's howl of pain was cut short in a tearing spray of red splashing against the cemetery wall.

Chris came home from work dead tired after his first day back to being a full human. In some ways being a werepoodle all night didn't tire him out. Whatever magic was used to make him a dog also left his human body refreshed as sleep did, or at least no worse for wear. His mind on the other hand had become much more turned on during those nights of the month, and his mind was exhausted and was looking forward to sitcoms, or maybe a buddy cop movie, or SpongeBob. SpongeBob would be cool right now.

What it wasn't looking forward to was Jake, which was a damned shame, because that was who was sitting there waiting for him in his living room.

"Hey, buddy! I ordered pizza; it should be here in about twenty minutes. Timed it so you have time to shower," Jake said enthusiastically as soon as Chris saw him.

Chris groaned, "Jake, why are you here?"

"Dude! It's your first full day back in the human world. I want to reassert my dominance as your number one friend. Also, I want to hear all about it," Jake enthused.

Chris groaned further, "You know what, I do want that shower, and then a beer. You're paying for the pizza."

"No prob!" Jake smiled. If Jake had no problems paying for something, this night together might take a minute. The concept of Jake not at least haggling over potential pizza payments meant Jake was focused on something else. In this case, that something else was Chris. More importantly, Chris's life as a dog. He was going to be pressing him for info... a lot, like an annoying amount.

Chris couldn't help but think about how disappointed Jake would be with the truth as he got into the shower and ducked under the glorious hot water. This meant that Chris had to stretch this shower as long as possible, at least until the pizza was already paid for. If Jake had time to press him too hard too early, his disappointment might bubble over into welching on the food.

He had just heard the doorbell ring through the door as he was drying himself off. Timing is everything in life. As soon as he came out of his bedroom he could smell the pizza Jake was setting on the dining room table. He looked up and saw Chris. Jake impatiently said, "I will let you eat two slices, but then I want deets."

"You said deets, nobody says deets anymore, nobody male has ever said it," Chris said as he went to get himself a beer.

"I just said it, I am male, and you have met all of my ex-girlfriends who also say it, your argument is invalid. Now, hurry the hell up," Jake said as he loaded three slices of steaming hot pepperoni onto his own plate and headed for the kitchen.

"You're not going to like it much..."

"What? Did you hump a dog?"

"What? No! What in the fuck is it with people and thinking the first thing anyone would do is hump an actual dog?" Chris demanded.

"Who knows, you can't say you're not curious," Jake shrugged.

"Yes, I can conclusively say that I am not!"

"You don't know, it could be the best sex of your life, and you're missing out because you're a prude."

Chris looked at him flatly, "I am so glad you don't have pets."

"I wouldn't say I would do it you freak! I don't turn into a dog. A when in Rome sort of thing. You could say it's just as gross for you to have human sex now since you turn into a dog for three days a month, and you are forcing bestiality on to some poor unsuspecting woman," Jake protested.

Chris went to say something further but froze a minute before replying, "All right, there is a very warped and twisted logic there, but it is still warped and twisted. But no, I won't be indulging in puppy love any time soon you weirdo."

"Well if it's not shaggy dog humping, why the reluctance to tell me everything?" Jake demanded as he slumped down on the couch and started shoveling pizza in his mouth.

"Because, it's boring."

"Boorung?" Jake asked around a mouth full of pizza.

Chris sighed, "Just as I said, man. It's boring, dog on a farm shit, that I know you don't want to hear about. Running around, chasing fireflies, fucking with cows, jumping in ponds. Nothing you could ever see Lon Chaney Jr. doing under a full moon. Also, talking with your mouth full is disgusting."

"Aww c'mon man, that's a total gip! I even sprang for pizza and everything," Jake protested after he swallowed.

Chris actually managed a chuckle, "Things have happened that were interesting, and the first time you actually stay awake mentally when you change is interesting, but really, we're just normal dogs mainly hoping that nothing interesting happens. When interesting shit happens to a dog the highway service has to come scrape them up."

"So, how are you keeping things on the down-low? It's got to be difficult running around town as a poodle, you figure women would be trying to adopt you left and right for the free dog."

"We were all in the city at first, there's a pack of us, we were meeting at the dog park…"

"I thought there was more shit in that place than normally," Jake interrupted.

Chris growled, "Do you have a single thought today that isn't disgusting?"

Jake was thoughtful for a second, "Yeah, I was thinking earlier that maybe I'd do better with women if I finally gave up on the Cockroach. So that thought is like, anti-disgusting"

The Cockroach was Jake's prized 68 Beetle. It was a terrible rattletrap of a vehicle. It smelled weird, the seats needed to be reupholstered, it rattled, it smoked, it was slow as molasses, and for reasons Chris had never been able to fathom, Jake adored it. Had since he had found it cheap when they were still in High School.

Chris nodded, "I am inclined to agree with that assessment. Women today expect more out of a date, air conditioning and seat belts for instance."

"I blame communism," Jake said firmly.

"How in the fuck?"

"People expect to have comfort in life now, and who gives them that idea? Communists!"

"Dude, communists burned their own cities to the ground and lived out in the woods rather than let Hitler have the place. Communism does not automatically equal comfort."

"All right, capitalists! With their bourgeoisie multi-fan climate-controlled ACs!" Jake snarled.

Chris was quiet for a second, "Actually, I think you're on much firmer ground here. Ridiculous ground, but firmer."

With Jake convinced that being a were poodle was much less exciting than it looked on film, life returned to normal, for a given value of normal of course. Chris was back to making halfhearted attempts at online dating, interspersed by accepting his failures at it and playing video games with Jake. It wasn't the most successful of social lives, but it was relatively placid. It was lonelier than he would have cared for, but considering the weredog thing, maybe that was for the best.

He had just settled himself in for a hard night of TV binge-watching when the doorbell rang. He hoped it wasn't one of the neighbors wanting to know if he knew anything about any strange dogs that had been digging up their marigolds, which was one of those concerns that had continued to weigh on him. "Just a minute!" he called as he quickly turned down his speakers, thinking that if it was about marigolds, maybe it wouldn't start on the right foot with the sound of that particular song being shoved in an elderly face.

He froze dead when he pulled open the door. Standing there looking sheepish was Suzanne!

She gave him a shy smile and said, "Hey. If you aren't busy, I think we have to talk."

CHAPTER 9

———————|———————

"We have met the enemy and he is us." – *the cooler cartoon Walt*

What do you even do in this situation? There is your ex-girlfriend, the one you had actually kind of fallen in love with even if you hadn't said it, but who one day just suddenly vanished from your life without a word? I mean there was a metric ton of stuff to unpack between seeing her there in the flesh and responding. It took Chris more than an awkward second of coming up with something to say before he spoke, and even then it was only, "Ummm sure, c'mon in." Which we can all agree was pretty weak sauce, right?

She slid past him into the house. When he had closed the door and turned she was standing in the hall looking at him. "Hi," she said meekly.

At first, he was stunned to see her, but some part of him reared up and reminded him how mad about this he should be, "Suzanne what in the hell? You vanish for months and then just show the fuck up one day?"

She let out a sigh, "Why don't we go sit down and I'll explain? You have every right to be mad, I'd be mad if I was you. But if you could hold off on yelling at me, which I deserve, I'll at least tell you why."

"So I have to be quiet and let you talk?"

"That's often the way explanations go, yes," she managed a little half-smile.

"Damn, I was hoping to go on a tirade."

"Let's sit, and once I'm done you can yell a bit if it makes you feel better."

"Well, now I almost don't want to."

Against his better judgment, Chris followed her into his living room. Suzanne sat down demurely on the couch; Chris sat across from her in his favorite easy chair. This had not been intentional, he had not been going for the power position of the easy chair automatically, it was just that she had gone for the couch first and he wasn't up for sitting that close to her yet. And if you don't believe that the lazy boy easy chair is the power position in any living room one resides in, I challenge you to find the remotes. You already know where they are.

"Why did you dump me," Chris decided to cut to the heart of the matter.

She shook her head and said sadly, "Because I was afraid I was in love with you."

He blinked at her, "Since when is that a cause for dumping? Usually, that means looking at bridal registries. Unless we're talking fattening food products, in which case of course you need to cut them out of your life for health reasons, but… "

"Let me ask you, what do you do with your time when the moon is full?"

Chris froze, it all swam into focus, all of it. He wished it didn't. With this new insight, he really wanted to start yelling, but somehow he couldn't look at her just sitting there looking so sad and follow through. It felt like it would be kicking a puppy, pretty literally he suspected. Instead, he whispered, "You... bit me?"

"I don't know… I wish I could tell you one way or the other. Why I left that night was to get away from you before I changed. I always arranged 'business trips' for that time of the month. I don't know for sure if I got away. You don't know what you did or are doing when you're hunting someone, the part of you that can stay rational normally goes away, and I know I have a blank spot in my memory. The problem with that ipso facto is that those aren't the only times you get a blank spot, there can be other moments when the canine takes over so completely you don't remember," she said quietly.

Chris actually felt mad about this, "So you didn't bother to check?

To see if I was all right? I mean, after the full moon was gone would have been when your business trip was over anyway."

"I told myself I couldn't have bitten you. I told myself that I must have gotten far enough away. I would have left you anyway at that point, you weren't safe from me, and I knew it. We all know what we do to those we love. Honestly, I've been moping about missing you and trying to convince myself that I'd saved you. And I almost believed it until I heard rumors about a new dog in town, leading all the little dogs. So I bit the bullet and I asked Sal. After what he said, here I am," she said with her head bowed.

"You know Sal?"

She looked up and nodded, "Quite a few of us at least know of each other even if we aren't pals. I had moved completely across town so you couldn't find me to keep you safe, but word reached me, so I called him. It wasn't that hard to figure out from there."

Chris was about to bitch about Sal not mentioning it to him, but as he thought it through he also realized that he not only hadn't mentioned an ex-girlfriend, he certainly hadn't mentioned her name. It was hard to find moral high ground starting with that kind of shaky material to stand on.

Instead, he said, "So, now what?"

She grimaced just a little before saying, "I, just don't know. If you want to hate me, you're well within your rights to do it. I'd hate me. I just wanted to make sure you're Okay, well as okay as could be expected considering. To let you know what I thought happened, and why I left. I don't know, just to make sure you knew I ran away because I thought I was protecting you, not because of anything wrong with you. If I did bite you, to let you know that I'm sorry for that too."

With that she stood up, "I guess I should have emailed it. At least that way I wouldn't be bothering you in person, I guess I'll get out of your hair."

Chris stood up quickly, he couldn't just let her leave like this, "Look, you don't have to leave right away if you don't want to. Maybe we could talk, or just hang out and watch a movie or something since you came all the way out here."

Suzanne managed a small smile, "I think I'd really like that, quite a lot actually."

Joey had heard about Koy's sudden and unexpected demise; it had been the talk of the big dog circuit. So even if he mostly stayed out of it news had gotten to him eventually. So Joey had heard about bits of Koy being strewn about the graveyard all right, Joey just didn't give a shit. Joey had thought Koy was a wanna-be canine Hitler, and could not even manage a small whine on hearing about the bastard's passing. In a lot of ways, Joey viewed it as an overall improvement in the world.

Naw, the way Joey had always figured it, it took all types. So, yeah, being a Pitbull might have made him one of the big dogs, but it didn't mean he had anything against the smaller ones. The way he figured; they were just trying to get by in a difficult situation same as him. Why in the hell should he make it any more difficult? As far as he was concerned there were no bad dogs.

Except maybe Koy. Koy had been a prick.

Koy had gotten some relatively nice guys, at least normally, to go along with his whole ethnic cleansing routine. Joey could only hope that all of that stupidity would die with the knucklehead who'd come up with the idea. He'd forgive the followers eventually, but eventually wouldn't be today, eventually would come when he knew exactly what each of them had done and where they stood now. Some things maybe you don't forgive at all.

In keeping with his no bad dog, other than the departed Koy, theme in life, he was on his way to hang out in a local junkyard where he'd developed a tentative friendship with the dogs kept inside to keep humans out. He worked his way diligently through the clutter he had carefully placed along one side of the fence when he was human. The other dogs had yet to figure out this way in and out was here and neither had people which told Joe he had done a good job of it. He was pretty sure that while the junkyard dogs didn't mind him, he didn't want them to follow his trail after he left. It took him a few minutes after he reached the right spot to wiggle himself under the small hole in the bottom of the fence that the clutter hid. Joey stood on the other side shaking dirt and grit off himself glad that he could enter his personal hidey-hole and get away from all the craziness of the world.

When all the bullshit between rival factions and just the craziness of being a loose dog in the city got too much for Joey, he came here. The smell of oil and antifreeze and rust assailed his nostrils as he began trotting into the yard, despite it being rank it smelled like safety to him. Safety and sensible company for the night. Other weres wouldn't risk junkyard dogs, too much unpredictability for them. Silence greeted him as he trotted into the yard, which was strange, usually once they heard him sliding in, the other dogs would come over to say hi, engage in a little butt sniffing among friends. The yard was silent tonight.

Joey sniffed at the air; nothing gave you the lay of the land quite like it. He immediately snorted in disgust; he could smell blood even above the automotive stench that hung over the place. He began tracking it immediately without giving it a second thought. If Joey was human maybe he would have turned right around and left, but there was enough of the Pitbull right now egging him on that he went where his nose was leading him.

The stench got stronger as he trotted along after it. It was so overwhelming he almost didn't want to look by the time it went around a stack of crushed cars. Almost. The dog in him had to know where it was coming from to decide if this was a flee or feast situation. A small whine came from his throat when he found one of the yard dogs, a normally vicious Pit and Rottie mix. At least, what was left of him. This was a dog that Joey sometimes worried would snap and go after him, and he actually worried because even with the ability to think more, he still wasn't sure he could take the brute. Something had taken the mutt pretty easily. He lay there with his blood pooled around him and his throat and belly torn apart.

Joey sniffed further, allowing himself to be sucked deeper into the yard. This was fresh! A growl rose from his throat, whatever had done this was probably still nearby. He managed to stifle the growl. If it was able to do this, he wouldn't do much better against whatever it was. Slowly he began to back away, his tail was tucked between his legs, and his hackles raised. His plan was to keep the scene and the way to it in front of himself until he hit the open stretch between the wrecks and the fence, then he was just going to run like hell. Backing up wasn't a dog's forte, but Joey was more than a dog.

Joey's head snapped up at the sound of a scrape along at the top of one of the piles of dead cars. There, silhouetted perfectly with the moon behind it, was the biggest damned dog he'd ever seen in his life. No, screw that, Joey had no idea how it had gotten here, but that sure as hell wasn't a dog. Something that big had to be a wolf! Worse, he heard it growling deeply and threateningly.

He was done with just backing away, he needed speed. Joey turned and ran as fast as his paws could take him. His breath already coming in pants, his tongue lolled out the side of his mouth, whipping slobber back over his face. He left nothing but dust behind himself as he ran at full tilt.

It just wasn't fast enough.

———————|———————

Suzanne and Chris were talking. They hadn't kissed or held hands or anything on the level of romance, but they were definitely talking, and they were talking in a way that seemed to open the door for the possibility of kissing and holding hands again at some point. Despite being the one hurt the worst in this, Chris was actually beginning to suspect he wanted to take that option at some point. For Suzanne, she felt like she was doing penance for some unbelievable sin, but weirdly, she was fine with that as well. Chris could have been a dick about it, and he was being the opposite. Chris had been a bit brittle at first, sure, and he'd earned the right, but the more they talked the more it felt like it was supposed to. She really did love Chris for all his goofiness, yet was also adult enough to admit that a little over a month of hanging out again was not quite enough time to forgive dumping him and completely altering his entire existence on this planet without so much as a by your leave. Those things took time, and as far as Chris was concerned he gave it another week as the correct amount of time before he tried leaning in for a kiss.

She was coming over today and Chris was tidying the house. He was lying to himself as well. He was saying that he was cleaning his house because, hey, who doesn't like a tidy house? He was actually tidying the house for the exact same reasons that he was thinking about leaning in for a kiss. It was funny, since she'd come back she was more honest and open with him than when they'd really been dating. He hadn't realized it at the time, but it was clear looking back on their relationship before that she'd always been holding something back. Now he knew why, she didn't want to get too close because of the whole biting thing looming over her head. On the plus side, at least that wasn't a worry anymore. Even if by some miracle it hadn't been her who had bitten him, the ship for worrying about it had long since sailed, that dog had slipped through the yard gate. He was vacuuming up the curly dog hair that proved he never needed to worry about the effects of a bite from her again.

He heard the front door open; they'd already reached the same point he was at with Jake, "if I'm expecting you just come in." He quickly threw the dust rag under a couch cushion and went out to greet her. One look at her face told him plenty, something was seriously wrong.

"Ummmm," he chose for an opening conversational gambit.

She sighed, "Let's go sit down, we need to talk."

"Are you dumping me again before we even did anything?" he asked dumbfounded as she pushed past him into the living room.

"Nope, though I might consider it if we don't do some of that something soon," she said over her shoulder before flopping onto the couch. The same couch where Chris could see the dust rag peeking out from under the cushion in an accusatory manner.

Chris had to force his libido back into the pause position and quickly, she seemed really upset about something, and he was house-trained enough to know that now wasn't the time to pursue and parse out that previous sentence for the innuendo it had contained. Instead, he said, "Okay, I'll bite, why the long face Mr. Ed?"

She gave him a halfhearted smile, "I got a call from a long-ago ex."

"What, is he a stalker or something?"

She shook her head sadly, "He says he knows you. Look I don't even want to beat around the bush on this. Let me just spit it out, the big dogs want to parley."

Chris sat on the easy chair in a flump, "Why in the hell would they want to do that?" After a very brief pause, he added, "And how the hell does your ex know me."

"I believe it was the way you almost bit Jerry's nuts off that created a lasting impression, and before you freak out, we dated a very long time ago. I was a lot younger and still thought that men who acted like macho boys had layers and depth that they in point of fact don't have. When I realized he was an idiot all the way through and through he became my ex-boyfriend, which is a state he remains in to this day."

Chris bit back a bit of jealousy, he wasn't in a position to be understandably jealous, and he had almost made the guy sing castrato. Instead, he asked, "Did he..."

She shook her head, "Nor I him, isn't life weird sometimes? He got bit after we broke up."

Chris gave a short nod, "All righty, so that does indeed fit the bill of weird. Why in the hell do they want to talk?"

"Well, he sounded kind of heavily stressed out about it, which is understandable. But, from what I gather from what he said, at least three of the big dogs in town have been ripped apart."

Chris was quiet for a second, you need a moment to process a phrase like, "ripped apart." You don't blurt out the first thing you say for the very simple reason that it will be the wrong thing. Even with the pause, all he managed was, "Ripped...apart...like...."

"Like by a wild animal. But the thing is, a normal animal shouldn't be able to do much to them. Certainly not kill them," Suzanne insisted.

"What about an even bigger dog?"

She shrugged, "How big would it have to be? One of the dogs that got killed was Koy. What in the hell could even do that to a mystical Rottweiler?"

"A wolf?"

She nodded, "The thought had crossed my mind as well. As in a werewolf for instance. But where did it come from?"

Chris sighed, "I'll call the others, but I can't see them liking the idea of meeting. It'll have to be when we're human. They'd get totally territorial about it during a normal get-together."

Suzanne smiled a little wanly, "That will have to do. I'm kinda freaked out by all of this. I'm thinking of joining you guys next full moon. Care to give a girl who could really use a hug a hug?"

"I can do that."

After joining her on the couch he let her flow into his arms like they'd never missed a beat. After that, a hug became a kiss. After that it became... Well never mind what it became you, nosy peeping readers.

"You must be fucking kidding me!" Sal bellowed into the phone.

This was about what Chris expected, so he had already held the phone away from his ear, "If you don't believe me, Suzanne is the one who talked to them. I think they're dead serious. They even agreed to meet in public as people."

"They are up to something, I fucking promise you that!"

"What if they aren't Sal? There are currently three dead weredogs, and big ones too. Including that nut Koy who tried to kill us," Chris insisted.

Sal was silent for just a second before he said, "Good riddance to bad rubbish."

"While I agree with that sentiment about Koy, it wasn't all big dogs that were following him that got torn up, but more importantly, whatever this thing is, it's picking dogs off when they're alone," Chris replied.

"Well, we ain't alone! Problem solved," Sal chuckled.

Chris sighed, "It's taken out a Pitbull, a Rottweiler, and a Pinscher, even with all of us together what shot do you really think we'd have against something like that?"

Silence again reigned while Sal contemplated it, "All right, I see your point. I'll call everyone else, but they ain't gonna like it."

"Sal, if it's any consolation, I don't like it, but I don't see what choice we have here."

"We could let them get eaten," Sal replied.

"No we can't and you know it."

"Yeah, I do, but let me fantasize a bit, huh?"

There were people already milling around as Suzanne and Chris headed into the park. One of them was definitely Sal, and all of them looked uncomfortable. Swell, this was going to go great, this would be FINE, Chris hoped that nobody was armed. Chris could see that they had split into their original groups, and the first thing that he noticed about the big dog's group was...well, that there was nothing to notice about them. They were just regular people, same as his group. To think that the people on the left had wanted to kill the people on the right because of some weird race thing… here and now with them all standing around as humans it looked even more patently ridiculous than when it had been happening.

Chris sighed; he knew how this was going to go. "Yo!" he shouted to get everyone's attention. "We might as well get this show on the road here, huh? Why don't we let the big dogs tell us what's going on and then we can go from there?"

Chris let out a bit of breath with relief when he saw his friends nod in assent to that.

"Jerry? Everyone kind of knows you, why don't you give it a shot," Suzanne said encouragingly.

Jerry, who kind of looked a bit like Todd, truth be told, started at that, "Me? You sure you want me to do it?"

"Sure Jerr, I'm one of the little dogs, and I know you're dumb but relatively harmless and easily lead by others, so maybe if you talk friendly like, the people you need to make nice with might believe it too," Suzanne said in a way where Chris heard the subtext, but looking at Jerry's expression, he didn't.

"Ummm okay, so, like you know there's something out there killing us, right?"

"Seems to only kill were-big dogs," Trish said coldly.

Jerry blinked for a second, before continuing, "Yeah, we kind of talked about that. The way we figure is, it's only cause he can't find you guys."

"He? How can you be sure it's a he?" Trish demanded. "Have you actually seen it?"

Jerry shook his head, "Not up close or nothin', I mean, I'm still talking to you right? But a couple of the guys caught glimpses of it, and if it's a girl, I don't even want to think about how big a boy is."

Sal cut in, "So let's get to the nitty and the gritty, huh? What in the fuck do you think we can do that you big tough guys can't?"

Jerry had the decency to look sheepish here, "We were kinda' hoping you could hide us. I mean there's only six of us left now, and he ain't gotten none of you. Clearly wherever you hid out from Koy, is hiding you from him too."

Chris saw the mistake there right away, so much as mentioning the former big dog Fuhrer was unavoidable, but he'd been hoping it would come up later. "Look, uhhh..." he tried to interject.

"Yes, Koy," Gavin cut in. "Why don't we talk about Koy?"

"Oh shit," Suzanne whispered under her breath.

"Yeah, you know why we got such a good fucking hiding place? Because we were hiding from that rabid fuck face and his buddies who were going to kill us. Some of those buddies are right here begging for our help. Give me one fucking good reason why we shouldn't say, 'Good luck with that,' and send you assholes packing?" Sal snarled.

"Well, for one thing, I hoped we were better people than Koy. It's a death sentence in the city right now," Chris replied before anyone else could.

Sal was about to snap out something else, but bit it off before he did.

"I don't know if it helps, but Koy was a really good talker, and we've talked about it, and we know we fucked up, and we're sorry," Jerry said with his head down.

There was a long silence before Vince spoke up, "I think we're all forgetting one important thing."

"Yeah, what's that?" Sal demanded.

"It's not our call, it's Todd's. I mean we could try and hash out our grudges all afternoon, and while I think that's a pretty good idea for going forward, Todd has the final say one way or the other," Vince replied.

All of the people who spent a few days a month as a little dog nodded. The ones who pissed higher up on the fire hydrant of life looked a little worried.

Todd saw all eyes on them, you could see him trying to puzzle out why before it finally dawned on him. Suddenly he sputtered to life, "Oh yeah, me. Bros I didn't go to school to help people get fit just to let them get dead, that's seriously lame. I mean we'll need some no mauling each other ground rules and stuff, but yeah, sure, I'll clear it with my folks."

CHAPTER 10

———————|———————

"I mean, he only tried to kill me once, but other than that…" – *Isaac*

"So, you're saying you're friends with them now, even though they tried to eat you?" Jake demanded incredulously.

"I didn't say we were friends," Chris protested.

"I could see you and Suzanne getting back together, she's hot, and I have no room to speak on the topic of on again off again relationships, but this seems too much live and let live here. Also, pardon me for pointing out your hotness Suzanne, I was not being a lech, even if it seemed that way," Jake replied.

Suzanne managed a chuckle, she had met Jake many times before so was used to his behavior, "No offense taken. But like Chris said, we aren't going to be buddy-buddy with them, we just couldn't sit by and watched them get killed. Someone has to be the better dog."

Jake shook his head, "I am not that dog. I will never be that particular pooch."

"You aren't any dog at all," Chris pointed out.

"Irrelevant to the point I'm making here, so stop trying to confuse me, you know how easy it is. How do you know you can even trust them?"

Chris sighed, "We don't. But Suzanne knows Jerry and says he's just a dipshit follower by nature. Something is killing them out there, and the first one it got ironically enough was Mr. Uber Dog himself, Koy. It would be major ironic if werewolves not liking dogs at all is why it got him, and it might very well be."

Suzanne chimed in, "And honestly I know what Jerry is like. It's weird even talking about this to a technically normal person, but since you already know I'm a were too... since for some reason my boyfriend tells you everything..."

"Best friends since we were kids," Jake interjected, "I tell him everything too."

"Regardless, I'm not a big dog either. I know Jerry, and despite the fact that I trust him to be an idiot sometimes, I also don't think he's smart enough to lie to me. If he says they're on the up and up, he believes it."

"Hey, I just worry about you guys," Jake protested.

Suzanne froze, leaving the rant she was about to deliver unsaid. Instead, she smiled, "Awww, that's so cute!"

"Don't let him fool you, if he's being that nice he's hoping we order pizza," Chris interjected reality into the touching Hallmark moment.

To say the least, the atmosphere at the farm was more than a little tense when they got there for the next full moon. Todd was fine, his parents were fine, there was a lot of fine coming from that part of the equation. Sal and Vince were not fine and were letting it show in belligerence. Chris understood what it was, it was fear being covered in bluster. And in Sal's case especially, Chris could admit it was a pretty reasonable fear at that. Jerry had been about to maul him at one point, or at least had been threatening to. How badly that mauling would have been was open to interpretation, but there was no denying something bad was about to happen before Chris bit the other dog's family jewels. The thing about being sympathetic to someone else's point of view was the simple reality that even if you can see the person's point of view, you could still wish they'd shut the fuck up, exactly like Chris was doing right now with Sal.

"Ain't there any way we can fucking leash them or something? They're big dogs, we put leashes on their human necks, who's gonna know the difference?" Sal demanded loudly, which was not helping the nervous group of people who would become full-sized dogs in a couple of hours overcome said nervousness at all.

"Sal, come on buddy. We already worked it out. They can change over in the hay barn on the other side of the pasture, we can have this one, nobody will have to have anything to do with each other if we don't want," Chris implored.

"Bro, this is like my place man, like my folks are here, chill some huh? I don't want my folks thinking I hang out with weirdos," Todd added.

"Well, you can't make me like it," Sal grumbled.

"Nobody is asking that much of you," Gavin smiled.

Just then Jerry came over, making Chris want to slam his hand over Sal's mouth.

"Hey guys, ummm Todd, look before we go where we'll be changing and stuff, I just want you to know how much we appreciate the hell out of this. I always kind of thought Koy was a bit of a bully and stuff, but you know, he was good at it, including with us, you wanted to please him. But last month really made me appreciate what he egged us into putting you guys through. If it's any consolation, again, we're truly and honestly sorry."

Everyone tensed waiting for Sal to explode. Amazingly he held his tongue. Instead, Todd said evenly, "Being scared sucks bro, I wouldn't wish it on anyone."

And that seemed to be that, the big dog group rode in a pickup over to their barn, and the other group started moving to theirs.

"I still think this is a bad idea," said Sal.

"Naw bro, home-field advantage. There's barbed wire and electric fences between that barn and here. When I was a kid our dogs wouldn't go anywhere near it," Todd replied.

Everyone looked at him gaping.

"What? I may be a nice guy, but I ain't a total idiot, brosefs."

They needn't have worried. Their little group of little dogs didn't so much as see the other dogs all night, or even hear the distant yip of one of their number who had discovered the electric fences or the barbed wire ones. Even Sal began to calm down and stop sniffing the air every few minutes for any telltale whiffs of Husky. Either fear had turned them into good neighbors, or it had truthfully been Koy driving them on the whole time. Not that it mattered at this point, what was done was done. Regardless of the whys, all of them couldn't help but feel like a weight had been lifted off their shoulders that this might work out without any bloodshed.

That still didn't exactly fix things, there was still a bigger problem looming. It didn't change what had caused this blessed peace between formerly warring tribes of weredogs. Somewhere out there was still something that would kill all of them given a chance, big dog and little dog it would most likely tear apart each and every one of them if only it could find them. For once a month, every dog on this farm right now was an exile from its home, a refugee fleeing for their little furry life.

This would need to be discussed as a group.

There had to be a way to at least get the full-blown werewolf to leave the area, or barring that, kill him before he killed all of them. Chris was not happy with the concept of killing anyone, but it wasn't like he was the one who had decided to start stalking the werewolf for fun, he wasn't really a stalking type of guy. If the guy who was doing this to them wanted to avoid these kinds of plots, it would have been pretty easy to prevent. Just play nice with the other puppies. Hell, even ignoring them would have achieved the desired effect.

"So what are you going to do about the werewolf dude?" Jake asked the next day as if reading his mind.

"You have suggestions?"

"Report him to animal control?"

Chris shook his head, "He'd probably eat them, and they perform a vital service."

Jake nodded, "Yeah, I hadn't considered that. I guess they don't make silver bullets standard issue just in case."

"Probably not, and we don't have opposable thumbs when we'd need them most. Well, since this train of thought hasn't been productive, how are things on the Hannah front?" Chris deftly changed the subject.

"Promising, she was over the other night for a booty call," Jake looked smug.

"A… booty call," Chris replied slowly.

"Yep," Jake smiled.

Chris nodded, "Let me ask you a question? How do you think Hannah would react if she heard you refer to her coming over and being intimate that way?"

Jake was quiet for a long moment before he replied, "Poorly."

Chris nodded again, "So, and keep in mind this is just a suggestion from your best friend, who frankly can't believe that she puts up with you, you should probably not get into the habit of referring to it that way."

Jake considered that. "Yeah, you're probably right. I figure she wants to break me of at least one more bad habit before she stops dumping me and wants to settle down. I need to start considering these things as I am not getting any younger, and as you noted on previous occasions, she's already out of my league. Thank God she thinks I'm funny."

"So what habit do you think you'll relinquish?"

Jake looked like a man who was about to dispense some sage wisdom as he said, "I was thinking picking my nose in public. It is kind of gross and there's no good way of getting rid of it if you pick a winner, you know?"

Chris nodded, "You are a thinking man. You do that, and maybe consider picking your underwear up from the living room before she comes over, no way she'll be able to tell you 'No way in hell,' if you present her with a ring after that."

"I spoil her, I really do," Jake agreed.

Today was another opportunity to further rebuild his relationship with Suzanne. Things were good, but even a few months in anyone's life makes them different, and that former "us" from then needs to be reshaped into an "us" for today. When those months involve learning you're a werepoodle, the changes are obviously more severe. There was a lot of work to do in their relationship for it to return to being a stable and healthy boyfriend-girlfriend thing at the level it had achieved before everything went to hell. The thing they had working in their favor is that both of them missed the stable relationship they used to have and were willing to put in that work to create something even better than that since they both hoped there were no longer major secrets. After admitting to lycanthropy, disclosing that you cheated on your eighth-grade English test seems a bit of a non-starter issue.

A surprising plus was provided by Suzanne living in a different part of town than she did before. If anything, that opened up new places to go together adding some variety to create new and untainted memories. Today they were walking through a park along the river that ran near her new apartment. It wasn't a grand park, or a grand river for all that matter, but the cool air coming off the water felt nice, and there were ducks. Who doesn't like ducks? Ducks are nature's eternal optimists, always willing to believe deep in their little ducky hearts that every person they viewed possibly had food for them. Suzanne had become addicted to feeding the ducks as a way of not feeling lonely without Chris, to the point that she had special order duck food in a bag in her apartment.

The happy little quackers swarmed towards them at the first sight of Suzanne.

"At this point, I think they'd miss me if I didn't come by," Suzanne said, as she felt Chris's raised eyebrow next to her. She didn't have to look at him, she just knew.

"I think at this point park ducks have evolved to look especially adorable. Survival of the cutest," Chris surmised, throwing some of the feed to their rapt audience.

"Well then you should last a long time," Suzanne smiled.

Chris managed a sheepish smile back, "Flattery will get you everywhere."

"Counting on it."

Chris's face turned serious, "Look, you don't have to butter me up. I'm getting over everything that happened, and really, I'm thrilled that you're back."

She managed a giggle at that, "So, can I just be complementary because I feel like it?"

"Well, of course, I mean..."

"In that case, you're still cute. If you weren't there'd be no point in buttering you up," she playfully thumped him in the chest with her finger.

"Oh, so you only like me for my looks."

She sighed dramatically, "I adore you, obviously, or we wouldn't even have all this drama to get over, but you, my dear, need to learn to take a damned compliment."

He looked sheepish again, "For what it's worth, you're more than a bit cute yourself."

"Now you're playing along correctly," she hugged him.

It was now month two of the new arrangement at the farm. By this point, some non-weredog communications had happened between people trying to create a better community, or barring that, a less hostile one. There had been a lot of apologies, because what Koy had led them to do had needed a lot of apologies, but it had reached the point that those apologies were almost being accepted. You start to talk to people and you realize you're all just people here. People who happen to turn into dogs once a month, but still, ordinary folks, except for that one majorly important monthly thing.

The exception of course was Sal, Sal intended to hold a grudge 'bout this for as long as he could, even if someone told him to shut the hell up. Chris was tempted to do just that, but the reality was maybe some little part of him wasn't quite ready to forgive and forget completely either. He'd been forced to bite another man's balls; you don't instantly get over something like that. The fact that the man in question used to date your girlfriend could be considered a mitigating circumstance and getting to do it a bonus win from a certain perspective.

Chris was trying at least. While Sal was off running around the pond with Todd, who found that sort of thing endlessly amusing, Chris was near the fence talking to a German Shepherd named Adam who worked in accounting at a company Chris's job did business with. It was like an awkward office Christmas party, with more fur and less hitting on Gail from accounting.

"So, how long for you?" Chris asked by way of an icebreaker.

"A couple of years now," Adam replied letting his mouth open in a tongue-lolling nervous pant.

The pause was deadly, dog conversation left a lot to be desired. They were more designed for knowing things and picking other things up by intuition and scent. Trying to talk like this with yips and growls and body stances for any length of time without an objective, like normal small talk existed for, was difficult. If it wasn't for the fence, and Chris's pride, they could just sniff butts and get on with it.

Chris had a sudden burst of inspiration for something friendly to do. "Race you to the tree over there and back!"

Adam's ears perked up immediately, his tongue pulled back in. "Awesome! Running man, it's what I was meant to do man!"

"All right, on three, one… two…"

Chris never got to three. An enormous shape seemed to come out of nowhere, like a part of the night itself had developed mobility and leaped out, landing directly on the poor shepherd's back. Adam had no reaction except a piteous howl of agony that cut off just as suddenly as it began. Chris himself let out an involuntary yelp of fear and scrabbled backward, his paws sending up sprays of grass in front of him. It was him! It was the actual werewolf! The beast actually looked him in the eye before he lunged down and bit down hard at Adam's throat, sending a hot spray of blood across the field. Some of it landed on the electric fence causing sparks and pops as the electricity arced that somehow made this all worse.

Chris snapped out of his shock and bolted for the barn, involuntarily howling and yowling for all he was worth to warn the others. He heard a zapping noise and a yelp, which told him that Mr. Werewolf wanted to have a discussion with him personally but had found the electric fence. After seeing what Mr. Werewolf had just done to Adam, Chris was bound and determined to forgo the pleasure of that conversation indefinitely if he could. He actually heard the monster land on the other side of the fence when he jumped over it a moment later, causing Chris to try and put even more paw to the road.

He hadn't even realized the full extent of how much he was yowling his head off until he heard all of the other dogs pick up the cry. It was nice to have some moral support here, but that wasn't going to stop the big bad wolf from tearing him apart. Chris forced himself to try and quiet down so he could have more breath to run, even if it went against his instincts. He figured if he could get to the house, there might be the slightest chance that Todd's parents might hide him. If he had been thinking at all straight and not so much like a dog, he would have considered that he was drawing a horrible killing machine right to their door, but that level of cogitation was well beyond his adrenaline-poisoned little doggy brain right now.

He could practically feel the hot air of the beast's breath behind him. He could see the porch coming up, but he doubted he was going to make it. "Oh, shit, oh shit, I am going to die, oh shit!" was his train of thought right before he was sent spinning by an almost casual swat to his rump from the bigger animal.

He was lying there in a heap, waiting for death to descend upon him when he heard the door to the house bang open. It was immediately followed by an explosion that was so loud Chris couldn't help himself, he yelped a little where he lay panting. Chris yelped a little more when the monster himself howled in pain. This time he yelped mainly because of how close the noise was.

Chris cracked open the eye he had no recollection of closing to see the beast had reared back up and away from him. Blood was pouring down its front leg from where it had been struck in the shoulder. The thing was absolutely enormous, its fangs alone…Chris peed a little. Coming back down on three paws it looked for a second like it was considering whether or not it was going to kill the prone poodle in front of it anyway.

The sound of a shotgun racking another shell into place split the air.

The werewolf chose the better part of valor and ran for it, well for the given value of running for it represented by its ability to do it on three paws that was. It was operating with not only three paws in this situation, but to add on there was blood loss and all... But still, it ran off into the night at a pretty good clip all things said and done, faster than Chris moved on four.

Everything was silent for a moment; everyone was too shocked to make a noise. Until Suzanne made a whimpering noise and galloped over to where Chris was still lying on the ground. She was so afraid for him that the dog in her took over, she started sniffing and licking at him vigorously. When she came to the claw marks that had scored across his rump she started to immediately lick harder at them to clean them.

Chris was touched, but he needed her back and thinking human some. "I'm all right," he groaned sounding exactly the way that older dogs always do when you move them or ask them to get up for a morning walk. Wincing from buttocks pains he got back to his feet.

"Chris, are you sure, you're bleeding?" she whined.

"Uh, huh, I'll be fine," he grumbled, at least she was thinking clearer now.

"Ummm, Dad?" Todd whined.

Crap.

"How'd you hurt the werewolf Dad; you need silver to hurt a werewolf, Dad. Why'd you have that handy?" Todd let out the idea in a series of whines before he suddenly took off yowling into the night.

"Son!" his dad shouted from the porch. "Come on back Todd!" He couldn't understand what the miniature Pinscher had yipped and yowled at him, but he knew it was upset and he could guess as to why.

Todd could be heard fading into the distance.

"C'mon inside Bill, you got rid of the bad one, and we won't be able to talk to him until tomorrow," Todd's mom pulled her husband back inside the house.

The next morning was awkward. With a major capital A. A Scarlet...

wait, different story entirely. Frankly, Chris wanted to thank Todd's dad for saving his life the night before, but with Todd more or less going to have a wailing and gnashing of teeth argument with his folks as soon as they all left, it seemed out of place. So instead he started picking up his clothes quietly and tried to think about how he was getting out of here before the fireworks.

Also, he had his own issues. Where the stupid werewolf had gashed his butt, he had three lines of fur when he changed back into a human. He was hoping nobody noticed, but he was wondering at the same time how on earth they couldn't. At least Suzanne had to have noticed, and if she hadn't noticed yet she sure as hell was going to notice the next time they were intimate. How in the hell did that even work? You got gashed by a werewolf as a dog and now you had fur there? Why? That was the problem with anything of an arcane nature, there was no one definitive you could ask, so the answer to your question always became, "Because, that's why."

"You were going to kill me," Todd suddenly yelled from right outside the barn.

Well, shit, so much for this part happening in private later.

"No, son, we planned to do no such thing," his mother pleaded with him.

Todd wasn't having it, "That gun you shot the werewolf with had silver shot in it. Why in the hell would you have silver bullets if it wasn't for me?"

His father shook his head, "Son, when you first turned, we tried to be understanding but we didn't know. Maybe one day you'd get it into your head to attack us, we only got it as a just in case. We hadn't thought about it in forever but with this werewolf coming around, we thought it might be a good thing to have."

"And see how right we were," his mother added.

Todd shook his head, "You'd rather have killed me than risk being like me?"

Todd's mother looked shocked and outraged, "Now don't you say that for one damned minute Todd! We didn't know if you'd get bigger, or what you'd do. We worried that you might kill us! If you don't remember correctly, let me remind you, you were like a wild dog at first. We didn't know what was happening so we took precautions. But don't you think for one minute we loaded that shot in that gun ever, ever until we found out about that werewolf killing other dogs."

"And even then son, it was to protect you and your friends," his dad added.

Chris didn't want to, but he felt he should intervene. Sometimes you need to be the voice of reason, even if it's never fun doing it. Nobody applauds the voice of reason, at best you just killed the party, like that reaction was the best you can hope for in life, at worse people take their anger out on you to take a break from the deeper emotions. Why guys do so much stupid crap is because none of them want to be the voice of reason and get called a wuss by the other guys for it.

Nevertheless, he said, "Todd, I know you're mad. But you know your folks wouldn't have wanted to hurt you. Hell, they've been running a sanctuary for us for months, and I'm sure they've been doing it just for you, and not out of any desire to have a bunch of dogs running around the place. And face it, they don't have those shells last night, nobody has me anymore. And I doubt that werewolf was going to stop with killing me, he sure didn't stop with Adam. I doubt he'd want to call it a night when there were so many other targets handy."

"I know but..." Todd began and then stopped by waving his hand.

Suzanne came up and put her hand on his shoulder, "I know it's a lot to take in. But really, them having that shot sort of saved the day for all of us. I mean it's not like you even knew it was there until today, it's not like they didn't have opportunity before today."

"Son, we love you. We did the best we could to never let you see it, but we were afraid at first. I mean heck, it's not like you can get pamphlets from the health center, 'So Your Son Is a Werewolf, What to Expect During the Full Moon' now is it? Once we saw what you were…I mean, we put the shells in a drawer and forgot about them. Thank God your mom reminded me we had the stuff when we heard about the mean werewolf. Double thank God the shells weren't too old, " Todd's dad put his hand on his son's other muscular bro shoulder.

It was Todd's mom who delivered the emotional coup de gras by reaching out and cupping his face in her hands, "Don't you ever think for one moment we meant to hurt you. I have loved you since the moment they handed you to me. Longer even, from as soon as I felt you inside of me. Think what would have happened if you becoming what you were had been something worse and you killed us? You'd have to live with that for the rest of your life. Why do you think we got buckshot instead of slugs? It didn't kill that beast, but it drove him off now, didn't it, my little Toddy?"

Todd was only human right now, so he responded in a perfectly human manner to the onslaught presented by a tempest of mothering. He responded by saying, "Aww mom," and then losing himself in the hug those hands promised.

"We love you, Toddy, don't you ever forget that," she said with her chin resting on his hunched shoulder.

"I love you guys, too."

It got mushy after that, so we'll just walk away awkwardly, which is what you do in this situation if you're a normal person and not some creepy emotional voyeur. Will you come the hell on already ya weirdo? We're moving on to the next scene.

Life as a full-time human was returned to at last. Not without some serious long-term and lingering worry though. The werewolf hadn't been killed. There was no wonderful closing scene here with the monster lying dead and people standing over it making quips, or in reality, dogs standing over it making quips that humans wouldn't be able to understand because they didn't have this book to translate for them.

Being back at work, with an itchy butt because of the fur, and no dead werewolf to quip over was just about as unsatisfying a scenario as you could have hoped for. Chris amended that in his head immediately. The most unsatisfying scenario was the one where Todd's dad didn't light the big bastard up with buckshot and instead the monster had caught Chris and turned him into poodle McNuggets. That was a much more unsatisfying scenario, especially for Chris.

Unsatisfied or not, he still needed to eat lunch. So, he found himself sitting in the park with his lunch which consisted of Indian takeout. The Styrofoam container annoyed him because it wasn't the most graceful way to eat Indian which tended towards runny. But it was a nice enough day out that it sort of balanced. He just needed to be extra special careful, curry stained the hell out of a shirt, and he had forgotten to replace his spare shirt at work that he'd already used from the time he'd found out exactly how badly it stained a shirt.

He was contemplating how he had never eaten chickpeas growing up, but now they seemed to be in everything he ate when he noticed a man staring at him. In reality, he was assuming the man was staring at him since the guy was wearing sunglasses, so Chris couldn't actually see his eyes. But it wasn't crowded in the park at the moment, and the sunglasses were pointed at Chris, so it felt like a safe assumption.

The guy had slicked back black hair that matched his goatee and mustache, it offset his pale face making the hair look even more dark. He was dressed in what appeared to be a very, very expensive black suit, the kind of suits that the bosses to Chris's bosses couldn't afford themselves but had just enough money to dream about affording one day.

That wasn't what really caught Chris's attention. What really caught his eye was his arm, which was in a sling…

Chris sat there gaping at the man, with a forkful of masala hovering near his mouth, the sauce threatening to cost him another shirt. As soon as the man was sure Chris had spotted him, he smiled broadly, nodded his head, and hurried away down the path.

Chris had one reasonable mental response to that.

"Well… fuck."

CHAPTER 11

————————|————————

"Well, I for one look forward to seeing Cuba again!" – *Wally Herndoink frequent flier and repeat hijacking victim, 1968*

What do you even do in that situation anyway? Do you run the guy down and tackle him? What if he's just a creepy guy with tennis elbow, then what? How do you explain that to the cops? Do you think they're really going to buy "Officer when we were both werewolves he tried to kill me?" Not to mention walking around with the cut of that suit, that kind of guy can afford the type of lawyers that make other lawyers not want to take your case on the strong principles of wanting to keep having a career.

All valid thoughts, but that wasn't the only reason that Chris stayed put, just sitting there gaping at the guy. He was afraid. In Chris's mind, this was still the great big werewolf, the one who would have torn Chris apart without some well-placed buckshot at the right moment. As people, Chris was actually a slightly bigger guy, and he had two arms to work with as well, but his mental perception of the situation was still twisted by what had happened.

Chris shook his head and realized he was being stupid. Unfortunately, the moment he did realize it, the guy was already out of sight.

He looked down at his food and decided he wasn't hungry anymore.

Jake already knew about what had happened at the farm. so he was in the loop, and Suzanne said she had shopping to do. Meaning that since

Chris needed someone to talk to about this latest incident he opted for his best friend. He needed to talk this out with somebody before calling the rest of the... well, extended and expanded pack, to tell them about what had just happened. The way Chris figured it, if Jake of all people told him he was being ridiculous, then he definitely was. Jake loved conspiracy theories, so that made him Chris's go-to when he worried about being paranoid about something. For the record, Jake didn't believe in any of the multitudes of 4chan butt blasts, he was just humored by the twists and turns of fractured logic people would go through to maintain a good theory. With his strong sense of disbelief that he brought to his fascination, it meant he was an expert on the symptoms of rampant paranoia and would spot it when he saw it.

"What's up fuzzy butt?" Jake asked as he opened the door. Chris had known deep down it had been a mistake to tell him that part, but despite his best efforts, the words had still flopped out of his mouth before he could retrieve them and put them back.

"Why are you like that?"

"What? I thought it would be like a cute nickname. Maybe Suzanne would like it, call you that as you lay together all nekkid and sweaty and stuff," Jake protested.

Chris sighed, "Your weirdness aside, I need an assessment from you as to whether or not I myself am being weird."

"You will have to narrow that down; I mean you do turn into a poodle for three nights out of the month. I mean what are the parameters of weird we're working with? Call it need to know information," Jake asked as he went for the refrigerator to acquire beers.

Chris excavated his spot on the couch, replying, "Valid. What we're aiming at here is especially weird for me."

There were two pops from the other rooms as Jake opened the bottles. A moment later Jake returned and passed Chris a beer, saying, "So, this ought to be good."

Chris took a sip before he replied, "Okay, I eat my lunch at the park on a regular basis..."

"YOU LUNATIC!"

Chris sighed, "Jake, please shut up or we'll be here all night."

"Sorry, continue. I was just hoping to say that at some point in this conversation."

"Thank you. Anyway, I'm having Indian today and I see this guy and he's just staring at me. I mean, you couldn't prove he was staring at me, he was wearing shades...."

"But you could tell he was staring at you through the shades," Jake interrupted.

"What did I say?"

"Sorry again, just thought I wanted that clarified," Jake replied.

Chris nodded, "I could tell he was staring at me because there was nobody else around. Satisfied?" Jake nodded back. "Good. Guy was dressed to the nines. Expensive clothing, looked foreign. But the thing was, he had his arm in a sling. Like, the exact same arm as the one the werewolf was shot in. As soon as he saw that I'd seen him, and had figured out who he was, he got a big shit-eating grin on his face and walked off."

"So, why didn't you go up to him if you were so sure?

There it was, the question Chris had been hoping Jake wouldn't ask. Because if Jake hadn't asked it, Chris wouldn't have had to say, "Because I'm fucking afraid of the guy, that's why?"

"What, was he huge or something?" Jake asked, going for the world record in questions Chris wished he wouldn't ask.

"No, I'm bigger than he is," came the annoyed reply.

Jake looked at him puzzled for a moment before he said, "Is this like a dog thing? He's dominant or something?"

"No! Well... kinda, yes. I mean the guy was going to fucking kill me. Then here he is stalking me. How in the fuck does he even know who I am without the fur? I mean I know in normal life I could have beat his ass, well, probably not, it's not like I'm a big fighter dude, just size-wise looking at him, but I was so scared of the guy from what had happened...."

"It just sort of carried over?"

Chris nodded.

"Are you even sure it was him? I mean perverts looking to score in the park can hurt their arms too you know," Jake said reasonably.

"I just...knew somehow. I was sure."

"Well then, if I were you, which I am not, I dress cooler for one thing, I would get over that fear of him. Dude, look at it this way, you just missed a golden opportunity to get you some back for the stripes on your ass. If he comes creeping around again make sure it's him and whup his one-armed crippled ass!" Jake enthused.

"Spoken like a true leader of men," Chris managed a smile.

"I have hidden qualities."

The next day Chris automatically texted Suzanne from work. He did it usually a few times a day, they liked to bitch about their jobs, obnoxious co-workers, that sort of thing. It was a great way to blow off steam, and it also let him communicate with who he'd rather be with right now more than anyone. It had become part of their new relationship routine. By lunch, he hadn't heard back anything. He was getting worried at this point, usually, her phone was always handy. Her statements the first time they'd gone out about not liking to return messages had been no more than a full moon ruse. Still, it wasn't a reason to panic, phones break. He'd checked Facebook, she hadn't been on, so it wasn't like she was ghosting him again or anything like that. On his break, he left a message on her home phone and sent her an email. He doubted that she'd get to either of those until she got home from work, but at least he felt proactive about the whole thing that way. You couldn't be justifiably annoyed about a lack of communication if you hadn't attempted to use every avenue available.

By the time he left work, the lack of any return messages was really starting to bug him. He knew she wouldn't be home from work, so he worked it out in his mind that he'd head over to her place just to wait for her. It'd be cute, he'd say he missed her, which he did, and offer to take her out to dinner or buy her a new phone or something. It was one of those, you didn't realize how much you just expected someone to always be available to chat until suddenly they just dropped off the face of the planet things. And since this had happened before, there was probably some underlying insecurity at work here as well.

Going up to her new apartment was a little uncomfortable, he really hadn't had time to get to know anyone near here yet. Hell, she'd barely had time to get to know people herself. There's just that feeling when you feel like people are looking at you suspiciously doing whatever you're doing, and they're debating whether or not to call the cops. It's usually only in your head, but it's just that feeling niggling at you. He had been here before. We all know that people pay almost no attention to things like somebody merely knocking on a door or going into a place with a key in a busy neighborhood, but the back of your neck itched anyway.

He went to unlock the door to her apartment with the key she'd given him, only to lock it instead. Clicking it back the door swung open. Thinking the door must have been unlocked, and maybe Suzanne was home sick, he tentatively called out, "Suzanne? Hun? You in here?"

Greeted by silence, he stepped into the living room and closed the door. They hadn't been back together that long and this was her new apartment, so it still felt a bit awkward being in here alone. She had the key to his place too and had used it, he liked to think that she'd felt a bit like that too when she did and that he wasn't just being weird about the whole thing.

Chris looked around as he waited for her voice to call out from inside, which was when he saw the envelope sitting out on the island separating the kitchen from the living room. Chris wasn't being nosy here, but he couldn't help but spot the way it said, "Christopher" on it in ridiculously ornate handwriting. He noticed the thing because he was supposed to notice it. Not in any way because he was trying to look at Suzanne's mail because he wasn't and you can get that idea out of your head, even if everybody does it sometimes.

The letter itself was sealed with a blob of wax with some kind of coat of arms pressed into it, which seemed weird. He just didn't see Suzanne as having a long and noble family that was so important to her that she had a signet ring to seal envelopes with, but not important enough that she had never mentioned it before.

He broke the seal, took out the letter, and read:

"Dear Mister Richter

Guess who? I'm sure you can see where I might wish to talk to you again. I certainly did not expect our first meeting to end the way it did, so, bravo for that. The silver has been removed, and over time I shall make a full recovery, I am sure. Thank you for any worry on my behalf. But alas, the silver meant we were so rudely interrupted before we could conclude our business.

Seeing you in the park, well, it made me reach a decision.

I do not wish to be interrupted again, so I have taken steps.

Speaking of taking, I have taken your lovely lady Suzanne with me. Where? I am sure you are asking just that. Well therein lies the fun, you won on your home turf, I would like a chance to see how I do on mine. I live near the mountain with three peaks that is also an old Slavic god. I will give you additional hints Mister Richter. I will be flying into the Marco Polo airport with your lovely Suzanne as a guest on my plane. We will not be dealing with customs at all, wealth has its privileges. The other is that you can expect to cross another border before we meet again.

Tell or bring whoever you want. In fact, I hope you bring them! I look forward to additional guests in my own lands.

Until we meet again.

Vukan"

Chris could only stand there for a long time, holding the letter, his hands shaking. A voice somewhere inside finally started to get through to him that maybe he should do SOMETHING. That the just standing there thing wasn't exactly lighting the world on fire in the helping things department. That led to the big question, the one he really didn't have an answer for, what in the hell could he even do about this? Where in the hell even was Marco Polo airport?

God help him, he needed to talk to Jake again.

When Jake answered his door, Chris just pushed his way inside past him.

Jake started to protest, "What the fu–"

Chris pressed the letter into his hands. Jake gave him a look that was still saying what the fuck, but took the letter and began to read anyway. His eyes got big as he went.

Finally, he said, "Fuuuuucccckkkk."

Chris nodded, "That is a pretty good summary."

Jake turned and began to walk around the room, it was something he did often when he was particularly deep in thought, despite the dangers inherent in not looking where you were going in his apartment. Finally, he said, "Well first off, let me fire up old faithful and do a little snooping on the airport's computers, even a private jet has to file a flight manifest."

"Wait, you can do that?"

Jake actually smiled, "Buddy, remember when you wanted to impress that girl at school by taking her to see Beyonce and it had been sold out five seconds after the tickets went online? Remember me getting you tickets? Trust Jakee-poo, my computer snooping kung-fu is strong young Jedi, I am the sound of no hands clapping."

"You mangled like five quotes there, how is that even possible?" Chris pointed out.

"Maddening isn't it?" Jake replied as he went to a desk in the corner of the room and brought his self-made computing monstrosity to life.

"So what should I do while you do whatever illegal thing you are about to do?"

"Grab me another beer and order pizza. I am helping you save your girlfriend, so you're buying," Jake replied already starting to click frantically.

Chris sighed and went towards the refrigerator.

Jake called over his shoulder after him, "And be grateful it isn't twenty years ago. You'd have to go down to the street and use a pay phone because the phone line would be tied up."

"Yes Obi-wan," Chris replied setting the beer down and taking out his cell to order.

By the time Chris got off the phone after ordering dinner, Jake was leaning back in his chair. "That was easy enough," he declared.

Chris gave it a minute before finally saying impatiently, "And?"

Jake started, "Oh yeah, I guess you'd want to know too, huh? Son of a bitch left in a Gulfstream a little bit ago, that takes money. The kind of money where nobody in their right mind checks your plane. It is registered in Italy, but he isn't from there. Damn, he has some money."

"Umm, yeah, who has some money?"

"Vukan, the guy from the letter dummy."

Chris took a deep breath before replying, "Vukan who? You never told me who in the hell he is!"

Jake looked offended, "Geez dude, no reason to get snippy."

"I'm a little tense."

"I can tell, have a beer for fuck's sake, we won't catch them today. Anyway he is Vukan Zver. Comes from a very old Slovenian family. Looks to me, just guessing here, he was one of the little entrepreneurs, which is an old Russian word meaning gangsters, that took advantage of the collapse of communism. Like bigly. With his family's background and connections, when everything was falling down he was able to snap up a ton of stuff all through the former Eastern Bloc. He's in deep with the Russian syndicates, and everything they run through from Poland to Chechnya. The mountain in the note is called Triglav, tri, three, get it? He has a place near it," Jake expounded.

Despite himself, Chris was impressed, "You did all that while I was ordering pizza? What, does the guy have a wiki page?"

"Nope, but once I had the name, a lot of stuff came up, I'm still going through it. One thing's for sure though," Jake replied turning back to his computer.

"What's that?"

"I'm coming with you when you go after him," Jake replied.

"What?! Are you nuts, I might be going to get myself killed over there!" Chris declared, and then found himself kind of shocked that he had already decided to chase after Vukan to get Suzanne back despite the fact that he might get killed trying.

Jake just laughed a bit, before he replied, "Dude! Have you looked at a calendar? I know when your time of the month is, I mark it off so I can make other plans, I know what I'm getting into. Hannah still hasn't figured out why I'm so attentive for three nights out of the month yet. But we'll need to take a break this month. You need someone to drag you back inside each night if nothing else. You will be needing a human handler. More importantly, you don't know somebody as good with computers as I am. This may require further need of my skills, I am betting it does. In fact, I'm betting that all you manage to do is wander around Slovenia with your thumb up your ass without me."

"I don't know, it's not going to be safe, I mean it's one thing to risk my own neck, but my best friend..."

Jake did something then he almost never did, he looked a bit pissed, "And how in the fuck do you think I would feel if I sat here all comfy and safe and my best friend maybe got himself killed by a fucking alarm I could have disabled remotely on my computer? Best friends goes both ways you know."

Chris knew he had lost the argument right there. But, because nobody likes to just be agreeable when they could throw out one last hail Mary, he said, "So what are you gonna tell Hannah? What about your job?"

"Hannah is going to be told that I'm going with you for moral support while you deal with some bullshit from some distant relatives you don't like. If you think about it, that's not an outright lie. My work, fuck, I work remotely anyway, and most of what I send in I bounce around so many IPs that work couldn't tell you conclusively that I'm not in Europe right now. As long as the work gets done, and I wear a t-shirt that isn't actively rude for Zoom calls they don't give a fuck."

"I wish I could say no here..."

Jake smiled, "I know you do. It's that attitude that has helped us stay best friends our whole life. You need a lot of selflessness to deal with me. After we eat, you should probably call a meeting of the pound puppies, they are probably going to want to know about this, I know I would in their situation."

"Well I'm coming with you, that's obvious," Sal said bluntly while sitting across from Chris at the restaurant they were having the meeting at.

"Why is that obvious?" Chris demanded.

"My wife has got family in that part of Italy. We get a base of operations at least for the first day, I get my wife the fuck off my back about visiting her sister. Like I said, obvious," Sal replied, managing to look smug about it.

"All right, but other than Sal, and his ulterior motives, nobody is obligated to come along. I didn't ask you all here for that, but I wanted to tell you in person what was happening," Chris quickly moved on from pointing out Sal's motives. Now he moved on to his next gambit, making others' excuses for them, "I clearly know I can't expect help here, I know it isn't cheap, heck, I don't even know who has passports."

"I'm coming," Jerry said quietly.

"Aww who the fuck said he could have a speaking part? Why is he even here?" Sal growled.

Chris held up his hand for quiet, "He's here so the big dogs know." He turned to Jerry, "Why do you want to come?"

Jerry looked thoughtful, "Well, first off, I'd be a dick if I didn't volunteer to rescue my ex. I know she's my ex, and she made it clear enough why we were becoming exes, so not a romantic thing, just a, she's still my friend even if she thinks I'm a dope thing. Secondly, I can't help but think none of this would have happened if it wasn't for Koy. Like it's all karma, we acted like we were big dogs and that made our shit the only shit that didn't stink, and then that made the world show us the hard way we weren't so big. If I help here, maybe it puts things right a bit."

"If my sister-in-law asks, you're my personal trainer," Sal replied glumly.

Chris was happy with Sal's response, that was one less fight.

At least until a second trainer chimed in when Todd said, "But bro, I'm going, and I thought you'd say that about me."

Chris turned to Todd, "Are you sure about this? That's a lot of money for a personal trainer."

Todd grinned, "Easy bro, my folks always wanted me to see Europe. I can tell the gym I'm going to investigate a hot new exercise technique or something. I'm hot right now, lot of clients, so I got some leeway if I say I'm researching stuff." Todd's face turned serious, "Anyway bro, I think after the whole gun thing, my folks might need a break from the whole werewolf thing. I mean if the big dogs aren't hassling the little ones, things can be normal here while we're gone."

"All right, but one thing, do us a favor and find out where your folks got the silver buckshot We have a civilian coming to be our evening face and computer whizz, I'm going to want him able to defend himself. At least a silver knife, but if we can figure out what's common over there, maybe we buy the bullets here and get the gun there or something." Chris couldn't help but note that Todd still winced at the mention of the gun.

Sal chimed in, "Let me worry about getting a gun bought. I'll have my sister-in-law buy one now, and we'll know what we need."

Chris turned to the last three of the original pack, "You guys going to be okay with that? Not having the farm."

Gavin and Trish nodded, Vince on the other hand said, "Well, I would be, but I'm coming with you. In fact, I'm financing this little jaunt."

The table grew silent as all eyes turned to Vince.

He smiled, "What? I'm rich. I mean not Vukan rich, I'm not enough of a bastard. But rich enough that I can finance our little rescue mission, and my accountant can probably figure out a way to write it off on my taxes."

Everyone still stared at him.

He shrugged, "Just because none of you ever asked, is no fault of mine you know."

"Do you have property we could have used?" Sal demanded.

"Well, I do, but I never thought to suggest it. I have people who would have had to be told... guards complicate things as well, like what to do with them while we're changed so I don't bite them, and NDAs, people violate those all the time. Until things got weird we were all having so much fun at the park and all and then Todd offered…"

Sal turned to Todd, "Congratulations, you are no longer the dumbest mother fucker I know. No offense."

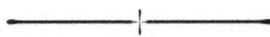

And now we get to find out Suzanne's side of things. It seems only fair.

Suzanne had not been happy, she was, if she was to describe it to somebody else at the moment, "Pretty fucking far from happy, so far in fact that happy cannot be found on a map. Happytown has joined Atlantis in vanishing off the map." There were pretty obvious reasons for her current mental state. Not the least of which was that the leather of the chair she was sitting in squeaked every time she moved. Actually, scratch that, it probably was the least of her issues at the moment.

If you had asked her yesterday if she thought someone could break into your house, kidnap you in broad daylight in the morning as you were getting ready for work no less, hustle you into a waiting limousine, and vanish with you into the morning air… Well first off, she would have said, "That sounds oddly specific." But the second thing she would have said was, "Oh get real, that kind of thing only happens in movies and poorly written books." To which this book says, "Hey! That's a mean thing to say!"

If you added in the bit about getting hustled into a waiting jet from the limo, with nobody in authority saying a thing she probably would have given you a dirty look.

She might have said all of that, she might have believed all of that, but it didn't prevent exactly that from happening to her.

This left her sitting in a leather chair, no longer bound at least, while a vaguely oily, yet handsome man with an accent tried to get her to try expensive foods and drinks. She was set free when the plane took off, and her captors figured she had enough self-preservation instincts to know that there wasn't too much she could do about the man and his three large bodyguards while unarmed and airborne. It had been a good guess on their part, she'd even tried a piece of cheese that had been proffered, which it pained her to admit was delicious.

The one with his arm in a sling who was obviously the boss here spoke once the plane was airborne, "The return journey to my homeland will be so much more enjoyable now that we have a beautiful woman aboard. My companions are stalwart, but they do not do much to liven up a room, or a plane for that matter."

Suzanne just glared at him as her hand moved towards the cheese of its own volition, well her stomach was a co-conspirator, but her brain wasn't. The men hadn't spoken to her the entire way to the airport. One of the... she was thinking of them as goons here, had just appeared like magic in her own house without making a sound, right behind her! Then he had gagged her, while the other bound her wrists as they moved her hastily from her apartment to the waiting limo, and then from the limo to the plane. Years of training by the army, costing who knew how much to the US taxpayer, and she hadn't even had a chance to so much as poke someone in the eye. That hadn't left much room for conversation, and after something like that who wants to talk?

"No questions? I assumed you would have many questions, how

peculiar," the man smiled with the kind of oily self-assurance that made Suzanne want to punch him. In the groin.

"Why?"

He looked bemused and asked, "Which part?"

"Any of it? Kidnapping me, hunting us, your aftershave, pick one, and run with it. Hell, add in a what or two to go with those whys, as in what the fuck is even your name?" she growled.

"Well, the last one is the easiest. My name is Vukan, and you are Suzanne, there, now we are acquainted and friends," he smiled. He leaned back and his face turned contemplative, "As to why for the hunting, have you ever... no, I don't suppose you have hunted a human. Let me tell you, we live, a very long time. Our curse slows our aging to a crawl. I watched the communists come, I hid my wealth, I watched them fall and I made more wealth. It is funny, no? On paper, I am my own father and grandfather. One needs entertainment in a long life, but hunting humans... pah! They are barely aware of their surroundings at all! Oh, we still do the traditional family hunts, but, really, the outcome is never in doubt. Then I heard about your American dogs, and I thought, well, it has to be fairer, no? A more robust hunt. And it was until silver was brought into the mix. I am still healing from that accursed shot!"

"I'm glad it hurt you. Just wish it had been aimed better. So that's it? Some 'The Most Dangerous Game' with werewolves crap? Don't you have better things to do with your money?" Suzanne sneered. In theory, she should be meeker here, she was on the asshole's private plane going to God alone knew where and he had goons. In her defense, she'd had a stressful day, and had more than enough of his shit at this point.

Vukan leaned back and took a sip of his drink, "No, it is not all. I wish that it were. You see, we do not make many werewolves the way it happens in your American movies. I think you can see why it would be rare. Few if any survive a werewolf attack you understand. No, most of our kind are born to it. We breed with women of our species and create more of us. But even a superior species needs numbers if it is going to wield its full influence on a country. If one controls even a single nation, it is amazing what one can do from there. I see the world as a wealthy man does, it runs on power and control, and who better to be in control than the obvious superior race? But we need well-trained pups from our women to fully achieve our destiny! In recent years though, the women of our tribe have grown barren, no new pups are born, their teats produce no milk for the puppies they do not bear us. And now I meet your new breed of werewolves, and I think, maybe there is hope for us yet. I chose you to be my bride because I know you are his, the one who escaped me. You will bear me fine litters and I will be able to continue my plans."

"In your fucking dreams, creep!"

"Wait. Wait until you see me remove the throat of the puny one you allowed to mount you. You will see, Vukan is a superior male, worthy of you," he smiled with the kind of self-assurance you just want to smack.

CHAPTER 12

———————┆———————

"I have the best maps known to man, no way this takes more than a week, tops!"– *C. Columbus*

Chris returned to Jake's later that night after things had settled down and everyone had gone home to get packing.

"So, what's the word, bird," Jake demanded as he let him in.

"We have five coming, another full human, Sal's wife," Chris replied breezing by Jake and heading for the fridge.

"All right, let me get my computer booted and miracle us some tickets," Jake replied rubbing his hands with anticipation.

"Hate to break it to you super hacker, but no need. We can do this part totally legally."

"You're saying everybody just has the cash handy to go to Europe? I know what your savings look like, this is gonna' kill you," Jake replied incredulously.

Chris handed him a beer and sat down, "Good thing none of us are paying. It turns out we got a money head in our midst who's coming along. Turns out further that he is a very, very successful dot-comer. Vince doesn't make the big top 100 Forbes list, but he can see it from where he sits."

They both silently took a pull on their beers while this was contemplated. They had both grown up middle class, like solidly middle, the concept of even knowing someone rich took some adjusting to their mindsets.

Jake had a thought, "So if he's rich, why in the fuck were you guys running around in a public park?"

Chris chuckled, "Sal had some words with him about just that. Quite a few as a matter of fact. To be fair, some of them your parents wouldn't have grounded you for using, like 'it' and 'or', the rest they still won't let on broadcast TV. It really came down to Vince hoping to put some distance between his very high-profile life as a wealthy person, and the fact that he's a wiener dog three nights a month. Hell, I've been paranoid about it, and nobody could sell my story to a major publication for my name alone."

"So what's the great and mighty plan when we get there?"

Chris sighed, "I don't know if we have much of one. I mean when we get there, we're staying at Sal's sister-in-law's place for a night, so I suppose that's a plan. Vince wanted to fly over in a private plane, that had to be vetoed because of exposure. Then he wanted us all up in first class, that was nixed next."

"Why?"

"Because right now Vukan is after me and Suzanne, which means he doesn't know Vince is one of us. Rich people cannot avoid getting into rich people pissing contests, it's part of why they keep making so much money that they don't need`, just to stick it up each other's noses. So, we want to keep the asshole from connecting me to Vince's money as much as possible," Chris explained.

"Assuming we get her back and vanquish the bad guys, no reason we can't come back on a private plane though," Jake replied thoughtfully.

"I suppose not."

"See! Extra motivation! I have always wanted to sip champagne on a private jet!"

"No, you haven't. You don't even like champagne," Chris retorted.

"Which is why I'd only sip it. See, I've thought this through far more than you've given me credit for," Jake protested.

"Well, we leave tomorrow, and we won't have access to champagne on the way," Chris sighed.

"All the more reason to wrap this up quickly, I want to get my luxury on."

They made for a motley crew as they waited at the airport. Sal's wife was not what Chris had expected at all, she was a thin woman, about the same age as Sal. But where Sal sounded and acted like he ran a deli in real life, his wife was polite and soft-spoken, with almost an air of refinement. If it ever came up Chris decided that he would love to know how the two of them met and how Sal had won her over. Vince, as a further act of subterfuge, was not speaking to any of them and was sitting some distance away with a laptop open working on something he had refused to discuss, Chris assumed it was business related. Jerry and Todd had actually arrived together, which was possibly not that huge of a surprise. Todd might be much smarter than he acted, but he still liked to act the way he did, and Jerry was right there with him pound for brosef pound normally.

Speaking of laptops, Chris had to physically stop Jake from opening his as soon as they got there so he could introduce him to everybody. "Hey everyone, before we get going, I'd like to introduce you to my best friend Jake." There was the usual round of polite greetings, so Chris pressed on, "He's going to be going with us the whole way. In case we need something done at night, or more importantly, what Vince can't just buy, he can probably fix it on a computer for us. Which of course leaves us free to hunt down a lunatic wolf, so less to worry about and all that."

"We made sure he's going to be safe around us?" Jerry asked.

"Well, I hope so. But there is a silver knife in his luggage like we planned. Since we hopefully won't turn without a full moon and on a plane, as long as they don't lose our luggage he'll have that," Chris replied.

Sal piped up, "Yeah, and I got my sister-in-law scaring up a piece right now to match the silver bullets that have already been Fed Exed over there at considerable expense that we ain't got to pay for because we had a possibly billionaire among us the whole time."

"You letting that go any time soon?" Chris asked.

"Not on your fucking life."

It wasn't until their flight was beginning to board that it dawned on Chris that although he'd had his passport for forever, and had always meant to travel overseas he had never actually done it before. It was going to be a very long flight, and he wasn't used to just sitting there doing nothing. He reasoned with himself that people did this all the time, how bad could it be?

A few hours later he had decided that intercontinental flight was the most boring human activity ever invented. He was fidgeting like mad when finally Jake said, "Here take these."

"And they are?"

"Ambien," Jake replied with a drowsy expression.

"Aren't these prescription only?" Chris looked worried.

Jake chuckled softly, "If you had known to go to a doctor, you'd have a prescription. All you need to say is 'Long flight' and boom goes the prescription pad."

"I don't know…"

"Trust me, you'll go nuts otherwise."

Taking a deep sigh, Chris downed the pills with some left-over Sprite from one of the pathetic little cups they gave you. When he turned to thank Jake for his concern, he saw his friend was already out like a light. He went back to reading a book he'd brought along, if it wasn't for being stuck in his chair he'd be enjoying the reading time.

At some point, he was jarred awake by Jake.

"Whuzzut?"

"Wake the hell up, we're landing soon and you need a minute to clear the cobwebs. Get some coffee from a stewardess while you got a shot," Jake replied throwing up his hand to get some attention from the crew.

"What in the hell did you give me?" Chris demanded muzzily as he put his hand up automatically as well for the flight attendant.

"It'll clear up in a minute, no worries, you slept long enough. Now really, just get some coffee from the nice stewardess."

"They're called flight attendants you neanderthal," Chris growled automatically.

"They are called people who can give you coffee, Mister Crabby," Jake sniffed.

Chris was moderately impressed with the airport once they landed, he was also significantly impressed when a limo showed up.

Vince managed to look contrite, "I don't care who he has hacking the flight records, there's no way he can look inside my limo. No way in hell was I hailing a cab here."

Chris took a good look at the cab situation at the airport. The limo and the taxis weren't far off from each other, the taxis were mainly Mercedes, but Chris couldn't see them all fitting in one. Or even getting one judging by the swarm of humanity. He just nodded, "Good thinking."

"Yeah, let's get a move on huh? My sister-in-law is waitin' on us, and she can be a total pain in the ass when she's waiting for something. Well, scratch that, she can be a pain in the as most times really, waiting just makes it that much worse," Sal grunted as he helped his wife inside.

"You know a limo can't take us all the way to where we need to go right?" Jake asked.

"Yes, which is why I have two very nice Mercedes waiting for us when we arrive at Sal's sister-in-law's. I told you to get your international driving permits for a reason. But it would look even weirder if I didn't leave in a limo, and frankly, I hate driving in the city, and this way we don't have to keep messaging to not lose each other," Vince replied as he waited for everyone to get in while the driver stowed their luggage.

Once they were mobile, Chris asked, "So where exactly is this sister-in-law anyway"

"It's in an area called Sindacalem dear, " Sal's wife responded, "it's a lovely part of the country."

"What she means is, it's in the sticks. Her husband, God rest his soul, inherited it from his father. Barely worth a thing, I mean it's a nice place, don't get me wrong, but nobody wants to live that far out. We asked around about selling it and getting her sister a place in the states with us. By the time you sell the place and move all your stuff overseas, there would've been nothing left for her to buy a place of her own. Our apartment is crowded plenty as is," Sal added.

"That's weird, back home, at least on the coasts, the country is what costs you anymore if you're near a big city except for LA and New York," Chris mused.

"Yeah, here, everyone wants to be right in the action. A good apartment in Venice proper will cost you more than the house, and her place has even got a little property with it, go figure," Sal replied.

The scenery had already changed, and it wasn't what Chris had been expecting. Every brochure or TV show featuring Italy, all you saw were cars whipping around mountain cliffs with the ocean in the background. Where they were going, in no time at all the sea had vanished from view, and it had not been replaced by any mountains. It quickly became nothing but relatively flat farmland.

"This, is not what I was expecting," Jake voiced Chris's thoughts for him.

"Most of the country ain't like the brochures kid. That's the other reason the place is cheap. Like I said, people want to be where the action is, where the movies get shot. But at the end of the day, someone has to feed all the people cruising around in their Ferraris, right? " Sal replied.

As promised, there were indeed two shiny Mercedes waiting in the driveway of the small farmhouse they arrived at. It was a blessing that there was something of a driveway for them so they could park the limo and that there was no other traffic on the road when they arrived. It's the kind of thing people talk about for years, and it's never in a good way, it's never "Oh look their rich friends came to visit!" or "Oh look, they won the lottery!" It would be dark rumors about drug deals or something of the like for sure, which is just one of those quirks of human nature.

Even before the rest of them could begin to extricate themselves out of the vehicle Maria and her sister were already hugging. Her sister looked like a fuller rounder version of Maria. Chris couldn't help but notice the dark looks her sister was giving Sal over Maria's shoulder the entire time. Sal had definitely made an impression at some point. Chris looked over at him, which he spotted, but responded with a little wave of his hand as if to dismiss it for it later in privacy.

Once the sisters broke their embrace, Sal quickly turned to everyone else, "Everyone, this is my sister-in-law, Anita. Anita, this is Chris, Todd, Vince, and my personal trainer Jerry."

Before she smiled and shook everyone's hands Chris easily spotted the look of disbelief that flashed across her face at the "personal trainer" part. So did Sal, "What? I want to get in shape. Y'know, better myself. Ain't no crime in that!"

After a night spent in an expensive house she supposed Vukan owned, they were on the road. Miles rolled by; the landscape had begun to change. There was still farmland, but in the distance, Suzanne could see the shapes of mountains through the tinted windows. There had been a border crossing, and any hopes she had of rescue there died quickly with it. The border station had barely looked at the limo as it drove through. She was guessing in this part of Europe getting lippy with the people with money enough to be riding in a limo didn't pay. Screwing with limo riders only paid for authorities in the states during prom season, truth be told.

There was a cold truce between them all now, as long as their roles were all understood. Vukan wasn't letting her go, and if she tried to release herself the hunks of meat along for the ride would hurt her for it. There didn't seem to be much in the way of grounds for a friendly mutual conversation. Kidnapping victims are renowned for their desire to not get pally with their captors in the short term unless it was to get special treatment, and except for the whole kidnapping to begin with thing, she wasn't really being mistreated. Of course, the intimation from Vukan was that he wanted her whole and healthy as a breeding bitch. After that, any good treatment from him and his men sort of fell by the wayside to be completely ignored since it was just an attempt at winning her over as an active participant. That kind of introduction is kind of hard to come back from except for certain exclusive clubs where leather and vinyl were popular. Suzanne was not a member.

They had turned off the main road and were heading directly towards a set of mountains up ahead.

Vukan watched her stare out the window, "We will be stopping by a family hunting lodge and staying the night before making our final way towards the castle itself. The roads....can be treacherous to the unwary since I tend to favor a few shortcuts. I would prefer if we started towards them in full daylight, and with time to take care."

Well, that certainly didn't sound ominous at all, did it? Nope, not in the slightest bit.

The lodge they arrived at later that day looked like something out of a movie. It was enormous for one thing, but despite its size, it was still built in a rustic log cabin style like some Viking fortress. No, wait, not like something out of a movie at all, like a big overpriced Aspen main lodge at a ski resort on steroids. Yep, that's the description we're going for here, and this book is proud of itself for thinking of a better analogy on the fly like that. But the Viking fortress isn't bad either, whichever makes you happy.

There were a group of men waiting to greet them outside of the place, Suzanne couldn't help but do a double-take at them. She wouldn't have been able to have told you last week how a gypsy dressed, but she'd be able to now. They dressed exactly like those guys in front of the place, they fit a picture she'd never known she had in her head of them. Leather pants, boots, embroidered vests, big poofy sleeves. Suzanne couldn't help but marvel at it. She was about to be held captive by gypsies in a ski lodge for Vikings, would wonders never cease. This also made her ponder over where in the hell they were. She had not been a wiz at European geography in class, even when they were drilled on it briefly in the army she'd been mainly indifferent since she knew she wasn't going there. That information would seem damned useful now.

She couldn't think of a mean-spirited gypsy joke off the top of her head, which made her practically unique in Europe, so instead, she went with, "You kidnapped me and flew me across the world to take me to an Oktoberfest?"

Vukan stiffened. "Do I look German to you," he growled.

Suzanne put on her best airhead voice because she knew it would annoy him further, "Gosh, I don't know. We don't get a lot of Europeans at home, anyway, I mean it's all Europe right?'

His face darkened in anger, which was more or less what she'd been aiming for there. She didn't harbor many hopes for escape, but she hoped that if she kept him off balance enough and pissed off enough, he wouldn't be thinking straight. Maybe there'd be a lapse in attention at some crucial juncture. Heck, it happened often enough on TV, maybe she could grab a gun or something. The fact that she was thinking like this at all really shows how far she'd sunk into desperation, nobody sensible expects something like that to work. She'd done a tour in Afghanistan; she knew all the way to her toes that the guy with the gun in his hand already was always the winner.

Instead of responding to her jibe, Vukan turned to his men, "I need to talk to the hunters. Take her to the special room, I want both of you to keep a hand on her until she's secure. If she resists, you may strike her, as hard as need be until she ceases to resist."

Suzanne's shoulders slumped involuntarily; she'd spent all this time pissing off the wrong guy. As two of the thugs pulled her out of the vehicle forcibly she mused that since they never spoke making these two irrationally angry didn't seem likely anyway. Overpowering either of them was out of the question, she had training, they had mass and numbers. Also, since they were bodyguards, possibly training.

They dragged her into the house while Vukan stayed outside. She'd attempted to walk normally and maintain some dignity, but the goons seemed even more intent on there being a dragging aspect to the whole affair. The first place they entered was a large open area, just like a lounge or a hall. There were trophies hanging in various spots on the walls which always look creepy. It took her a moment to notice something vitally important about them though that made it way more creepy. It was a real doozy of an important thing to notice. What was that thing this book hears you screaming? Glad you asked! That thing was that not all of the heads technically belonged to animals. There were absolutely some that you could have asked what time it was and have expected an answer in the not-too-distant past. She looked twice to make sure before she was dragged out of the room and down a hallway, yep, no doubt about it, one of them looked like the guy had been an accountant.

It's not often you feel grateful to be shoved forward by two enormous gorillas that had been wedged into suits and taught how to walk upright, but this was actually one of those times. If Suzanne had been given the opportunity to stare at the grisly trophies she might have started screaming. Instead, she'd just have nightmares about it while maintaining her dignity. Once they were out of sight and down the hall, she was able to process the bizarre scene she'd just witnessed better and she almost made a mental shrug. She was being held captive by werewolves, werewolves who had come to America with the intent of hunting other werewolves. Their family hunting lodge wasn't going to have squirrels on the wall. She'd have to teach herself not to react, which would let them think she was weak. She refused to let these assholes get to her, that was the road to quitting.

She was just making peace with the heads when was shoved again brusquely into a darkened room. Before she could even turn around to complain the door was shut, and she could hear the lock clicking shut. Suzanne had a brief moment of panic, thinking that they'd be leaving her in this darkened room alone when something dawned on her, she hadn't actually checked the lights yet. Reaching out carefully until she found the wall next to the door. She started to feel about her hand snaking up and down blindly fumbling to find the switch.

Speaking of blindly, her eyes had exactly enough time to adjust to the dark when she found the switch. Momentarily blinded was exactly what the light did to her. It was more than a moment before she finished blinking and she got a look at her new digs. It was nothing grisly this time, just a small bedroom, the kind of thing you'd expect from a hunting lodge. There was a bed, a dresser, and a space to walk between them which led to what looked like a small bathroom. It wasn't luxury, but they hadn't thrown her in the "cooler" either. This was amply survivable all things considered.

That left the issue of currently having nothing to do, except for using the bathroom of course, which seemed like a good idea after the drive. But even that activity involves lengthy moments of nothing. It was a long trip; we don't need to go into details since that probably doesn't need explaining and this book is too proud to go into potty humor literally. We are a proud book, and consider ourselves to be much higher quality than mere toilet humor, unless we get low on jokes later in which case all bets are off.

One thing that caught her attention was that the soap smelled vaguely of honey, which she thought was interesting, and counted as a positive. You needed to count the positives in a situation like this to keep your chin up. Suzanne decided to give her face a vigorous rinsing using the soap, again, it had been a long trip. She was just drying her face off with a towel that could probably have been used for sheet rock paneling in a pinch when there was a knock on the door.

"Just a minute, I'm..." she began.

She never got to finish that thought because the door opened, and there stood Vukan in all his smarminess, smiling at her like a cat... wait that's a really tired metaphor. Like a... well, like someone who was really smarmy and smiling. There, that's better.

"I hope you find the room to your liking," he grinned at her, in a way that could be best described, as, we don't know, let's go with smarmy again here with a side order of smug. Smarmy's a good word, very descriptive, lots of character that word.

"It's hard to have a high or a low opinion, it's private, it has a bed, it has a bathroom, I haven't seen any roaches, so those are the plusses. The minus of course is me being held captive by a creepy asshole."

"It pleases you to jest..."

"Who said I was kidding."

Vukan's eyes turned dark, leaving his frozen grin on its own for the moment. Finally, he said, "I wish to point out some features of this room. There are bars on the window, so you will find no escape there. The base of the door, you will see, silver, the same as the bars. I do not know if your American weredogs can change at will, or even if you change before the full moon, but you will see that it won't matter if you do. You are quite secure here. I have other things to attend to, so before I leave, is there anything you require that you don't have?"

Suzanne couldn't repress the sigh she let out. She hadn't even considered escape until he said something, but contemplating it, and plotting it would have given her something to while away however long she was stuck in here. The sigh was because he'd just said the impossible thought that would have formed in her head and shot it down preemptively. It's amazing the things we didn't even know we wanted until someone tells them we can't have them.

Finally, she said, "A book would be nice."

"Excellent, I have many books here on Slovenia, it will give you an opportunity to learn about your new family and homeland."

God, but she wished she could kick his ass right now. It would be a great opportunity to use all that army training in a constructive manner that her current day job didn't. The problem was the thugs and the denizens of the lodge that would come running to his aid the moment he so much as squawked. But dear lord it would be gratifying to knock the look off his face.

CHAPTER 13

──────┼──────

"Enjoy our welcoming brisk winters!" – *Russia's 1941 tourism slogan*

The next morning had almost become the next afternoon before anyone had achieved any level of functionality. Exhaustion from the flight had them fully in its grasp, and everybody slept in as long as they could before their rooms got too hot. Yes, there was a goal, there was urgency, but it was agreed that once they left and entered Slovenia itself time to take a breather might be at a premium. Instead of making them breakfast, their gracious host Anita had graciously reserved her yelling about lazy bums to only include Sal, and had gone right into making them lunch before they left on the next leg of their journey. When they got to the dining room. Everyone except for Sal could only stare at the amount of food on the table in awe and disbelief.

Sal finally leaned in, "In Italy, lunch is like a big thing. So there's a lot of food. Hell, we're going to be moving quick in Slovenia by tonight, I say eat the fuck up, we won't eat like this again for a while."

Chris replied, "I've never eaten like this in my life, my family's Protestant."

After they had stuffed themselves it was time to make their goodbyes. Sal hugged his wife for a long time. It was quite sweet, Chris figured he wanted to leave a good memory. Because if their stay with his sister-in-law had been any indication, Anita would be trash-talking the man to his wife the entire time they were gone. He couldn't help but notice that the way Maria hugged him back was just as fierce. He had to concede that it was also possible that they were a couple unused to spending time apart. He was kind of hoping it was the former though, that would make him feel like less of a dick for dragging Sal along on this ridiculous adventure.

As they walked to the two cars that would take them the rest of the way Jake called out, "I'm driving!"

"Why does he get to drive?" Jerry demanded.

"Because I called it, you snooze you lose," Jake replied smugly. "Always wanted to drive a Benz."

Vince turned to Chris, "Well, he's your friend. Will you vouch for him?"

Chris saw the expression on Jake's face. For whatever reason Jake really wanted to drive, and Chris didn't have the heart to be completely truthful here so he just said, "I kinda don't think I have a choice here. I mean, he'll cry if I don't."

With that settled, their little wagon train moved on into the Italian countryside.

They had only been driving a little while when Chris noticed a white car behind them. He noticed it because it always stayed the same distance behind them, and had taken the same turn as them the last three times they'd needed to work their way towards the big highway leading to Slovenia. Finally, Chris said, "Hey Sal, do you recognize that make of car?"

Sal turned in his seat, "It's a Skoda from the looks of it. Why?"

"It has been exactly there through three turns. Where are they made?"

"Czech Republic I think," Sal replied, his eyes going a little wide as he worked it out.

"Ah, so not an Italian brand, more of a former Eastern Bloc country just like where we're driving towards brand, cool," Chris replied. "I'm going to text over to the other car to get Vince's opinion."

"Texting takes too damned long. Why don't you just fucking call him and talk directly? " Sal demanded.

Jake snorted with disgust, and Chris just replied, "That would be weird. Look, you know the area better than us. Start thinking of somewhere we can lose them."

A few minutes later, Chris's phone pinged. He glanced down and read the incoming message before he said, "Vince also thinks it would be a wonderful, marvelous idea to lose whoever the hell that is. Any bright ideas back there Sal?"

"Yeah, maybe, but we'd have to be on foot. It don't work if they don't get out and follow us," Sal replied.

"Here, text Vince the directions," Chris said handing him his phone.

"So what's this great idea of yours, Sal?" Jake asked.

"Bar I go to sometimes to get out of the house to get away from my sister-in-law. The owner knows me, and there's a back way out," Sal replied.

"Won't they get suspicious that we parked so far away?" Vince asked as they all got out of the Mercedes.

"Naw, first off you can't park in front of the bar. Secondly, there is a house of… ummm… negotiable affection next door. So, while the place we're going is a nice quiet bar for older guys, those selfsame older guys won't park anywhere near it if they drive. Not to mention, the street it's on really is too narrow to park on, these side streets will barely pass a car. Somebody parks there it's a roadblock," Sal replied.

Once they got away from the wide-open plaza where they'd left the Benzes, they could see that Sal had been exactly right. The ancient village they were in had been built with carts in mind, cars could barely fit down most of the streets that branched off from the plaza before snaking between the venerable yellow buildings. Glancing over his shoulder, Chris was not at all surprised to see the Skoda pull in and park on the other side of the plaza from their Benzes.

"Our friends are back," Chris said.

Jake turned to look like he was talking to Sal, instead, he looked over the older man's shoulder, "Jesus, it's clearly goons that were told to trail us. I mean wait until these guys get out and you'll see. I mean we all agree with that, right? I've never been subjected to hired goons before. But damn, whoever it is isn't even good at it. We made them way too quick."

"Here's hoping they're dumb enough to follow us on foot," Vince replied.

As if on cue they heard two car doors open and close.

"On a plus note, at least now we know how many there are," Jerry said.

"Not necessarily," Vince replied.

"How do you figure that, bro?" asked Todd.

"One of them could have stayed with the car," Chris explained what he'd just figured out for himself as well.

"Well, crap," Jerry said.

"No big deal," Sal cut in. "Even if there's one left in the car, I doubt he leaves his buddies hanging like that when we go to leave without them on our tail. He won't take off without them. Anyway, we can find out for sure when we double back. We can get a look at the car from the alley."

They had just passed a door with a light bulb in a lit ornate globe over it when Sal suddenly turned a right. Chris hadn't even seen the alleyway until they were turning down it. A little in the distance he could make out wooden chairs and tables in front of what he could only assume was their destination. Before turning the corner Chris risked a look back. About fifty yards back there were two slabs of grade A beef in Armani loping along behind them. Somehow Chris didn't think these guys had suddenly decided to pop into a nondescript town in the countryside of Italy for an afternoon beer.

Sal called back over his shoulder, "We ain't gonna be in the bar but a minute, as much as it breaks my heart."

The little bar was dimly lit, the walls showing bare brick. The few drinkers this early were all older men, some sat in chairs outside the place taking the sun but the majority were inside taking their drinking seriously. Sal veered off from their little group and went right for the bartender, speaking quickly to him in Italian. Chris had no idea what he was saying, but considering what they planned, he could figure out the gist of it. While he waited Chris turned and looked at the room, trying on a brittle-looking smile. His smile was not returned by the men littered about, hunched over beers and wine glasses. He gave up and turned back just in time to see a set of bills trade hands between Sal and the bartender.

Sal turned back to the group, "All right, that's taken care of, follow me."

"What did you say to the guy?" Jerry asked.

"I told him we were being followed, and to tell the big hunks of dope that'd come lookin' for us that we weren't here and that he figured we must have gone into the whorehouse next door," Sal replied as he scurried towards the back of the bar.

This was greeted with moderately horrified silence.

Except from Jake, "Smart thinking. Wish we had time to prove you right."

Chris smacked Jake on the arm.

"What the fuck dude?" Jake demanded.

"We're rescuing my girlfriend," Chris replied.

Jake looked disgusted, "Well, we aren't doing it the entire time!"

"YOU have a girlfriend," Chris pressed.

"Umm, not today I don't. Turns out she was mad about me coming over here without her," Jake shrugged.

"Well, you will when you get home, she'll forgive you. Try and remember that, huh?

Sal went behind the bar and passed the bartender as he headed towards the kitchen through a small door behind him. He paused for a moment then waved for the others to follow. It was dead quiet in the kitchen except for an older woman sitting in a rocking chair near a large wooden stove. She smiled when she saw Sal and said with a thick Italian accent, "You hiding from Anita again Sal?"

"Not this time Sophia, some big dumb ugly bastards been following our car. No, I don't know why, but we'd prefer if they didn't keep doing it," he replied.

The woman sat bolt upright, "You bring Policia into our bar, Sal?"

"Not unless Italian police drive Skodas. Naw, we're driving Mercedes, I think it's some border trash trying to rip us off," Sal replied.

"Well then get the hell out of here. I don't want no thugs smashin' the place up. You know the way," she thumbed past her to a dark wooden door in the corner.

"A pleasure as always Sophia, you look lovely as ever," Sal replied before making for the door.

"She speaks English really well," Chris noted on their way out the door.

"In my experience, most Europeans speak English better than anyone in the Bronx, the American south, or Scotland for that matter," Vince replied.

Outside in the alley, they all paused while their eyes readjusted to the bright light of the day. But only for a moment before Sal said, "Come on, let's get back to the car and get gone. At least this time we're gonna go in the back way so we can check to see if they left someone."

"You know, for an alleyway, this is really immaculate," Jake noted. "I mean this is cleaner than an American tourist area."

"Yeah, these little towns, they get bent out a shape about litter. I learned that the first time I came out here," Sal replied. "I'd hate to be an Italian werewolf, not a lick of trash to get into."

"They probably all pretend to be sheepdogs and spend their time out in the fields," Chris replied.

"Oooh hadn't thought of that. In that case, I'm sick of being an American werepug. Course, I'd be useless out here. No sheep is gonna listen to a pug." He stopped dead in his tracks before hissing to the others, "Now everyone shut the hell up and stay the hell put. I'm gonna go check their car."

The group of them sat in the alley feeling foolish. The way it had twisted and turned, they were out of sight of the mouth where Sal was, but nobody felt comfortable talking either. So instead they all tried to find something to stare at while they were waiting. There was a dearth of those things in the alley, mainly because of the cleanliness noted earlier, so they ended up staring at different walls in a manner that would be totally inconspicuous at a convention of the blind, and even then only maybe.

Except Jake that was, he already had his phone out, whispering, "Will you look at that? I never thought a Kardashian would date him!"

"Will you put that thing away? We might need to move in a hurry," Chris hissed.

Jake did so grumbling a little.

A moment later Chris asked, "So, who's dating who?"

"Not telling, you were mean to me," Jake sniffed.

Before Chris could reply, Sal was back. "Bad news, there's one of them left in the car."

Todd smiled, "No problem."

Before anybody could reply he started walking out of the alley. Each of them scrambled a bit to get a view of what Todd intended to do about the remaining goon. As they watched, he walked confidently up to the Skoda where it sat parked with a clear view of the Mercedes parked across the plaza. Todd rapped on the driver-side window.

"Excuse me!" he said loudly enough that they could all hear him clearly.

The window rolled down. None of them could make out what the man in the car said. Not that it mattered much since the second the window was completely open Todd reared back and punched him with what they could guess was an amazing amount of force judging by the way the guy's head completely vanished from view and didn't return.

Todd turned to them and waved. Then he started shaking his hand in pain.

"I think that's our cue to get the fuck out of here," Jerry said.

"Hold on a sec," Jake said.

"For what? Let's go," growled Chris.

When he turned to look at his best friend he was holding a largish silver knife. Jake smiled, "I made sure to get this out of my luggage since you told me to have it for protection. Bet they don't drive very far on four flats."

"Good thinking," Vince said. "But as soon as we have a chance, that goes in the secret compartment in my car with the gun and the bullets until after the border crossing."

"But how am I going to protect myself from you weredoggies?" Jake protested.

"We've still got a night before the full moon," Jerry replied.

"But Chris is mean to me sometimes," Jake pouted as he started stabbing tires.

"Am not, anyway, your mom always took my side," Chris retorted.

"I wonder what crossing the border is going to be like?" Jake mused.

"Aww, it ain't gonna be nothing. Since the EU, the borders are more or less open to member countries. I think the old border patrol building has a restaurant and a duty-free shop in it," Sal answered him confidently.

"You been out this way much?" Chris asked.

"Every damned chance I get. It gets me away from Anita. I tell her I like to shop over there for stuff, I tell her it's cheaper. She says it's shitty, and she's right, but hey I ain't gonna admit that," Sal replied.

"You spend a lot of the time away from the house when you're here, you know that Sal?" Jake said.

"You seen the way Anita looks at me. Wouldn't you?"

Chris could tell already that sometime in the near future their landscape was going to change. In the distance, he could already see mountains beginning to loom up. He figured he should get used to the idea, he'd looked at the maps, mountains were going to be a constant soon enough.

Traffic was moving at a good pace when they approached the

Slovenian border. The former border crossing buildings that weren't selling things looked neglected. At first, it looked like they would just drive in without incident. But, just as they had passed the restaurant that Sal had mentioned, the car was flooded with flashing lights and a siren went off behind them.

"What the fuck did you do Jake?" Chris demanded.

"Nothing! I was going the speed limit and everything," Jake protested.

"How the hell do you even know what the speed limit is?"

Jake looked at him like he was stupid, "I make sure the number on the sign matches the one on the speedometer dummy."

"Kilometers or miles per hour?"

Sal interrupted, "Whichever it is, you better fucking reduce it and pull the fuck over!"

Jake pulled over, and Chris already had his phone out to call Vince to tell them what was up. He needn't have bothered, as they were pulling over a second Skoda police car whipped by, its lights flashing as it pursued Vince's Mercedes.

"This, don't look good," Jake said quietly.

A moment later a Slovenian police officer was at their window, he had the smile on his face that is almost the universal symbol of, "I am going to enjoy telling you exactly how screwed you are,"

Nope, not good at all.

Chris and Jake were in a jail cell together. That sounded bad, but to be fair, it was much nicer than an American jail cell. It wasn't a large holding cell/drunk tank or just a creepy dark individual cell. There were actual windows for one thing. They were made of chicken-wired glass and it was barred outside, but still, there was natural light and then a street light as the day turned to night. There was a wooden chair to sit on, two beds, and not much else as far as décor, but hey, they were soft beds. But still, if you were traveling in Europe and rented a room as you went, except for the bars on the door you probably wouldn't think to complain.

"But we weren't smuggling," Jake complained again.

Chris waved his wand back and forth.

"Well *we* weren't," Jake replied.

They both sat back on their bunks and stared at the ceiling. Finally Jake couldn't take it any longer, "So what do you think this is even about? We weren't smuggling and they had no reason to think we were."

Chris looked at him and said quietly and levelly, "How much influence do you think billionaires have on the activity of the local police back home?"

Jake looked dumbfounded for a moment, but Chris could see realization dawn on him, "Ohhhhh, you think a certain puppy dog just pissed on our tires."

"Yep."

Jake considered it for a moment before he said, "But why? I mean he *wants* you to follow him."

"Well, for one thing, it slows us down some. He's probably at his mansion, or castle, or whatever you want to call it, by now laughing about what he did to those dumb Americans."

"And the other thing?"

"Huh?" Chris looked perplexed.

"You said, 'for one thing,' Well, what's the other thing?"

Chris nodded, "Well the other is, he now knows the name of everybody who's on this jaunt."

Jake fell back on his cot with a thud, "I hadn't even considered that."

Chris sighed, "So now everybody is in danger. I didn't even consider he'd pull this shit. For what it's worth, I'm really sorry."

Jake looked over and actually smiled, "Hey, I wouldn't have come along if I didn't think we were gonna kick his hairy ass. And I wasn't naive enough to think he'd make it totally easy."

Their conversation was interrupted by yelling outside between two people. The back and forth seemed to be happening in Italian and very loudly. Chris and Jake looked at each other with worry. The yelling seemed to be coming in their direction, and frankly, they weren't exactly in the most kick-ass position ever to defend themselves if that yelling had something to do with them.

Both of them visibly shrank back a little as a guard appeared in front of their cell. Behind them was a little man clutching a briefcase. Both the briefcase and the smaller man's clothing looked very expensive. Chris couldn't help but think that with the money he'd spent on clothes the guy could have afforded a better hairstyle which was trimmed short and prematurely gray yet somehow included bangs.

The cell door was unlocked. A moment later it clanged open. The guard pointed at first Jake and then Chris, saying gruffly, "You! You! Out now!"

When Chris and Jake didn't immediately step to and instead clutched at the sides of their bed in fear, the smaller man managed to work his way past the large brutish-looking guard. He smiled at them and said with only the slightest of accents, "Excuse this lout, he knows that he will be hearing about this later and will not like what he hears. He is understandably upset. I am Meester Vincent Forth's personal attorney in this region. There has been a misunderstanding of course, but in my experience when misunderstandings happen to a man of Meester Forth's resources, many, many people hear about it later. Would you come with me please?"

With no real options, they did exactly that. It wasn't like they were married to spending the night in their cells, unless it was the guard who was the one demanding they follow, in which case they were not only married but thinking of kids and a nice house in the suburbs. The attorney moved with precise and efficient speed as he led them out of the holding area. The guard trailed lackadaisically behind them. He probably felt that there should be some official presence while they were in the jail area, but also didn't want to draw any attention to himself for when the 'hearing about it' part came later, figuring if he kept a low profile hopefully he wouldn't be pointed out by name.

Vince, Jerry, Todd, and Sal were waiting for them in the lobby that the lawyer led them to.

As soon as Jake and Chris cleared the barrier between the lobby and the rest of the station the lawyer whipped around and stuck his finger in the face of the shamefaced officer who was manning the front desk, "Since I know you damned well know English, I shall use that language so everyone understands what I am going to say next. I expect the rest of Meester Forth's stay in your beautiful country to pass without further incident. Since you obviously have the license plate numbers, if anyone in this country so much as even thinks of pulling Meester Forth over for anything short of a murder there will be even worse consequences than what will come from this incident. I am not talking about complaints to your country's interior department next time, you'll have to deal with them tomorrow, oh no, I am talking complaints to the EU itself. In fact, even if there is a murder, I strongly recommend you weigh how much you needed that particular citizen, and even then I expect you to call me first. Do I make myself clear?"

The forlorn-looking officer manning the front desk nodded.

"Good, then we will take leave of you. Goodnight gentlemen," the lawyer snarled before leading them through the front doors and out into the night air.

"Well, what now?" Jake asked as they flowed across the lots towards their cars that had already been brought out of impound.

"It's gotten late. I'll arrange for us to stay nearby and then we can see about getting rooms somewhere closer to the target for tomorrow night," Vince replied. To his lawyer, he said, "Thank you for your timely assistance Signore Bottino. Hopefully, I won't have need of your services again, but please, if you would be so kind, leave your ringer on."

"It is no problem Meester Forth. Things like this, this is why I charge as much as I do," the lawyer smiled before making for his own very expensive-looking sports car.

Vince had out his phone leaving the rest of them to mill about.

"I'm surprised," Jake finally said over the sound of the lawyer peeling out of the station's parking lot and roaring away.

"About what, bro?" Todd asked.

"For all the dumb shit I've done in my life, that is the first time I've ever seen the inside of a jail cell. It wasn't as bad as I expected," Jake supplied.

"Let's not make a habit out of it, okay? If TV is any judge, American ones aren't as nice," Chris grunted with leftover annoyance.

Vince had snapped his phone closed and rejoined them, "All right, there's a casino not far from here. I have us rooms there for the night. They are the best rooms they have available, but to be frank, I had us booked in a countryside manor for tonight, which I have had to cancel, so I'm a bit bummed about that. I have no idea what we'll do for tomorrow night."

"I think that's gotta be our main goal for tomorrow. We need somewhere out of the way to lower our profile. So I think we're going to be spending the day looking for quaint village inns. Also, quaint inns that we pay for in cold hard cash will be less likely to be traced by Vukan," Chris replied.

"Yeah, and getting supplies," Jerry added.

"What for bro? I've seen plenty of stores," Todd looked confused.

"Here, sure, but we're right near the border. If we want to be safe to change tomorrow night, we better be in the middle of fucking nowhere," Sal explained.

"Yes, I may be rich, but I don't want to be paying for that kind of damage to a hotel room if it all could have been avoided," Vince agreed. "I had scouted online during the flight a little, and I've been here before, there are a ton of bed and breakfasts as well as cabins and houses littered through the country. It's Alpine and that means hikers and such. We can look them over tomorrow as a group and figure out the best one. As long as we stay away from the park around Triglav itself where he has his chateau we should be out of his more direct sphere of influence. What we do from there is anyone's guess."

And that was the problem, it was anyone's guess. Chris had to wonder what all this spy game crap was even going to accomplish. He had to get his girlfriend back, and that meant going to where Vukan was sooner or later. He was kind of hoping to avoid running into him werewolf to were-silly-looking-dog if he could avoid it. But other than that small hope that Vukan slipped up somehow, his options were kind of limited here. The guy was filthy rich, had a castle from the sounds of it, and they were in his country. Even though Vince said he was working on something, he wouldn't say what, and for all Chris knew, what he meant was he was working on a business merger. How on earth they intended to get him to come out and bring Suzanne with him when he did was beyond Chris. Worse, he had gotten everyone else into this, and he had no idea how he was getting them out.

It had seemed so obvious at the time, Vukan had her, Chris simply had to get her back. He had been thinking like an American the whole time, fast and to the point, and with laws he understood. But now that they were here, nothing seemed obvious at all.

CHAPTER 14

———————|———————

"I ain't that type of princess buddy!"– *Boudicca*

They had left the lodge behind that morning. It had been quick and efficient, breakfast was brought in at almost dawn, and she had been told to eat and make ready. Watching the miles go by she was discovering the difference between expectations and reality. Suzanne had seen the sign for "Slovenia" and just assumed that all "ia" countries that had belonged to the former Warsaw Pact were muddy old-world villages with donkey carts. They might have that kind of region in the country, she had no idea how big the place even was, but she hadn't seen any of that so far. It made her feel her dumb American conceits towards the rest of the world, the view out the window forced her to have to take them out and examine them a bit.

What she had been able to see whipping by out the windows as they sped off deeper into the heart of Europe looked more like what she thought of as Alpine, like Switzerland or Austria. Her complete blanking on more knowledge of Europe than that was not helping her here, since she began to wonder if the people here also wore wooden shoes and she suspected that was completely wrong. Suzanne at least had enough of a grasp that she also began to wonder what kind of sausage was popular in the region, so, she got that part right on the nose.

Mountains loomed up all around. She had thought she had understood the concept before from books and descriptions, but frankly, the Alps loomed far more than she had life experience to relate it to. Back home mountains didn't really loom, they more rolled along next to you cheerfully. These had begun their looming off to the left at first, and before too much longer they found themselves driving among them, following roads cut through miraculous valleys barely wide enough for one jagged mountain to end and the next to begin. That was some serious looming, it was wonder enough sun got down here for anything to grow.

Suzanne was more than fully aware by this point that she was also hopelessly lost. Between the turns they'd taken, and the way the roads kept changing their direction to accommodate passes and valleys, even if she did escape at this point she had no idea where she'd even run to. Away was still a pleasant option to consider and work toward, but not nearly as pleasant as it would be if she'd had the slightest clue where she was.

Finally, she had to ask something that had begun to bug her, "How do you even expect him to find you out here?"

Vukan smiled, "I am a very rich man, who owns the only castle in the region that isn't a museum or a tumble-down ruin. Between your... google, and simply asking, I am sure he will have no problem finding Grad Volk."

"Man, you don't like a fair fight at all, do you? I'm supposed to fall madly in love with someone who cheats? Why don't you ask him to tie one hand behind his back while you're at it?" she sneered.

"What do you mean, cheat? Once he finds the castle I intend to give him every chance to best me!" Vukan blustered at her; Suzanne could tell instantly that she had actually managed to score a direct shot here. He added quickly, "And tying his hands won't be necessary to make it fair, we werewolves heal quickly, I will be out of this sling by tomorrow."

She pressed on, "Oh sure, a fair fight in your backyard. Where you're used to the terrain, and you know where everything is, and your buddies are protecting you in case it goes south and you start to lose. Even if you kill him, you're still a loser in my eyes."

"We shall see," he replied cutting off that avenue of discussion off. He wasn't done talking, unfortunately, "But soon, you will see something else. Soon we will be at my castle, and maybe that will impress you."

As they rounded a bend she finally saw Grad Volk as it sat in a little valley at the foot of the mountains. Despite herself, Suzanne had to admit she was impressed. Not that he owned it, but that the place existed at all. She had known fairy tale castles existed in Europe, she'd seen pictures online, but she thought they all existed in Germany. If she somehow got out of this alive and sane, she'd have to write a book, "It Turns Out I Don't Know Shit About Slovenia." She could just fill it with observations for other Americans who don't pay that much attention to Europe except what they learned in school, which she would point out in the foreword, tends to skip a lot.

What she could see of the place from the car was a high stone base surrounded by a stream. Above that were whitewashed walls with slotted windows, and finally, a roof topped with red slate. It seemed that all of the structure was like that, from what she could see she guessed that it was three long walls connecting the turrets that soared above everything. Suzanne couldn't say for certain; she couldn't even see all of it as they drove across the first of multiple stone bridges that led to the rocky outcrop that it was built on.

Vukan could see her gawking, "I see you are impressed. Unfortunately, I cannot say that I built it. It has been in my family going back to the time of the Duke of Carinthia, which seeing as you are an uneducated American, I am sure means nothing to you. Suffice it to say, we are a very old family. Unlike the other Grads, Volk seemed to be a rather tough nut to crack for various invaders and usurpers and it remained with my family."

Suzanne could see why. It was isolated, to begin with, there didn't seem to be a village that it lorded over so there seemed no good reason to attack it for another thing. The walls were in very good condition, certainly, that fact detracted from its attractiveness to an advancing army. And, and this last important point was the one that probably had done it, it was full of werewolves. Taking a castle is tough, but when every person who manages to breach the walls instantly gets his throat ripped out, well it tends to take the will out of an army. When you looked at it all combined, you could see the communists had probably just viewed it as more trouble than it was worth and had just turned a blind eye to it. The Germans had probably done the same in World War 2 for similar reasons. Some hornet's nests just weren't worth sticking your dick into. One total massacre would have been enough to get the word out.

They entered the courtyard and as the cars pulled to a stop the wooden gate was pulled shut behind them by servants who had appeared as if from nowhere. At that moment Suzanne got a real deep-down feeling of how absolutely screwed she currently was. Like, in the middle of nowhere, in a castle, in the mountains, in a completely foreign country, a prisoner of the kind of guy who actually owns a god damned castle and has thugs and servants and a gate to close and everything. That is a level of screwed most people cannot even begin to comprehend. It makes going home for the day and realizing you forgot a major report that's due tomorrow look like freaking Disneyland.

The door to the limo was opened for them. Vukan stepped out and held his hand out for Suzanne, "Come my beautiful bird. Come see your golden cage."

Suzanne got out without taking his hand. Standing next to him was a largish man, the type rich guys usually have standing next to them to encourage other people to fuck off. Vukan ignored the insult of her not taking his hand entirely and said, "This is Janez. He will take you to your rooms in the castle. There are changes of clothing for you, and if you use the bell pull, food will be brought up. You will be happy to know that we have indoor plumbing. I have personally never been fond of baths, I prefer the crisp cold water of one of our mountain's streams, but I find it makes it easier to entertain business guests. So, you will be happy to be able to wash as well."

Janez took her arm rather forcefully before turning and starting to walk in a manner that indicated that she was coming with him regardless of her own opinions, it was a matter of her own dignity as to whether she walked or was dragged.

Vukan called after them, "Janez, I feel I should remind you; I do not want her bruised. Purple is an unattractive color in skin."

The man grunted, but his grip on Suzanne's arm lessened somewhat. Instead of responding to Vukan, he said to Suzanne, "You come with Janez, Janez no hurt."

As Suzanne stumbled to keep up she replied, "I can tell the conversation is going to be scintillating"

The interior of the castle was all white plastered walls, and either wood or stone floors. Various historical instruments of human mutilation were hung on the walls to give it a homey, cheerful Count Dracula feel. Along with the instruments of decapitation, there were shields depicting the same coat of arms in every room. Suzanne would have been pleasantly surprised if those shields had not had a wolf incorporated into the design. She was not pleasantly surprised at all. To finalize the motif of creepy castle, there were various taxidermied animals hanging on the walls looking ambivalent towards their fate as they stared out at the world through glass eyes. On the plus side, there were no giant candelabras dripping with wax, and there wasn't a cobweb anywhere to be found. In fact, for such an enormous place the appearance of the rooms was almost spotless. So it was a tidy castle of doom at least.

Janez finally let go of her hand, confident that she had gotten the idea by the time they got to the first set of wooden steps leading up. The stairway itself hugged tight to the wall like it had been used for defense as much as any formal entranceway. The wooden stairs weren't really large enough for him to drag her, so it was probably just being expedient rather than him relenting any. If he hadn't heard her feet on the steps behind him, he'd have probably grabbed her all over again and possibly just slung her over his shoulder.

One set of stairs became a second. Finally, on the third floor, Janez opened a door into a long hallway.

"So, you gonna' be stuck up here babysitting me?" Suzanne asked.

The large man just kept walking in front of her until he came to a door that he pulled open to point inside. "In there."

"Wait, what about the bathroom, the shower?" Suzanne protested.

The big man was quiet for a moment, probably trying to puzzle out the few words of English he knew, to not only understand what she asked, but then to manage a reply. He went with, "Also in there," before putting a meaty hand on her back and shoving her inside.

The large wooden door slammed shut behind her.

Suzanne immediately whirled and tried the handle. The door pulled open easily, she was able to lean out and see Janez's retreating back. That would seem good at first blush until you realized that what it really meant was they weren't particularly worried about her escaping. The consensus would appear to be that the building and the landscape around her would do a fine job keeping her a prisoner. Why bother locking the door or leaving a guard when there was nowhere she could go?

Now with that disheartening fact driven home, she gave up on escape for the moment and took stock of her room. There wasn't all that much to take stock of. It was dominated by a huge four-poster bed, there were a few rugs on the floor, and an enormous wardrobe sat against one wall. There were a few chairs and a vanity as well. There were windows, and she was sure the view was magnificent, but frankly, by this point, she didn't give a damn about the view unless it opened to an airport. To her left, there was another door. Opening it she breathed a sigh of relief. A bathroom, with a huge clawfoot tub, and a toilet. Which meant taking care of a pressing need and sitting down and contemplating the world for a few minutes, it had been a long drive again, and Vukan must have an amazing bladder. She realized, not for the first time, how dependent she'd gotten on her phone for potty amusement, she wondered what kind of books they had in this place for future trips. On the plus side, this room meant a glorious and wonderful bath. She hadn't been able to soak and relax for forever it felt by now.

She was reminded that Vukan had said there were clothes in her size as well. She made her way over to the wardrobe and threw it open. Inside were a series of dresses. It didn't matter what size they were; she was not wearing them. She didn't wear a dress normally unless someone was dead or getting married, to begin with, but considering the sexist motives for there being ONLY dresses she damned well wasn't wearing one of these. These were frilly girly dresses, as in all of them were frilly and girly, a frilly and girly all over, with no variation, she could see the mind at work here. With fear and trepidation at what she was already expecting she pulled open one of the drawers inside. The contents confirmed those suspicions, the underwear was all from the "Victoria Secrets Men Buying Them for Their Girlfriends Collection." Yep, she might consider some of those occasionally as a treat for when Chris had been an especially good boy, but she was double-dipped damned if she was wearing them here.

Suzanne was going to have words with someone about this. Until then, she'd see how many days she could stretch out her jeans and blouse. The bra and the panties might be more of an issue. Suzanne figured she might have to entertain the thought of washing them in the tub. It would be worth the bother because she was not getting dressed up in a fairy princess dress while wearing hooker lingerie underneath it strictly because Vukan liked it. No shot in hell.

Suzanne would worry about that later, but for now... she needed a bath.

Later she was redressed in her old clothes and was well on her way towards getting bored when the door to her room opened without a knock. A very pretty brunette woman dressed very similarly to the dresses that had been left for Suzanne walked in pushing a lunch trolley. She took one look at Suzanne and said, "I would have thought you would have wanted to bathe after your trip."

"I did get a bath actually. You are?"

The woman ignored that and instead demanded, "But you are still in the clothing you came here in? Why?"

"Tell Vukan it will be a cold day in hell before I dress up like a Cinderella princess for him, and that includes the underwear he picked out. I can only assume it was him, no sane woman chooses underwire for another woman. Again, you are?" Suzanne replied.

The woman smiled a bit, "I can see that you and Vukan will get along splendidly, and I will be sure to tell him all that you said. My name is Adja, I am Vukan's bitch. Well, I was at any rate. I bare him no more pups and see what he does."

Suzanne saw the anger she must have felt towards her and Vukan immediately, "Look, I have no interest in your man. I have my own. This has not been a willing European vacation on my part. And I am definitely not giving him any children, or pups either, or even a kiss on the cheek after a nice date to the movies."

The woman actually smiled a bit more at that, "I suppose we shall see about that, Vukan is very strong-willed, even if he is not very bright."

Suzanne tried to press the friendship angle further, an ally could go a long way here, "You speak English very well. I mean you have an accent, but other than that... did you go to college somewhere?"

The woman's pale face took on a slight look of melancholy, but only for a moment, "I studied abroad. My father was a man who had made money working for Vukan, but he still owned his own company. He had no sons, so with only a daughter to leave things to, he insisted I be educated in England. I did not meet Vukan until I came home to help with the business. We first met at a business luncheon."

"Fell in love over the books?" Suzanne tried on a smile.

Adja shook her head, "More that he became obsessed with me. Demanded me. My father was so dependent on his loans and business he pressured me into it. But obviously, he had sold me off to no normal marriage. Thank the gods we only have the two children."

"I'm sorry to hear that, no really, that sounds dreadful. Maybe it would have been better for you if I were here for your man. But as bad as I feel for you, still no dice, not happening."

Adja nodded, "It's too much to hope for. Still, I can probably help you with the clothing, frankly, Vukan is more interested in hunting than he is with the castle, he won't notice if I get some things sent from a local store. With the full moon up soon, his mind will only be on the days of change, and probably a bit of an obsession with killing your beau. He's very single-minded."

"Thank you, I mean except for the killing Chris part. I'll get into a screaming match with Vukan about everything if it comes to it, but it's already been a rough couple of days and I could use some clean clothes," Suzanne said gratefully.

"I understand. Just because my husband is an ass is no reason for me to be one. Before I leave to go to town to see to that, will you require anything else? Do you take any medications for instance?"

"Only birth control," Suzanne shrugged.

"Oh, well since I'm sure he didn't let you pack; do you know what you take? I am also sure you don't want to miss too many days," Adja said with a truly sincere smile.

That night Janez came into her room without knocking. He didn't even say anything he just stood there hulking. Suzanne's heart rate went up immediately. She had no way of knowing how loyal Vukan's underlings were, and she'd been rude to Janez earlier. For all she knew, he wanted to get some incredibly personal revenge on her and had come to collect.

"Yes?" she asked, cursing herself for the way her voice faltered.

"You come eat with Vukan," he grumbled.

Suzanne didn't bother to say something sarcastic. Of all the myriad of horrible reasons Janez could be there, dinner with a complete asshole barely even rated. She just got up and followed. When Janez finally opened a large wooden door and indicated she should enter, she was in no way surprised that they were dining in a great hall. Vukan was exactly the type of obnoxious shithead who would want to show off how exorbitantly wealthy he was to her by dining like this. There were probably half a dozen normal dining rooms in this place, but none of them were as pompous as this one.

He, because of course he did, sat at the head of the table.

Janez lumbered into the room and pulled out a chair near Vukan. Suzanne was forced to walk past the other guests to her seat. The men were all dressed in very expensive suits, the women in the same style of Sleeping Beauty reject clothing Vukan had thought he was going to get her into. She noticed that Adja was also next to Vukan, across from where she was expected to sit.

"Did you not have time to change?" Vukan started right in as soon as she was seated.

"No clothes," she said bluntly.

Vukan pretended to look shocked, Adja if anything looked amused at the exchange. "I was sure that I had ordered that there be clothing for you," he said in one of the worst acting performances in history that didn't involve Nicholas Cage slumming through a paycheck film.

Suzanne didn't even blink, "Yeah, must have been a bunch of stuff left over from your last kidnapping victim. Bunch of dresses and frilly Victoria's Secret undies, nothing I'd wear if my life depended on it."

"It might," Vukan growled.

"Still not wearing it," Suzanne replied sipping some of the soup that had been waiting for her at her place at the table.

Vukan stared hard at her for a moment, seeing not even a flicker in her expression, "Very well, we will have to see about something more congenial for you to wear."

"Please, I can only wash this outfit in the tub so many times," she replied, she was gratified to hear Adja have to choke back laughter. Adja had brought up her clothes and her pills earlier in the evening, but Suzanne had decided to make a point.

"In other news, you will be pleased to know, your boyfriend is indeed foolish enough to chase after you. I had him arrested at the border this afternoon," Vukan changed the subject so smoothly you could hear gears grinding.

Suzanne spluttered a bit at that. Some part of her hadn't even considered the idea that Chris would follow her. The part of her that loved the big goof was hoping that he'd be smart enough to stay the hell home and try to forget she'd even existed. She recovered enough to say, "Doesn't seem fair if you just go and attack him in a jail cell. Not very impressive."

Vukan smiled. "It turns out your beau has a powerful friend of his own. He should be out of custody shortly would be my guess. I cannot help but wonder, is Mr. Forth a friend who is helping, or is he one of your little pack?"

Suzanne had no idea who he was talking about since everybody just kept things to a first-name basis among the pack. Thankfully she didn't have to feign bewilderment, "I have no idea who you are talking about."

Vukan chuckled, "It doesn't matter. We have plans for any humans your boyfriend might bring along. If they knew what they are getting into, their hope should be that we just kill them."

The next morning started very slowly. It was not Chris' fault. Frankly, it was nobody specific's fault. The easiest place for them to find to stay after they were released from jail had been a casino, which had distractions. They had also been arrested earlier that day and had spent time in a jail cell, not to mention having to dodge the thugs in Italy. Take a bunch of men, who have had a major shock to their system that only a jail cell can provide, and release them into an atmosphere where alcohol can be found in plenitude. Watch what happens, we dare you. The fact that nobody had gotten alcohol poisoning or arrested again was the real achievement here. The place had its own brewery for the love of God, them even seeing morning was a minor miracle.

Chris was not too bad, he'd had a few beers, so it wasn't like he was being judgmental or anything. Exhaustion had just set in earlier on him and saved him from himself. Too much crap had happened that day, and really, he hadn't been sleeping well even before that because he was worried about Suzanne. They'd been trailed by mysterious Slovenians who absolutely meant them ill, they'd been arrested, and he hadn't even been in Europe for 48 hours yet. So, while the rest of the crew seemed to be just getting started, Chris had packed it in.

After ordering up breakfast for himself that mainly involved strong coffee, fruits, and a croissant, he took a gloriously hot shower to wash the detritus both inside and outside left over from yesterday. Clean, fed and caffeinated he packed up to leave. He wasn't in a particularly great rush, because he had serious doubts about what condition everyone else would be in. With nothing else to delay him, he went in search of the hungover and miserable to revel in their misery as you do. They had been the ones "having fun" last night, so you owed it to yourself to have yours now.

He found Todd first, who was neither hung over nor miserable but was already waiting in the lobby. Chris wasn't shocked, Todd was big on the whole, "My body is a temple" thing. He was also having a few, but at some point in the evening it was bound to dawn on him how many carbs were in these European beers and unless he switched to something harder, he would have gone to bed.

"Hey bro!" Todd smiled when he saw Chris.

"Hey yourself. Any word on the others yet?"

"Vince called down a while ago, said he had just gotten up."

As if on cue, the elevator opened and a worse-for-wear Vince entered the lobby with Sal in tow.

"You bros ready to jet?" Todd said brightly. This made Chris suspicious. Like, it was a little too bright and cheerful. Like maybe Todd actually had a sense of humor under everything and was enjoying the hard drinkers from last night's misery a bit.

"Not quite yet," Sal groaned. "I need to get some more coffee first."

"Also, we're down two yet. So while we wait, if you'll excuse me and Sal," Vince added.

A few minutes later Jerry came down. He didn't look all that terrible, but he still looked grateful when Chris pointed to where Vince and Sal were hovering near the enormous coffee tureen. This place knew its customers.

Chris gave it a few more minutes before he went over to Vince, "Since you're paying for the rooms, they should be able to open them up for you."

"I guess, why?" Vince looked confused.

"Jake appears to be sleeping in. We need to get going, don't we? Go get a card and let's retrieve our final team member. I need something, I'll meet you there," Chris smiled as he headed for the elevator.

A few minutes later Vince was standing in front of Jake's front door with a key card. He saw Chris coming, "All right, why do we need to enter the room?"

"Did you knock?"

"No, is there something wrong?" Vince looked worried.

Chris brought around the ice bucket he had had behind his back, "No, but most likely he wouldn't have woken up if you'd knocked. We've been best friends most of our lives, and he was well on his way to plastered when I went to bed." Chris smiled, "Just open the door Vince, and let me handle it."

Vince's finger rose after he swiped the card as if he was about to say something, but Chris was already in the room. He deftly lifted up the blanket that was covering Jake's sleeping form and tossed the ice cubes under it. He then stepped back and waited.

A few moments later, Jake's muffled exhausted voice said, "You know, I really hate you right now. You know that, right?"

"No you don't, you're still under the influence of copious amounts of alcohol. So, you getting up?" Chris replied cheerfully.

The blanket was flung back, Jake blinked at him, "Yes, but just know that I would hate you even more if I was even remotely sober."

"I will take that under consideration. Want some help getting to the shower?"

"I'll manage, you evil prick."

Chris turned to Vince, "We'll be down in just a few minutes. Go enjoy your coffee." Turning back to Jake he said cheerfully, "Guess who isn't driving the Mercedes today?"

"Why was my best friend replaced with the devil?" Jake moaned from the shower.

CHAPTER 15

—————⋅—————

"Be vewwy, vewy quiet." – *E. Fudd*

Once Jake was put back together enough to be trusted inside a motor vehicle without throwing up or releasing any unfortunate odors, they set out on the next leg of their journey. Despite promises that he was fine, Jake was still stuffed into the back seat by himself and Sal sat up front with Chris who was driving. Trust only went so far when vomit was a possibility. Todd had surprised everyone by more or less demanding he be allowed to drive the other car, since he normally didn't really ever demand anything. Jerry and Vince hadn't put up much of a fight though, while they weren't in the same deplorable condition as Jake, they could see it more clearly, blearily really, from where they stood than they could see Todd's bright-eyed and bushy-tailed demeanor.

The landscape quickly changed as they drove down the highway. Any of the previous soft flat land and farms were quickly replaced by the foothills and solid rock of the Alps. By the time they reached the capital city of Ljubljana, the Alps were nearby and dominated the view. It should be beautiful, but Chris felt that it was kind of ominous. Like instead of rising majestically, they were thrusting up with sinister intent. He knew that somewhere in those mountains that he assumed had been featured on so many postcards, the jerk-off that had caused all of this was lurking. A spider in his web just waiting for them to step onto a strand so he could devour them.

Ljubljana itself was a gorgeous city. Almost like something out of a fairy tale, it even had a castle on a hill overlooking it to complete the Lord of the Rings feel. Chris wished this trip was for pleasure, he wished Suzanne was here to see this with him, he wished that there was a holy hope in hell that they wouldn't have to flee this entire country and never come back again when this was all over with. And fleeing with Suzanne in tow was the good version, the one he was trying to focus on. He had to believe that when they did flee, it would be with Suzanne when they did it, otherwise, they might as well just go back to Italy now to be overfed by Sal's sister-in-law.

They were sitting in a nice restaurant. Nice enough to have plenty of shadows promoting romance. Thankfully the place dealt with the tourist trade here and the menu was available in English. In fact, the waiter could speak it as well, scratch that, probably better than Jake had been managing at about two AM last night. Dumplings figured heavily into everything, as did really large numbers next to every item on the menu, which Vince had told them to not worry about because he was paying. Chris being solidly middle class by nature worried anyway.

The big goal of the moment was trying to figure out where in the hell they were going to stay tonight. Since nobody wanted to just park the cars and hope for the best with the moon tonight, especially with Jake along, it had a particular urgency. They had canceled last night's original reservations, and they didn't want to stay in the city since it was sure to be watched. But being spied on wasn't the most important factor in their decisions, though not being spied on definitely had preference. Tonight was going to be a full moon. They wanted somewhere where they could roam free, and say they had been enjoying a nighttime hike or something if anyone asked. They needed a place to come back to int the morning with a little privacy. There being six of them did not help matters one wit. There were plenty of places in the mountains, but they had to have six rooms open tonight and be isolated enough that five of those guests could vanish into the woods for the night without getting into any kind of major mischief. It wasn't an easy get even with so many choices available and even with Vince doing some pre-scouting. All of them had their phones open and were going through google except for Jake, who had his laptop out.

"Oh, this is maddening," Jake growled.

"What part? You've got plenty to choose from," Chris replied as he toyed with his dessert dumpling, which was a delicious hazelnut

CURSE OF THE WEREPOODLE | 193

concoction. He would have loved it if he wasn't already feeling a little heavy from all of the dumpling-based food.

"That's the problem right there! Finding a place. I mean there's plenty to choose from, but last minute and everything… and you guys are going to want to be able to go roam tonight…"

"Have there been any favorites?" Vince asked.

"Well there's a few near this lake, you can rent a whole apartment. Hell if you had enough money you could rent a building or two adjoining…" Jake shook his head.

"Please, may I look at your laptop?" Vince said.

"Yeah sure, but…"

Vince looked at the pages that Jake had up flipping through them quickly before he seemed to make a decision. A moment later he took out his own phone. He pressed the screen once, almost instantly he was talking, "Hello Robert. Yes, still Slovenia. Look I'm going to email you some pages, I want them rented out for myself and my traveling companions, pay what you have to. Six of us need to sleep with our own rooms. Arrange so my name isn't anywhere near it. Great, text me when it's done."

After pressing a button he handed Jake his phone and said, "Here, send those links to this email, please. Head it as 'Urgent from Wolfie,' Robert will know it's me."

"You seem pretty positive that…" Chris began as he waved his hand.

"Actually Jake hit the perfect place, it's in the mountains, lots of space to roam, and there are a bunch of those mountains between there and Vukan's castle. We won't accidentally be bumping into bigger and badder puppies that way. The nice thing about my kind of money is I could buy the place if I needed to, short notice won't be an issue," Vince said with a smile.

Chris wondered if he could get a job working for Vince.

To get to the lake they were staying near took them away from seeing mountains in the distance to seeing them as a constant presence. They had driven for quite some time through what appeared to be a long flat valley between massive upthrusts. Nestled inside the valley there was a major highway and the numerous small pull-off towns you'd expect with the highway. They'd also passed another castle on the way; castles were way more common than in America it would seem. Apparently, Slovenia had a proud and lengthy history of sieges. Chris wondered if maybe there had been disputes over dumpling recipes.

After spending some time on the highway they had turned off the major road onto a road that while still well maintained dropped to two lanes and took them in a slightly upward direction at first, into yet another intersecting valley carved out between the behemoth mountains that had become constant companions. It was possible that there were mountains this high in the Appalachian Mountains they had back home, maybe even higher in the Rockies or something but they didn't feel like this. Those mountains back home had a completely different vibe to them, you could get homey and become friends with the mountains back home. These mountains spoke of violence in their creation, and of the violence that could happen to a man if he got too clever hiking at their highest most brutally upthrust spots. The view was frankly breathtaking while at the same time more than a little intimidating.

After the drive became steeper for a while they arrived at the lake that was the main local attraction. It wasn't a particularly large lake, but it was crystal clear and gave them commanding views of the nearby peaks. A little town of rental chalets had grown up around the place, Chris figured skiing was probably a really big-ticket item come winter, at least if all the James Bond films he'd watched as a kid hadn't lied to him that was. For the rest of the year, a lakeside chalet would probably be just the thing to make for a dream vacation for someone. Jake was taking pictures with his phone like mad and had to be yelled at repeatedly not to post anything until this was over, especially considering that posting a bunch of pics would more or less be telling the bad guys exactly where they were if they were spying on his social media. And considering they had Jake's name, you had to assume they were.

From the little village of chalets, they needed to carefully navigate up an increasingly narrow road to get to the place where they were staying. They had two cabins rented, built next to each other at the end of the road deeper in the forest than any of the more popular lodges and hotels below. There was already a car in one of the teeny spots in front of the buildings when they pulled up, so Chris had to be extra careful pulling in behind it. Thankfully the thing was only a Fiat 500, though how the thing functioned in these steep mountains was a miracle of automotive obstinance. He was happy to see it, it meant there was ample room to park the cars on this tight little dead-end street. A Mercedes S Class might not be the big things they used to be, but space was still at a premium with a mountain on one side and a drop on the other.

Standing out front was a middle-aged man that could be best described as weedy looking; scrawny would have worked, short, pint-sized would have also been in there as well. Rat faced might have worked additionally as a descriptive. Basically, Fredo from the Godfather had a Slovenian relative that they could have used as a stunt double is what we're going for here. He looked nervous as all get out, but then again, if he had figured out who he was renting to, or even the kind of people who had rented these cabins from him, well, nobody likes to be sued into non-existence, so that does cause nerves. Chris could understand the guy's demeanor, one day you haven't gone up to the rental place in a minute, it's been slow and it's empty, and you figure you'll clean it at some point, but no rush. And then out of the blue some very lawyerly type people call and say they want the place tonight; cost is no object. It would throw anyone off.

His frightened eyes could have sued his mouth for libel over the bright smile it portrayed when they got out of the cars. He clapped his hands together and said with forced joviality and a bit of an accent, "Welcome, welcome! So nice of you to choose to stay here!"

Vince walked forward and shook the man's hand with a smile, "Thank you for being able to accommodate us on such short notice. I do apologize for that; I didn't expect the layover. If I ever have opportunity to come again, I'll certainly book further in advance."

The nervousness was explained in an instant when the man replied, "For you Mr. Forth it is not trouble. You honor my home! Please, let me show you the houses!"

Vince's eyes went dark for a moment, Chris could see the annoyance at the man knowing who he was, but thankfully the man himself was oblivious to Vince's irritation. Shaking everyone's hands, the little man directed them to follow him so he could show them the cabins. The tour didn't take long, there wasn't all that much to show. There were bedrooms that looked comfortable, a living room with a small TV, a dining room.... even with showing off the almost non-existent amenities of the spartan bathroom and kitchen it could only be stretched out so long.

The man stood by the front door and said, "Well, I have payment already. If you need me for nothing else, I will leave you be."

"No, I think that should be all, and thank you again for having us on short notice," Vince smiled again.

The man scuttled off to the car while most of the group were still exploring the house some before they went out to the cars to get their bags. Chris was looking out his window trying to take in his situation some in a bit of a daze. He was standing in a cabin in Slovenia, chasing a werewolf, it seemed so unreal and ridiculous. While he watched, he was surprised to see the caretaker pull out his phone before he even got into his car. Probably he noticed it more because he was just as surprised that they had signal out here, about the only thing he could see was trees and mountains, so having service was kind of amazing. As Chris watched, the man got into his car he seemed to be involved in an animated conversation with somebody. Chris couldn't help but notice he still looked shaken, which was odd considering everything he'd already gotten through with this rental, and it going that easy. You'd have thought he'd be relieved to have survived this meeting. Who knew, maybe running tourist places was particularly stressful in Slovenia for some reason.

"So, what do we do now?" Jerry asked the room in general, shaking Chris out of his reverie.

"Well, first I call my office to find out how the man knew who I was," Vince said with a growl. But then just as quickly it was replaced with a smile, "After that we unpack, and then I take you fine gentlemen to dinner. I already checked, we have choices."

Suzanne let out a sigh of relief when after dinner Vukan excused himself and Adja had walked her back to her room. Not having to talk to Vukan was a blessing, what do you really say to a kidnapper? Lovely weather in this place you dragged me to? Adja was also a vast improvement over Janez who frankly scared her. Adja was quiet, but it was a calculating quiet as if the woman was trying to make some kind of decision about Suzanne. Suzanne on the other hand hoped it wasn't worrying about Vukan's plan to convince Suzanne to be a polygamous bride that was causing her concern. That, was not happening, the castle had very high windows if it came to that.

Finally, Adja left Suzanne in her room without a word. Her empty room, miles from home, away from everyone she loved and cared about, in a castle owned by a total creep.

Sleep took its sweet time in coming.

It would be a misnomer to say that things had looked better in the morning. How in the hell could they really? She was still stuck in a castle being held by a psycho who wanted to murder her boyfriend and then rape her. To make matters worse, which shouldn't even be possible, it would be the full moon tonight. A life dream, to turn into a little dog in a castle full of wolves. What could possibly go wrong with that? Okay, that was a bad train of thought, maybe she'd be better served by thinking of places in here that she could hide for the duration.

Breakfast has been waiting for her when she got up. She was not particularly happy that people could come in here quietly enough not to wake her. You would have thought that enough time in a combat zone would have cured that, so she had to think they must move amazingly quietly. But, there was coffee with that breakfast, and it was still warm, so it wasn't a total loss. The rest of it consisted of sausage of some kind, cut fruit, and some kind of oatmeal. Since it wasn't quite the oatmeal she was used to, she hazarded a guess that it might be porridge. It was food, and since she wasn't big on breakfast anyway as anything more than fuel, it did the job.

When she got up to get dressed, she checked the big wardrobe that had been full of stupid dresses the night before. She brightened when she saw that it was full of blouses. A check of the drawers showed jeans, some dress pants, and normal human underwear right down to running bras. Adja had delivered the goods as promised. She might not totally trust the Slovenian woman yet, but she definitely owed her one.

She contented herself with a light workout that could be done in the room. After that, a shower and dressed later she tried to consider what in the hell to do with the rest of her day. She didn't have a phone, didn't have a computer, there was no TV, there weren't even any books in here yet. She'd been so concerned with the clothing situation she'd forgotten to ask for books. Hell, she couldn't even write a book to amuse herself since there wasn't a pen or paper. The night she'd spent at the lodge had been one thing, it felt like a wilder situation, to begin with, like a real camping kidnapping. This was the lap of luxury with none of the luxuries she took for granted. She'd had breakfast waiting for her this morning, it had involved fruit, you shouldn't be without TV or books in a place that served you sliced fruit for breakfast, it didn't seem natural. The pampered clashed with the prisoner aspects of her life and did it hard.

After the fifth time looking out the window and trying to enjoy the view, it dawned on her that she hadn't even tried the door. She just assumed it was locked, but then she remembered that assume broke down to ass u me and figured why not. It hadn't been locked before, why would it be now? It pulled open easily. Revealing Janez. Who was mainly hulking there quite effectively. So maybe someone had developed a fear of her fleeing overnight.

"What you want?"

"A book or something, I'm bored," she replied.

"You are prisoner, prisoners get bored," he shrugged.

She couldn't argue that, so she decided to try another tact, "You should be nicer to me. I might be Vukan's new bride soon."

The big man let out a rumbling chuckle at that, finally, he replied, "Ask Adja how much we care what she thinks. Go inside like good pretty little girl. If someone comes by, maybe I let them take you to library."

Suzanne did not know how, but someone was going to pay for

this.

Thankfully Adja came with lunch right about when Suzanne thought she was going to lose her mind from boredom.

"Oh thank god," she burst out before she could stop herself when the door opened.

Adja looked a bit taken aback by that, "I did not expect such a warm welcome. But, hello!"

Suzanne smiled, "Are you kidding, with nothing but that big lug outside to keep me company, and nothing even to read in here, you are a breath of fresh air, a burst of sunshine into my otherwise dreary life"

Adja laughed a little at that, "If only more people here were that happy to see me. I want you to note that it's amazing what money can do, especially when your husband doesn't understand computers enough to look over your shoulder. If you look under your plate you'll also see I had your prescription filled out for you."

"You're a godsend. In fact, you're the only person who is nice to me in this place. Which, is kind of odd when you think why I'm here."

Adja nodded, "A little suspicion would do you good here. But you can trust me on two things. I absolutely do not want Vukan to get you pregnant. If you can hold him off or get out of here this month all for the better, but if you can't you'll note you have next month and some day after pills as well. Secondly, I am as much a prisoner here as you are. Believe me, if I could even get over the border to Austria or Italy right now. Well, if I could take you with me, Vukan wouldn't have to worry about leaving two women unsatisfied and miserable because we'd both be gone."

"That bad?"

"I curse the day I met him. It is like being married to my grandfather. No, I take it back, my Great Grandfather, all the sexism, all the old superstitions, all the second-class citizenry for women. I'm an educated woman, Vukan thinks if I think too much my brain might get overheated," she practically spat.

"Ah, so, something to look forward to then?"

Adja looked up at her in shock for just a moment before they both began to laugh. It felt so good to laugh and to feel a connection with a single human being for even a moment. The tension of the relationship that had been constructed by this ridiculous situation between the two of them finally seemed to dissipate completely. Suzanne could see where maybe Vukan would be smart enough to want Adja to be friendly to Suzanne to maybe weaken her opposition, but if he did, Adja had gone off script quite a bit.

"Well, I feel better for that, "Suzanne breathed.

"I would rather we spent the rest of the day like this. Unfortunately, our Lord and asshole expects us at a party this afternoon," Adja replied before letting out a sigh,

"What on earth would he be celebrating that he wants me there?" Suzanne looked perplexed.

Adja shook her head, "I assume it can't be for anything good, but he didn't bother to tell me. He just left word with a servant that I was to see that you were presentable."

"You know, he really is a douchebag," Suzanne snorted.

Adja smiled, "I don't know that word, but I can sort of guess from inflection there. Rich men are all pampered fools, but he is a rich man who is the head of an ancient pack of wolves. So it is, what did you say? Douchebag? It is douchebag squared."

They heard a car door slam below them. Suzanne went to the window. She caught a flash of a dark-haired man being ushered inside. She could also see that tables were being set out along with chairs for whatever this afternoon's festivities would be. Teens wandered around talking to each other, probably children of the pack. She considered for a moment making a run for it now during the bustle and confusion and immediately thought better of it. In a few, all too short hours this castle would be full of wolves, and she would be a cute little dog that got carried by rich women with one hand and got called Snookums. Unless something happened that changed the dynamics for her, she had no idea how she was going to escape this place. Sure, Chris was supposed to be coming for her, but really that was just a trap. A trap that couldn't be sprung if she wasn't the bait, bait that at the moment felt completely screwed.

Suzanne turned back to Adja, "How does he feel about makeup? Do you even have any? I could protest and not do anything, but I haven't been able to wear makeup in days. I'm torn here, part of me just wants to look like a slob to say fuck you to him, part of me wants to look like me to say look you haven't broken me. I don't know, what do you think?"

Adja nodded at that, "Well, yes I do have makeup. I would go with the second one. He would love to see your spirit crumbling already. It would give him all the excuse he needed to make you feel like a princess, by force if necessary. Of course, he thinks a princess is an airheaded nincompoop who sits around all day waiting for a big strong man."

"Have you two considered marriage counseling?"

"I'd poison his food if there was any silver in this place. Maybe I will buy some soon since our children are nearly grown anyway," she snorted.

Suzanne laughed as well, "Well, we have definitely found a common denominator. Our hatred of Vukan."

While they were talking, more people were filing in across the bridge that led into the castle. Inhabitants of the castle were out and mingling, drink, and food was just now being set out. The oddity was that most of the guests looked just like normal people. The cars that pulled up were what you'd expect to see on any street, and the people were the people you'd expect to own them. Vukan was rich, he was very rich, and from what she could gather his family had been rich for a very long time. It seemed off for him to become a man of the people in this particular situation.

Adja looked over Suzanne's shoulder, "Well, I suppose you should eat up. Vukan will be unbearable if he needs to send someone up to fetch us. I mean, more unbearable than normal."

After putting on some makeup and some of the light business formal clothes she now had, Adja and Suzanne went out to the wide and open courtyard where the party was being held. The inhabitants of the castle seemed happy enough. That couldn't be said for the normal people who were in attendance for today. Even though they seemed to be drinking more than enough, the guests still looked pensive.

Suzanne leaned into Adja as they came outside through a nondescript side door, "Who are these people?"

"Locals mainly, nearby towns and villages. Vukan loves to pretend he's still some medieval lord for the area and that these are his peasants. Of course, if he's to be believed, he remembers a day when their grandparents honestly were his family's subjects. I don't know how long the extended life of a werewolf is, but for one who was born to it like him, it's supposedly considerable," Adja replied.

"Oh great, if I don't find a way out of here, I'll be stuck with the asshole for decades," Suzanne sniffed.

Adja looked thoughtful at that, "You know, I don't really know if it affects those who are just infected with it that way. Considering my own situation, maybe I should ask around a bit. If it doesn't it would give me something to look forward to."

Vukan appeared with a flourish, exiting the castle through a set of double doors that led into the castle's main hall, his hands raised as if he was greeting an adoring public. It received strained applause from the locals and more enthusiastic claps from the inhabitants of the castle. Funny that. He looked so happy, not for a second noticing that not all of the applause seemed sincere as he stepped onto the stage, mugging for imaginary cameras like he was the star of Evita.

Vukan did the hands thing indicating the crowd should drop the applause, you know, the thing where the person looks like a three-year-old waving who hasn't gotten side to side down and they're just waving their hands up and down in front of themselves? Okay, maybe the book just knows weirder three-year-olds than you do. Willing to concede that.

Adja leaned in and whispered to Suzanne, "I will translate, he will want to know you heard his grand speech. If not, he will only make you sit through it again later."

Vukan finally decided he had everyone's attention. He said in a loud voice that carried around the courtyard, "Welcome friends! We are here to celebrate an ancient family tradition. Tonight, is the night of the hunt!"

Suzanne couldn't help but notice that the applause that broke out was definitely even more divided this time.

A younger lean looking man had joined Vukan on the stage his face showing a ton of nervous energy. Where everyone else was dressed in what seemed to be their Sunday best, he was dressed in a tracksuit and trail running sneakers. Vukan continued once the applause had died again, "As you know, tonight is the opportunity for one of the local poor to become a very rich man. In ancient times the prize would be a plot of land, when being a landowner was the height of wealth. Times have changed, of course, your farms, many of which your families received from the hunt, well, they are nice, but maybe that doesn't make you wealthy these days." Vukan smirked as he said it, and it received the polite laughter it aimed for.

Vukan waved his hand expansively to work the crowd, "But now, we make you a rich man in another way. A million Euros!" More applause erupted, this time even the locals seemed enthusiastic. Vukan waited and then added, "But even if young Miha fails tonight, never fear, his wife will receive a lovely house and a plot of land, and his children will be cared for all through and including the cost of their schooling. It's win/win for our Miha! So please, enjoy our hospitality this afternoon, and except for Miha, be sure to leave well before dusk!"

With a flourish Vukan left the stage after that, leaving the poor Miha standing there trying to figure out what he should do next. After a few minutes of realizing that was everything he was needed for at the moment, the poor man just slunk quietly off the stage.

Everyone else returned to the food and drink made available by Vukan. The party filled the rest of the afternoon and filled the revelers with drink and food. Except for Miha. Miha looked everywhere, his eyes darting over to almost every corner, Suzanne even felt them flit over her briefly. Satisfied with something, the young man just started walking. Like, he walked right out through the gates, looked over his shoulder for any kind of pursuit, and then just booked for it as fast as his legs could carry him. Within moments he had vanished into the surrounding woods.

Suzanne tugged on Adja, "Umm hey. Hey, should the guy Vukan brought on stage just a minute ago be making a run for it like that?"

"If he knows what's good for him he will," she replied.

"Huh?"

Adja sighed, "He's what they'll be hunting once the moon is out. They think it's funny to let him have a head start like this to give him false hope. The old tradition is if he gets away and they don't kill him, they owe him a fortune. If they do kill him, his family is always taken care of. They scout the slums, they find a man with a wife and children, maybe a man who owes a lot of money to the wrong people. For him, it's a way out that takes care of his family for them it is a fun diversion and a tradition. And who knows, maybe he lives through the night?"

"How often has that happened?"

"Twice that I know of," Adja frowned.

Suzanne frowned back, "So, it's more or less a party to celebrate tonight's murder."

"Well, when you put it like that... I suppose it is. Anyway, we should get you back inside. The party is about to wrap up, and you don't want to be out here when it does," Adja took her arm as she spoke.

Suzanne could see she was right. Already the locals were getting in their cars to leave. She couldn't say she blamed them. She didn't particularly want to be here herself come sunset either. If only one of the retreating villagers had offered her a ride she'd be out of here while the wolves were busy tonight. She turned back to the courtyard before she went inside and saw the sun beginning to make its way over the mountains. It would be beautiful if it wasn't the harbinger of something so horrible.

CHAPTER 16

———————|———————

"So enough about me, how was your night?" – *Ash Williams*

The sun was beginning to set already as they climbed further into the mountains. Jake had been left back at the hotel with silver weaponry in the form of a loaded gun and a knife and strict orders to not open the door for any canines of any kind. Even if they did look adorable which was the case with Sal. People just have a soft spot for pugs, so this needed to be stressed repeatedly.

"This is gonna be great!" enthused Jerry as they stopped by a recognizable outcropping of rocks where they were expecting to change.

"How da' fuck you figure that?" Sal demanded.

Jerry shrugged as he folded his clothes to put in their agreed-upon stash area, "You know, we'll get to run around an entirely new place! I mean really wild and stuff, not fenced in at all."

"Yeah bro," Todd agreed enthusiastically, "who knows what they got to chase up here."

Sal snorted with disgust, "Listen to the two of you. We'll be lucky if we don't end up on the menu in these mountains."

"How do you figure?" Chris asked.

"They got bears here kid, they got lynx, they got real wolves in this country. Do you know what I would do to a lynx if I ran into one?" Sal demanded.

"No, what?" Chris returned his question with another.

"Give it terrible fucking gas and maybe the shits, that's what," Sal replied.

"Hmmm maybe it's not too late to go back to the cabin and get drunk first," Vince mused.

It was too late, and it was no little trepidation that they saw the sun set over the mountains.

Suzanne cracked her door as the sun went down. She didn't want to be trapped in this room with a castle full of werewolves all around her. It was so far from her to-do list it was below cleaning the grout in her bathroom. She had little hope of outrunning the monsters, simple physics worked against it, but if they turned nasty while she was trapped in her room she had no hope at all. She had to figure that if Chris could open his door back home, these beasts could operate the simple ancient latch mechanism on the door. How could she even hope to keep them out?

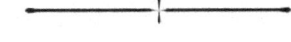

Jake watched the sun going down from the back deck of the cabin. He'd have to go to his room soon so he wanted to enjoy the view and the early evening air at peace with a beer. He was at peace that is, beer is usually all fizzy and stuff. That he'd have to go in soon was kinda lame. He figured there might be some nightlife down there in town that he was completely missing. Maybe hot Slovenian chicks who dug Americans or hot Swiss stewardesses on vacation who also dug Americans. But he'd promised Chris, and he could see his buddy's point. For all he knew, werewolves could catch your scent on the breeze. How do you even explain being in a bar and suddenly having a poodle bust in to savage you? Better to stay in his room just to avoid that kind of embarrassment if nothing else.

Janez carefully parked the car along a wooded road. By nature he did everything carefully, he was a large man, and so many people and things were so fragile. Here in the woods, it was already almost dark and he didn't want to attract attention. He needed to hurry to be ready in time. Still, it didn't do to be messy, he carefully folded his clothes as he took them off and set them inside the vehicle to await the coming of the moon.

Vukan stood naked in the courtyard, attended by his favorites. Even before the change he could catch the slightest hints of Miha still lingering on the wind, the man's fear was like a beacon of sweat and adrenaline in the air. It would be a good hunt tonight with mandatory attendance from the entire pack. Vukan wanted to show the pack he had no lasting effects from his injuries. Miha looked like he might be able to move quickly, and he didn't seem particularly stupid. Hunting a human wasn't perfect, but what was? Tonight might even be a bit of a challenge!

Oooo, now that was some good writing wasn't it? Juxtaposing all of them watching the sun going down like that? Seriously, go back and re-read how we did that there! You don't see that in any damned Twilight books! Unless it was there because frankly we didn't read them and we're just making a cheap joke. Someone go read one and report back. Look... okay, we'll stop now. Back to the story.

Chris had to admit that the mountain air was invigorating. His curly fur actually seemed to have some function up here for a change, instead of something that made him look stupid like it usually did. If it was just him and Jerry they'd probably have a blast just tearing through the forest primeval and everything. Jerry often did just that, taking off ahead of them, leaving it to Chris to slow down on his own so Sal, Vince, and Todd could catch up. Eventually, it would dawn on Jerry that he was alone, and he would come galloping back dumbfounded that a Pug couldn't keep pace with him.

If Sal had had the energy to do it with, he absolutely would have bit Jerry after the third time.

And the thing was, while Chris felt bad for running ahead to be with Jerry his body just wanted to run. He wasn't even sure if he liked Jerry yet. Jerry was his girlfriend's ex; he'd bit Jerry in a very sensitive location. It was a lot to just get over in not that long of a while. Chris couldn't also help but think that it felt weirdly unsafe letting the husky shepherd get too far out ahead of them by himself. Chris knew deep down they should all be within barking distance for safety reasons. Technically they had an entire set of very large mountains between them and the werewolves that wanted to kill them, but considering the very fact that those werewolves did want to kill them, those mountains didn't seem nearly big enough.

The other problem wasn't just that Jerry was faster than Sal, there was the fact that Jerry was faster than Chris. Maybe he was naturally faster, or maybe instinctively Chris was holding back a bit so he wouldn't get too far out ahead of the smaller dogs. He felt stuck acting like a bridge between Jerry who wanted to run like hell, and the other three who were running as fast as their little legs could handle trying to keep up and failing miserably.

Chris had lost Jerry yet again and had paused to wait for the others to catch up. Frankly, he hated being alone up here. Being up here with the others was great, it was invigorating, alone was spooky. When the big dogs had been threatening the werepack, the experience had created a mindset of wanting to stick together, and that mindset had stuck. Just because they didn't think there was anything particularly dangerous on this particular mountain, despite Sal's misgivings if something did happen it just felt better to have the group handy to try and think it through. They weren't home where they all knew how to deal with things, they should try harder to remember that. Sometime soon he was going to have to find a way to rein Jerry in for the rest of the night.

His hearing could just about pick up the smaller dogs coming up behind him, they'd be here soon. He'd also noticed Jerry seemed to be heading back as well, he could hear his panting and footpads approaching. What was weird was, every other time he'd realized he'd lost the others Jerry had just trotted back a little sheepishly. This time it seemed like he was running full-bore in this direction.

At first, it didn't even look like Jerry was going to slow down as he approached. The dog slid to a halt and growled, "We have to run!"

"Why?"

"Hunters!" Jerry whined.

"So?"

"They're hunting us! They saw me, pointed a gun, shot at me, and then let a bunch of tracking dogs loose! We have got to get the hell out of here!"

Nothing needed to be said after that, both Jerry and Chris whirled and started running back toward the others.

Chris barely slowed as he barked, "Run, we have to run, dogs, hunters coming for us!"

That was enough for the smaller dogs. Even Sal whirled and started running the way they'd come. It was frustrating for Jerry to stay with the pack, but Chris managed to get the idea across that the two big dogs should stay in the rear. If there were hounds on their trail, Chris and Jerry could fight back. Sal would have no shot at all.

As fast as the little dogs tried to run on the uneven terrain as they dodged rocks and trees, it didn't seem to be fast enough. Already when Chris looked back he could see spotlights shining through the night, and he could even begin to hear the baying of the bloodhounds as they closed in on them. Something was going to have to be done, and soon. Chris didn't know why in the hell there were crazed Slovenians chasing them, but there absolutely were and he wasn't in the right shape to try and talk any misunderstandings out with them.

A gunshot went off behind them, followed almost immediately by a yelp of pain from Sal. Vince turned to see what had happened and immediately lost his balance, tumbling down the hillside away from them.

"Vince!" yelped Todd.

"My ass! They shot my ass! That was silver!" yelped Sal louder.

Chris made to go downhill to see if he could rescue Vince, but Jerry nudged him. "No time, look."

Chris could see he was right. The lights were almost close enough to reveal their little pack to the hunters. The bloodhounds would be here any second. Chris made an executive decision. "Grab Todd!" he barked before picking Sal up by the scruff of his neck with his teeth.

Jerry got the idea, Chris could tell by the way Todd whined, "Awww not cool bro!"

Sal only whined, "Who shoots a guy in the ass like that?"

Chris didn't know where he was going by this point, other than away from the hounds. It was kind of worrisome that Jerry seemed to be following his lead since he really wasn't leading as much as fleeing. It worried him, even more, when he saw that the lights and the hounds had stopped. Right about where Vince had fallen. The hopelessness of it set in, there was nothing they could do for Vince, they might not even be able to save themselves tonight. Those assholes had definitely been looking for them or someone like them. It meant that once they were done with Vince they'd be back on the remaining dog's trail They'd only grazed Sal, but he was still bleeding a little, Chris could feel the occasional drop hit his paw as he ran. The hounds would have an easy trail to follow.

The baying of the hounds had started in their direction again. He could only hope that he could find them a place to hide, and he was also hoping against hope that they hadn't found Vince.

That was when he had the best idea he'd had all day, well night really. There was a lake and a river right below them. All they had to do was make it down there, survive until dawn, somehow get their clothing back, and figure out what to do about Vince. Oh, and try to get Suzanne back after that. Easy.

Suzanne was not happy. It had been a constant state for a while now, but right now managed to be worse. She was a small dog, in a huge castle, so that was already too much for her, everything dwarfed her far too much. It was an unnatural feeling the way everything towered, there was too much empty space that just seemed to swallow her up. It wasn't outdoors where open air was to be expected, she was still indoors, and indoor rules are strict in the minds of dogs. It was so open it felt like it should be outside, but outside didn't have furniture. Speaking of which, she wanted to be outside. She wanted to run on something natural. She had already gnawed on numerous things to try and calm herself down some but it wasn't doing the job at all. Mind you, she was quite proud of the damage she'd done to the one post of the bed.

She began to work her way through the door. Her nose was going a mile a minute, there were a lot of wolf scents, so they each had to be tasted and gone over. Suzanne needed to be sure if they were residual or fresh. Because the last thing she wanted to have happen as she began to creep down the hall was to find out that some of the wolves in this place had been banned from tonight's hunt for any reason.

Suddenly in the distance, a howl broke the quiet night, it was picked up by others echoing up and down off the mountains. Suzanne couldn't help it, she piddled right there in the hallway. After an all-over body shiver that rustled her fur, she picked up her pace. Wolves were like the bad big dogs on steroids, and she had no desire to meet one tonight.

The stairway presented a bit of a challenge. Each step involved a little hop to reach it, which wouldn't be that bad if the things weren't worn smooth by centuries of feet walking up and down them. Eventually, she settled on going far to one side where at least the stone was a little less polished and gave her claws some purchase. Castle full of werewolves and none of them had thought to put carpeting in to make this easier, Vukan was obviously in charge. Suzanne was only thankful that she didn't go tumbling down them, even if she was panting heavily by the time she reached the next floor down. By the time she had reached the first floor she was wondering if they kept any water bowls out and handy for the denizens of the castle for those times when that would be what they'd prefer. Maybe they drank out of the toilets, who could tell them, "No! Bad dog!" if they wanted to?

Suzanne had no game plan here as she trotted out into the courtyard. How could she? She was miles from anything, she was in a foreign country, with no passport, no money, no anything, hell, when she woke up tomorrow morning she wouldn't even have clothes. Escape was not the goal. Getting out of that room and maybe running around the courtyard some had been the goal. A little doggie adventure, a little exploration. Anything was better than sitting trapped in that room, especially since the howling hadn't stopped since that first one and she couldn't bear to think what would happen if one of them caught her in that room. She was going to be severely embarrassed about that puddle tomorrow that was for sure.

If it hadn't been for the howling, and where she was, this would actually be pleasant. She wished Adja was here, but the other wolf had probably been forced to join the hunt. The air had a mountain chill to it that city air never had, even in winter. It just felt clean and crisp. Not to mention that for once her long coat didn't seem like a bother, it actually felt like an asset. She felt comfortable in her own fur as she trotted around the courtyard, sniffing here, piddling there.

She had almost made a full circuit and was right in front of the open gate that led to the road. There were a lot of logical reasons why she should just get back up to her room now. The night was passing, there was no real way of telling when the werewolves would return. She absolutely did not want to be out here in the open when they did. Vukan might have told the wolves to leave her be when they had all been human, but she didn't trust them to remember that when they were wolves.

There were lots of logical reasons to begin making her way back. It was a shame that was when she heard the very human scream pierce the night. At that point, her paws acted on their own, and logic could fuck off and go straight to hell. She bolted down the road and into the woods in the opposite direction from the screaming.

Jake was so fucking bored. He had gone past bored, through fucking bored, and was now at DefCon so fucking board. He had been trying to amuse himself by hacking into various spots in Vukan's financial empire and shaving off funds here and there in ways that might not be noticed for months and then secreting those funds in places where he could decide what to do with them later. He wasn't doing it for the money, Jake was normally never as gauche as all that. Besides, that kind of hacking could cause you bad troubles later back home if you got tagged, and he made fine money already. But he was bored, and that douche was the enemy, so it passed some time and he was burying everything where it couldn't be touched, not unlike where Vukan thought he'd hid a lot of his money in the first place, Jake was just much better at it.

He could hear music wafting up the mountain from the lake. This was insanely unfair. He was technically single at the moment, and from the sounds of it, alcohol was flowing down there. Most likely with fine-looking Alpine tourist girls who would not look down on him for his mode of dress, but instead assume he was doing something romantic like hitchhiking across Europe. Come to think of it, he could buy a lot of drinks with some of Vukan's money...

He froze in mid-fantasy. He could swear he heard something outside. He doubted it would be anybody he knew; they were out having a doggy adventure frolicking among the Alpine Forest right now. No way would they be back already. Then he heard it again! There wasn't much of a wind out there, but he definitely heard something rustling through the pines. Nervously he reached for the silver blade that had been entrusted to him by Chris.

He got up and opened his bag and started rooting around for the gun with the silver bullets they gave him. If he had been thinking straight for once in his life, he would have had the gun out and ready to fire as soon as they left. But Jake tried to forgive himself a little, it hadn't been a problem up until now, and it probably still wasn't. He was just keyed up from being left alone here on the mountain was all. He found the gun and set it on the bed.

Which was when the window exploded!

Something landed heavily on top of Jake shoving him down on the bed, closing his eyes with the force of the blow. His eyes snapped open as his breath woofed out and he looked up to find himself staring at the largest wolf in the history of wolves. This wolf used to pick on the Big Bad Wolf in wolf school! In reality, he was mainly staring at the largest wolf jaws he had ever seen outside of a Howling flick. They managed to take up all of his vision and filled it with sharp teeth, but he could assume that anything attached to it was pretty big as well. Jake did the only thing he could think to do, he stabbed it with the knife.

The beast yelped loudly and tugged away from Jake, leaving a trail of blood from its retreating body to where gore still clung to the knife. Jake realized quickly that he might have wounded it, but he certainly didn't kill it. The beast stood its ground on the floor, its hackles raised as it growled and snarled at him. Jake's hand fumbled around the bed, trying desperately to find the gun while keeping his eyes locked on the creature which was currently taking all of the available space in the room.

As his hand continued to grope, the monster bunched up and launched itself at him again. Jake's hand closed on the gun and brought it around in one swift movement as he fired. The beast landed directly on top of him.

Jake's eyes were closed for a long moment, scrunched up expecting painful bites and slashes and then screaming death to occur. It took him a second to realize that it was, in point of fact, not occurring. He was not, in further point of fact, currently being maimed in any way. Not only that, the beast wasn't breathing anymore. Not only that not only that, but blood was seeping all over him, gross! Also, speaking of breathing, the damned thing was heavy!

It took a massive effort on Jake's part to worm his way out from under the equally massive, dead wolf. He really wanted a shower and a room with a window that wasn't shattered for that matter. Also, less adrenaline, so he could think rationally, would be nice. Holy shit! He'd just killed a werewolf! No, wait! That wasn't the calm down and think rationally train of thought, try again.

There was something important about that killing a werewolf part. He seriously needed to calm down a little and think.

While he was waiting for his brain to start functioning again, he shoved the massive beast off his bed. It hit the floor with a great thud that shook the room. Then he checked his laptop. Luckily, it barely even had any blood splatter on it. His bedspread on the other hand was completely fucked. Come to look at them more closely, this set of clothes was probably going to have to join the blanket and sheets in the trash. Which was a shame, because this T-shirt was from a con he'd talked Hannah into going to, so it had sentimental value.

As logic returned slowly but surely it just dawned on him what was so important about the dead werewolf. Other than it busting through his window, almost killing him, and being dead. All the werewolves were supposed to be miles away from here! So what was this one doing in his room, right above a tourist trap lake?

Jake reached to pick up the gun and held it very close. He was going to go sit in another room for the rest of the night, one with less wolf for instance. He just prayed it would stay that way.

Vince woke up in a cage. Specifically, he was inside a dog cage in a building. He heard men's voices in the distance, and then he heard a door slam. It took him a minute to run through what he had been doing before waking up in said cage. Once he'd replayed the entire sequence of events that had ended with him falling violently down a little gully on the mountain and cracking his head, he came to one conclusion. He, was seriously fucked here.

Vince started to whine.

And stopped after just a moment. Whining wouldn't get him out of here. Panicking was not the answer, that was a dog reaction, and he was more than a rat-catching hound. He'd heard the men leave right after he came to, which meant if he could get out of the cage he'd be home free. Of course, cages were sort of made to keep things in, so he could see where he was starting this exercise from a disadvantage. Vince tried first to just bang into the cage door itself, hoping against hope that maybe it hadn't been latched all the way. It was, but you had to go about these things methodically. He couldn't help himself, he let out a yipping bark of frustration to find out that they'd done a reasonably good job latching it.

Next, he tried to get a claw through the bars to maybe flip the latch up. It was fiddly work, and dachshund paws were built more for digging than they were for this kind of careful delicate endeavor. He growled and yipped the entire time in growing frustration.

After that, he tried to get a hold of it with his teeth, which reduced him to just growling at it.

A voice called out, "Just hold your water, I'll be there in a minute."

A voice that had been more of a bark, as in another dog!

Vince heard clicks and clacks coming from another room. It was another dog, those were claws! Of course, why he would think a human would be barking at him, and getting the intonations just right to be understood was a question for another day. Vince could just make out a shape coming through the doorway from a hall beyond, a relatively large dog. Not a wolf thank God. Vince's excitement would have snuffed out like a candle in a hurricane if it had been.

A long, jowly face appeared in front of the cage. Not all of the bloodhounds were out with the hunters right now it would appear.

"Got yourself in a bit of pickle, eh?" the big dog woofed.

"Please! You've got to let me out, I am sure they're going to do some not nice things to me if you leave me," Vince yipped hopping up and down on his front paws to drive home the urgency of the situation here.

"Yep, I'm sure they will," the dog agreed. Vince started to whine piteously and the old hound quickly added, "Now don't worry, I'll get you out. Just need a second to see how to do it. They've never caught anyone before today. Trust me, I'm on your side, just never expected to have to do this."

Vince practically vibrated with nervous energy as he watched the other dog contemplate the latch for a second. Finally, the hound made a decision. First, he used his teeth to get the latches turned in the correct position, then he nudged them over with the crown of his head.

The instant the second latch clanged open Vince rocketed towards freedom, banging the door off the hound's head in the process.

"Ouch!" the dog complained.

"Sorry! Sorry!" Vince yapped. "Bit nervous, you can probably guess why."

"Yep, they're werewolf hunters and you were wearing trousers at noon today," the hound agreed.

Vince froze, "You know?"

The bloodhound looked so amused it almost grinned, which was an impossible feat with the enormous jowls it was blessed with. "Who do you think rents these idiots this cabin? And why do I know they're idiots? Because for ten years now I've been renting it to them while they're in the area, barely even laid eyes on them at first frankly and all I said after I got bit was, 'Don't mind my dog, I leave him there, I love him, but my wife complains about the smell. Just don't take him on your hunts, he's too old for that, he'll just come and go as he pleases. Don't know how he does it.' They think of me as a mascot. They have lodges all around the mountains they rent, haven't seen them here in months though. "

"If they're idiots, someone must have tipped them off that we were there," Vince growled. "They were right there as we were running around the mountain. We just got here today, so it wasn't like they got reports of dogs being sighted in the area."

"Well, be that as it may be. Thanks to old Jakob, they'll fail again tonight. I'd vacate the area tomorrow during daylight if I were you. Come along, I don't trust these fools to walk me, so I have my own exit."

With that, Jakob trotted along one of the wood halls and hopped down a set of stairs. It led to what looked to be a finished basement, with a television and a dart board, the whole thing done in wood paneling which someone must have thought matched the real wood of the rest of the house when it was installed. They were wrong about that, but Vince could see no other logical reason for it.

Vince followed close behind the bloodhound as he squirmed into a corner, between a couch and a love seat. It wasn't until they came up close that he noticed the seams in the wood paneling itself. The other dog nudged it with its nose revealing a doggie door.

"This leads to a deer trail, it will take you close enough to the village, you should be able to find your way back to where you're staying when the sun comes up."

"Won't they wonder how I got out and find this?"

The bloodhound almost grinned again, "No, because I can also crack open the front door, I built this house after all. They'll be so relieved to find me asleep down here, they'll just assume one of them left the door cracked and you figured out the latch. When I'm human I tell them all the time how much my dog means to me, and how mad I'd be if it got hurt in any way. They'll be so happy to see me they won't think it through much, not that they think a lot, to begin with. Now, I'd get moving if I were you, stay on the trail and keep your ears and nose open and you should be fine."

CHAPTER 17

———————|———————

"I did what last night?" – *L. Godiva*

The dogs sat in the river directly below town. All of them were shivering vigorously, even Chris and Jerry. The group huddled together looking the kind of miserable that only wet dogs on a cold day can manage.

"Fucking great idea, I think my balls are the size of peas," Sal complained.

"But you stopped bleeding," Chris pointed out reasonably through chattering fangs.

Sal turned and looked where a bit of silver shot had left a shallow furrow along his hindquarter, "Well, there is that I guess."

"Bro, stop whining, I got an even thinner coat than you dude bro. You don't see me complaining," Todd added in response to Sal.

"Yeah but I can see your little ass shivering and I can hear your teeth clacking," Sal retorted.

"Anyway, it's getting lighter. Figure it will be dawn soon. Hopefully, they give up by then, or at least we can see well enough to avoid them," Jerry cut them off.

"We need to get up there before anyone can see too clearly, being as once we change we'll be nude," Sal replied.

"Which means we should be quiet and stop drawing attention," Chris said.

They sat at the edge of the frigid stream for a while longer before Chris said, "C'mon, it's going to get light enough to see soon. I think we can start making our way along the edge of town to the house. I told Jake to leave the back porch door open that goes to the basement of the one house and to shut up everything else tight. At least we can get to where there's heat."

"Thank Christ, maybe I can get some feeling back in my paws," Sal growled.

It was a tourist town that had imbibed the night before so that none of the villagers were waking up early to get up before the sun so they were able to move free of prying eyes. Still, their eyes and ears, and noses were on high alert as they crept back home through the woods. There was no saying for sure that the hunters weren't still out there somewhere, watching and waiting to hunt them down, hoping to catch them before the change. Once they were up from the banks of the river, it was a silent troop that made their way through the edges of the sleeping town back towards the houses they'd rented.

Their fears and worries got worse when they got closer to the cabins. They didn't have to communicate it at all, they all smelled wolf. Chris whined a little, he couldn't help it. He wanted to check on Jake, to make sure he was okay, but that probably wouldn't be a good idea. Jake might be fine and dandy at the moment, but once Chris got within five feet of him getting bit by a full-sized poodle would probably blow that okay feeling right out of the water. He only hoped that having to shoot his best friend might be considered marginally worse by Jake than getting bit by him, but it still made it a poor hypothesis for field testing.

All he could do for the moment was join the others in slinking into the basement. It would be an early night, and one that ended without the clothing they'd hidden up in the hills. There was still at least an hour to go until sunrise proper which meant they had some time to kill. Chris was at least happy to be somewhere safe and inside at last. His only regret is that they'd been so up for the idea of exploring a new place as dogs, none of them had thought that maybe it was everybody's interest to just stay in one house and leave the other to Jake. Of course, Vince would have probably have still wanted to go out, he'd have been on the hook for anything that had gotten broken by the trapped and rowdy dogs. Also, there was the argument he might have made that no one likes cleaning up their own poop the next morning. Still, if they had stayed in, maybe Vince would be here, and maybe the wolf smell wouldn't be.

What abouts weren't going to change anything. Chris decided to do the only sensible thing, join the other dogs in a pile on the floor, and call it a night.

Chris was woken the next morning by a nudge in his ribs.

"It's your turn to make breakfast Jake," he grumbled and turned over in his sleep.

The toe found his ribs on the other side.

"For fuck's sake," he growled, rolling on his back and opening his eyes to see...Vince!

Chris was on his feet and hugging Vince like lightning.

"Buddy," Vince chuckled, "I'm happy to see you too. But I do feel compelled to point out we're naked."

Chris let Vince go very quickly, and took two steps back for good measure.

The others were beginning to wake up and started to slap Vince on the back, with "Holy shits and "Thank Gods and "No shit Bros.

Finally, Chris was able to say clearly, "But how the hell did you get away? Did they just not find you where you fell, or what?"

Vince laughed, "It would turn out, there's a viper in the hunter's midst. The one bloodhound in the cabin they stay in wasn't purebred if you get my drift. He let me out when they went back out to hunt for you guys. Speaking of which, how did you get away?"

"By freezing my damned balls off is how," Sal grumbled. He turned around to look at where he'd been pierced by shot last night. "Oh, fuck! Would you look at that?"

Sal whipped around so fast none of them had a chance to avert their eyes. All of them could see there was a streak of fuzzy pug fur in perfect correspondence with the wound he'd received the night before right near the crack of his ample ass.

Before Sal could say anything, Todd said, "Bro, I can get you a good deal on like a really good shaver."

"I may take you up on that."

Chris suddenly remembered something important and started running for the stairs.

"What the hell is up with you kid?" Sal yelled up at him.

"We smelled wolf last night! I gotta' check on Jake!"

The others quickly followed him. Vince grabbed the spare keys.

"JAKE!" Chris called once they were inside the other house. Not waiting for an answer he bounded up the stairs to Jake's room and froze at the sight of the very large, very dead wolf lying on the floor.

"JAKE!" Chris practically screamed in terror.

A bedroom door opened, "Dude, what?"

It took a long time for Chris to stop hugging his best friend.

"Dude, you are like totally naked right now," Jake muttered sleepily, but allowed himself to be hugged, frankly he felt he needed a hug after last night and might even take another one if his best friend would finally put some damned clothes on.

What finally broke it up was Vince, "They knew we'd be here. I suspect the realtor, but whoever told them it doesn't really matter, they knew we were here. We have to leave now. The Austrian border is an hour from here, and in Austria, I have power of my own." He saw the others staring at him as all of this sank in and added, " You can hope things go peacefully and easily and we found a way to sneak in and get her, but... Anyway, I've already made phone calls to arrange some things before we got here, just in case things went....well like they have. You don't keep the kind of money I have without making some contingency plans, I would suggest that this would be a great time to take advantage of them."

"Look, leave me the one car. I need to at least scout out the area around the castle he has her in. Who knows, maybe I get lucky, or I find a way in," Chris replied.

"Now Chris...." Vince began.

"No listen, I just can't. We've traveled halfway across the planet to get here, I can't just go running off to safety when we're this close. You hear me? I can't! And look, if I screw up too badly, whatever you have planned as a just in case can get Suzanne out of there," Chris cut him off hotly.

"But really, Chris, I have…" Vince tried again.

"I appreciate that, I do, knowing you're up to something gives me some confidence to try to get her before you can get back. At least I can think there might be a plan B. Which would be great, since I still don't have a plan A. But I just can't go running to another country without at least looking."

"Well, I'm coming with you of course," Jake said matter-of-factly.

"Jake you don't have to…"

Jake laughed, "Of course, I do dumb ass, I'm your best friend. If I won't follow you into certain death, then who the hell will?"

Suzanne guessed that waking up in a field was probably going to be a problem. Well, it wasn't the waking up in a field part, it was more the "being naked when waking up in a field she had no idea where" part. The military had spent some significant funds to assure her that she'd be able to function anywhere she woke up in this world, they had not mentioned nude even once in basic training. She got to her knees to get her bearings while trying to keep her breasts covered. A glance gave her an overview of where she was when her doggy self had run out of gas. On the positive, she didn't appear to be near one of the main roads, so at least she was not currently being ogled most likely. Of course, calling any road around here a main road stretched the definition by quite a bit. The flip of that was on the negative side, in that it meant she was in the middle of nowhere, nude, in a country she knew almost nothing about, where she didn't speak the language.

At least the term field meant a building would be somewhere nearby, hopefully, at least a barn, something. A building could additionally mean clothing even if it was a set of coveralls. She was mostly out of sight down here in the grass-covered furrow, but that was getting her nowhere fast. She had to get up and get moving if she wanted to finish this a free woman. As she got to her feet, she could see a cabin a short distance away, and despite her best hopes, there was a road nearby that the trees had hidden. She needed to do something about the clothing situation first and foremost, and the house was her only option, she would just need to hurry and hope.

As she crossed the field in the morning dew that had settled on what she was guessing was wheat soaked her naked legs. She wondered exactly how she should approach this. Stark naked is no way to start a conversation, well it is, but not with a stranger at any rate, well not someone who would hopefully stay a stranger. People got ideas. She hurried to a light jog as she went, nothing about this was ideal, but having a car pass at this moment would be even less than ideal. The only way things could end up being ideal is if that house was empty, except for a change of clothes and maybe a light snack.

When she got closer she smiled before hurrying forward even faster to a run. The day seemed to be taking a turn for that ideal, there wasn't a car parked anywhere nearby. The place felt empty just looking at it, that feeling you just get where you know that not only is nobody inside a building, nobody will be any time soon. Which left a quandary, knock, knowing that if you were wrong and if someone was in there, you'd have to explain the nudity situation, or to just find a way in, hope the place was empty, but still try to move quietly enough not to wake anybody who *might* be in there until you could find clothing. You could explain your presence *way* better without your tits distracting people.

Suzanne went to the back to look for a door or an open window in the rustic-looking structure. It didn't look fully abandoned, more like a rental property that was currently empty, some kind of upgrade over a rustic cabin. The first door she tried opened immediately and easily. Getting over her surprise, Suzanne quietly stepped inside and looked around.

Nothing inside looked even remotely personal, the room she stepped inside of looked like a generic kitchen. Like these were the things that are expected to be here but nothing with any person touches generic. Stepping into the next room she found a generic dining room, even the living room consisted of a table, a fireplace, a couch, and a recliner, along with a television, but no clutter that spoke to occupation. Her instincts seemed to be correct as to the nature of the place, this had to be a place for tourists to stay. Well, she was a tourist, sort of, and she'd be staying here, at least until she found something to cover herself with.

She quietly went from there up the stairs to the second floor. The first room she entered at the top of the stairs turned out to be empty. Prodding at the worry that she was breaking into someone's house like it was a sore tooth she decided to check the other two rooms immediately for signs of life. She almost sighed with relief when they revealed another empty bedroom and bathroom with a little stand-up shower stall as equally devoid of personality as every other part of the house. At least if there weren't any clothes, she could hopefully find a towel, or barring that, she could always do something with the shower curtain.

A search of the set of drawers in the first bedroom almost brought a burst of happy tears. She was able to find a dusty ill-fitting pair of pants and a t-shirt in a bottom drawer. She'd still be doing without underwear because there was absolutely nothing else except extra sheets and blankets for the bed. Suzanne could live with that. She went back to the bathroom taking a towel out of the closet. It was practically as thin as paper, which was perfect, she could use it as a makeshift belt to hold up the pants.

Regardless of the poor fit, this was an improvement, at least, she had clothing on, she had shelter that it looked like nobody was coming to any time soon, so she was ahead of where she woke up. With the mountains right nearby there were probably a lot of these rental places in the area for tourists. She should only thank her lucky stars that someone had forgotten some clothing in the one she broke into. Now all she needed was wheels and shoes and to get the holy hell out of here and back to civilization. Of course, where a woman's size 8 pair of shoes were just going to fall out of the sky was anyone's guess. Maybe they were in the back seat of the car she didn't have.

Vukan was not having a good morning. You could tell he was not having a good morning by all the screaming he was doing. You probably wouldn't be able to tell exactly what he was so mad about if you were there since he was doing the screaming in an older dialect of Slovenian that really doesn't get used anymore even by Slovenians. But on top of that, drool and slobber were involved and slurring his pronunciations because of all the not having a good morning he was doing and him taking it piss poorly.

So we should probably just tell you the gist of what had gotten his panties in a bunch. He had a list, and it was far too long for him to still be rational about it since anything over one issue usually taxed his patience to begin with. Firstly his hunters had one of the dogs, just like he had set them up to do, but it had gotten away somehow. It had just vanished out of its cage in their hunting lodge without a trace. Then of course there was the fact that his kidnap victim who was to be the mother of his future pups had escaped, also without a trace. Since she hadn't been allowed to bring any or had any perfumes purchased for her yet, she hadn't left a scent strong enough for them to even follow now that they were human. And then there was also the problem that Janez had not reported back in from his assignment the previous evening, which was not like Janez at all, so that did not bode well for how it went. Any one of those things most likely would have sent him into a screaming rage. Combined, well....he was more or less incoherent. Let's see which one he decides is the most important thing to yell about first when he calms down a bit, shall we?

After letting him rant and rave for the last half an hour, Adja decided she'd had enough and slapped him. He froze.

"Stop it Vukan! Screaming helps nothing," she noted, her voice flat and calm. It should also be noted that she enjoyed that entirely too much, if he had been more lucid he certainly would have noticed that a smile had darted over her face while the slap was still ringing in his ears. He didn't realize it, but for an observer, it would seem like it was entirely possible that she wasn't so much interested in helping her husband as she was in shutting him the hell up for a minute.

He blinked at her repeatedly and then rubbed the red spot on his face before he nodded, "You are right of course, my dear." He was about to bark for Janez out of habit before he caught himself. This caused a moment's pause where he had to recompose himself to keep from going on another tirade.

Finally, he stood up and turned to his various underlings who were cowering nearby, "Alright, I want people out there on foot and more importantly driving the roads. If she has any hope of getting out of the area it will be by car, and since she didn't drive herself here, she'll have to find a car which will be difficult but not impossible. If we don't have her by nightfall, if she's foolish enough to try and go overland by foot, well, then it will be easy. We run faster than a little dog, and her scent is fresh enough for us to follow when we're wolves. It will be a bonus hunt. Don't hurt her overly much please, our plans remain the same."

"I still say we should have gone with Vince," Jake said.

Chris shook his head, "Your objections have been noted. But look, we only know theoretically where this castle is. We've never seen the place and we're supposed to be leading a daring rescue from it. I have no idea what Vince has waiting for him in Austria, he wouldn't say and really I kind of didn't think to ask too hard after I made up mind to do this. But it might be useless if we don't know the layout of the place. We're in a car for the love of God, we get off to the side of the road and get a look or something, act like lost tourists, how hard could it be? "

"Famous last words there compadre. What if there's only one road in. These roads are tight, we'd be sitting ducks," Jake pointed out.

"Well, we'll get close and pull off and walk or something. People are hiking all over these mountains, from a distance we'll just look like two more," Chris reasoned.

"This, does not seem like a well thought out plan."

"It's not your girlfriend who's trapped there. I said you didn't have to come."

Jake chuckled, "Oh no, I am forced into this by the best friend's code of honor. There are some things I just have to do. Like, I have to get you drunk as fuck the night before your wedding. Also, your significant other has to put up with me despite finding me repulsive, and in exchange for getting away with being repulsive, when you get a dumb idea in your head like this I have to have your back. If for no other reason, so when your significant other yells at you for it you can blame me. That's how this all works."

They rode in silence for a while. Chris didn't have any real response to that and didn't want any distractions at this point. It was a level of loyalty that it was easy to forget Jake was capable of due to Jake's easy-going irresponsible nature. Chris loved his best friend and sincerely wished he was back home in America while at the same time he was grateful Jake was here to keep him sane. Google maps had given up on directions a while ago, and at this point, they were navigating off of screenshots they'd taken off of the 3D map. Reception had been excellent for a lot of the trip, but as they neared the mountain itself, it had decided to go spotty for some reason. Who knew, maybe the plan that came with sim cards they'd bought in Italy didn't have good coverage here, or maybe the USB that was running from Jake's phone to the laptop that enabled it to use roving data was being wonky, who knew?

"I'm going to pull over in front of that house up there, it looks like it has some kind of a driveway or something, also there's a pull-off. Let's look at the screenshots again," Chris said.

"Yeah, hold up, let me bring them up on the computer," Jake replied.

Once they were stopped, Chris had Jake flip through them while he scanned over them again, hoping to get a better feel for the area and an idea of how close they were. He didn't even look up when he heard a car pull up near them.

To Jake, he just grunted, "If they get out, just ask them if it's their driveway we're blocking."

A second later Jake replied, "I think we're pretty close to the castle now in fact."

"Why do you say that?"

"Can you think of any other reason why they'd be pointing guns at us?"

CHAPTER 18

"I could totally kick her ass" – *John Fastolf 1429*

Suzanne heard the car pull up and risked a glance out the window. It was a really nice-looking Mercedes that had pulled off the road in front of the house. She really, really wished and hoped, and on top of that, prayed while she was at it that these weren't the homeowners come back to claim the place. Or renters who would be wondering what in the hell she was doing here for that matter. She was undecided about what to do next in any case. While she could really use a ride, starting off asking for one after being found inside their house while trespassing wasn't a really good ice breaker. On the plus side, at least she wasn't nude anymore. Always look at the positives.

Looking out the window as she tried to decide, she squinted to get a better look at who was inside the car so she could decide on her next move. If they were younger maybe they were just renting the place and might be amenable to giving her a ride somewhere just to get her out of their hair. She could explain that she'd gotten lost hiking or something. It was entirely plausible, except for her not having any shoes, but it was a good opening gambit.

Huh, that was funny, she found herself thinking, the passenger in the car almost looked like Jake from this distance.

She saw the black SUV pull up a moment later.

A few minutes after that she was sure she wasn't mistaken about it being Jake when she saw Chris and Jake get out of the Mercedes with their hands up. They didn't look happy as they got into the SUV which immediately drove off in a spray of gravel. Worse, she recognized the SUV and the men who had gotten out of it to grab Jake and Chris from the Mercedes. They worked for someone she hated, they worked for the bastard she was desperately trying to escape. These guys were about to become Vukan's employees of the month.

God closes a door, but he opens a window. Or in this case, God solves the car issue, but now she has to go back to the castle she just escaped to rescue her boyfriend.

"Well, this kind of sucks," Jake said.

"You know what? I'm not even going to argue with you. You were right, I was wrong, we should have stayed with the others, and yes, this sucks," Chris replied.

Once she got to the car, she wasn't surprised to find it still unlocked. They were at gunpoint from the looks of things when they left, that's no time to really worry about closing up shop before you go. People get impatient when they have a gun pointed at you, and the people who are getting impatient might shoot you. But even better than just being unlocked, the keys were still in the ignition! Chris really must not have wanted to make any sudden upsetting moves once he saw the guns. Best of all, Jake's laptop was open. She could message somebody! Now the question was who?

To her eternal shame, the phone number that came to mind immediately to text was Jerry's. Chris would so not be happy to know that she still had her ex-boyfriend's email and phone number memorized. At the same time, it would be used in the service of saving his ass so any complaints would fall on deaf ears. She didn't know who was in the country with Chris and Jake, but she knew from them getting arrested that Jake and Chris didn't solo this trip. Not that Chris wouldn't have tried to do just that, but she just couldn't see the other dogs in the pack letting him, which had been more or less confirmed by Vukan with his arrest prank. Jerry might not have been one of the group that had come over, but he would have the emails handy of those who did.

She could see that the signal was weak here, so with no game plan on how to rush in and save the day Suzanne turned the car around and started heading back the way they'd driven up. Hopefully to something approaching civilization. She had to find out who was here in the Alps, she had to see what kind of help they could offer her in getting Chris back before it got dark tonight. She was smart enough to not go rushing in, but if help wasn't available she'd have to consider sneaking in. She really needed that help now, not later, because after dark tonight it wouldn't matter who was here, Chris would be a dead man, dog, hybrid, poodle thing, well it wouldn't matter to Chris what you called him by that point. If no one was here, then she'd try and think of something. But she really needed to feel like someone would be able to help. Otherwise, she'd feel like crying and she didn't have time for that right now.

Once she reached a small town nearby she glanced down to see the laptop had signal and sent out a message to Jerry.

She almost cried when she got one back almost immediately saying, "Oh thank God! Vince says to head to Ljubljana, we'll be there in a little while."

"Is that on Google maps? And in this country?"

Chris was not happy to see Vukan. He couldn't think of any time he'd be happy to see the Slovenian strong man normally, so there was no reason this time would be any different. This time managed still to be far worse than what would normally be bad, this time the asshole was gloating. And he had pretty good reason to gloat, which helped nothing. When people are pointing guns at you, and the guy who seems to hate your guts for some reason has a look on his face that says he's just won life, well, that isn't good. You are completely justified in your displeasure on this one.

"So good to see you again, and just in time for the moon!" Vukan boomed happily. "Welcome my guests!"

"Fuuuccckkkmeeee he's just like you said," Jake groaned.

To Chris specifically, Vukan said, "If I want the lovely girl to come back, it is you I need. Tell your friend to be silent and not draw so much attention to himself. We hunted last night, but we would be happy to have another hunt tonight."

Chris turned to Jake, "Umm he said..."

"Got it," Jake replied.

"Good, we understand each other. Now you will be taken to a nice and cozy room in the cellars where I will not have to worry about you. Since I know there was a very wealthy man traveling with you, I will have my assistant message him to let him know you will be staying with us indefinitely." Vukan clapped his hands and large burly men grabbed Jake and Chris, "Normally I would have Janez escort you, but, he is not available today for some reason."

Their destination was of course a cell, Chris had known it was going to be a cell when Vukan had said it, and he was not disappointed. What was worrisome was the lack of dust down here. This area got used way more than you would expect in the 21st century. There weren't even cobwebs.

As they were pushed inside one of their escorts said, "I bring food later, if I not busy."

As they heard his footsteps vanish in the distance and looked around their dank and dimly lit surroundings, Jake said, "You know, I liked the jail at the border a hell of a lot better."

"This sucks," Chris replied.

"I told you that earlier."

They had been fed at some point, some fruit that was actually fresh and bread that wasn't terrible or moldy, so at least starvation had not been added to their woes. While both of them were rightly worried about what would happen to them that night, boredom was starting to set in. "I spy" wasn't working because the answer was always either "bars" or "stone." Boredom was better than excitement, but it was a neck and neck race. Neither of them was thrilled when their boredom was unfortunately relieved when sometime in what they guessed was early in the afternoon their cell door was approached by their bulky previous escorts.

"You are to come out. Vukan wants," the spokes-thug said.

"For style, for personality, for a lot of things," Jake said as they got off the cots they'd been resting on.

"Shut up Jake, you're going to get yourself killed! Remember, low profile?" Chris hissed.

"Sorry, I just can't help it!"

They were led up to one of the numerous large rooms in the castle.

This one was decorated as a study or a library, with lots of dusty books, and very nice hardwood tables and desks. Vukan was seated in the most comfortable-looking wing-backed chair in the place waiting for them.

"Ah, Chris. I am sorry to have kept you and your pet monkey waiting. I am a very busy man. Please, sit," he pointed to two overstuffed antique chairs that were nice, but definitely not as nice as the one he was in.

Once they were seated he reached over to Chris with a phone in his hand, "I know you Americans always check your messages. So what you will do is, you will message or email Suzanne to let her know of the situation here."

Chris took the phone and opened up messages and entered her number, he quickly typed, "don't come trap" and his thumb hovered over send before looking up at Vukan, "What exactly is the situation here?"

"If you want to live, you will tell her that she must come here. I have no use for you otherwise. If she does not get the message, well, we will keep trying. But, when she answers, it had best be to say she is on her way. Otherwise, we have tonight and tomorrow night to hunt."

Chris deleted his original message.

Vukan had left them sitting there after having taken the phone back. Neither of them had a clue what they should be doing with themselves, they didn't even want to talk in case someone was listening. The way both of them figured, the less attention they brought to themselves, the less likely they were to go back into the dungeon. Escape wasn't an option, yes they were left unattended, but it was in a random room in castle with a lot of big strong guys between them and the only door they knew about that actually led out of here.

Chris had started to drowse, but he woke with a start when Vukan came back into the room a short while later, "My congratulations Chris. My men say that there is a vehicle coming up the road. It looks quite like the one you were driving earlier. If only my men had known she was so close, why I wouldn't have needed you for the message. We could have just hunted her down tonight. But whatever you said must have been quiet convincing."

He nodded to his men in the room, who immediately seized Jake and Chris. "Come along, she must see that I do indeed have you. And she must see there is a penalty for disobedience to me."

Chris wanted to make the man drag them out there so he didn't seem so complicit in his own demise. Unfortunately being drug hurt, and the man had no issues with dragging him at all and even fewer about hurting him. Finally. he just walked to save the wear and tear. They arrived in the courtyard just in time to see their Mercedes get surrounded by Vukan's men, the cloud of dust it raised coming up to the castle was already settling onto the trees that crowded the road. Suzanne got out suddenly, the violently opened door wailing one of Vukan's thugs who stood too close, causing the guy to hop away cursing in Slovenian.

As soon as Vukan saw her he shouted across the courtyard, "Did you enjoy your outing my dear? An old friend stopped by unannounced to visit!"

"I thought you said you wanted to fight him Vukan? Where's the big boxing match?" Suzanne demanded.

"Oh, but I will fight him, I will give him a fair fight tonight," Vukan laughed. His men all laughed with him.

"In other words, you'll cheat. Alright then, fight me, and do it now. Unless of course, you're as big a pussy as I've been saying all along," Suzanne sneered.

"Dude, has your girlfriend lost her mind?" Jake hissed at Chris.

Chris shook his head and whispered, "I don't think so."

"And why should I damage my beautiful new bitch!" Vukan's voice boomed.

As if on cue, which his refusal kind of was, gunfire erupted from just outside the gates. All eyes were instantly locked on the newcomers that stepped into the open once they had their attention. Vince, Sal, Jerry and Todd stood just outside the gates trying to strike manly poses near where the gunfire had come from. Well, maybe not all eyes were specifically on their three friends, maybe more all eyes were more on the heavily armed men that flanked them. To be fair, Todd was in pretty good shape, but he wasn't hired muscle "in shape," or holding what looked to be a military-grade machine gun either. Now that we think about it, it was probably the machine guns that had really riveted everyone.

"Lady says she wants a fair fight," Vince called out. "Before you tell your boys to fire, just keep in mind, I had these bullets special made, if you get my drift. So, I suggest you take off that suit jacket and give the girl a fight for her and the two boys. Hell, I wanted to just shoot you."

"You would use silver against your own kind?" Vukan snarled.

"You used werewolf hunters against yours, and they damned well had silver, so let's call it a draw." Vince laughed.

"You will never be my own kind," Vukan yanked off his suit jacket and tie. Despite what Vukan said, a few grumbles were heard coming from his people at that revelation.

"And there we have it," Vince nodded.

"Why do you not just take them and leave? You have the stronger position here, why fight at all? Vukan demanded.

"You know, I suggested just that. In fact, I planned to do just that if we couldn't just sneak her out somehow when she was the one stuck in here. I told Chris I was working on something, and this is the something, so let's let this play out. After the bullshit you pulled with those hunters, who I remind you were packing silver, I really wanted to come in here all guns blazing, but," Vince smiled, "the lady said something about specifically wanting to kick your ass before we left. I deferred to her righteous anger."

A space cleared quickly as Vukan walked toward Suzanne. Having guns pointed at them with actual silver in them got the attention of Vukan's men very quickly. Where before it had just been thugs, the sound of gunfire had begun to bring some of the teenage werewolves out along with many of the wives, including Adja.

"Fine, if the bitch needs to be taught her place, so be it. The stakes are simple, you win, you leave. You lose, you bear my pups for me as my new bitch, I haven't decided on killing your beau." To his own people, Vukan added, "I was planning to discipline the uppity American female for running anyway. She will be all that more obedient for it later!"

"No killing Chris, sorry, all you get is me," Suzanne replied.

He stood in front of her and thumped his chest, "Come, take your best shot."

"How's your arm?" she asked sweetly.

He growled, "Never mind that, let this farce be over with. Swing already, so I can get back to business matters."

Suzanne nodded in acknowledgment before walking straight up to him, feinting a straight left in stride. When his hands came up to block it, she followed it with a right hook that made Vukan stumble just a little. He looked at her with shock for just a moment before covering it with bravado, "The kitten has claws, I like it." He called over his shoulder, "Jakob, cancel my two o'clock call with Zurich, I want to enjoy this some!"

Immediately after speaking, he charged at her trying to use his weight to grapple with her. It would have worked better if she hadn't seen it coming and swatted down the still weaker outreaching arm before stepping to that side while tripping him. Vukan went down hard on the cobblestones. Not waiting for him to get up, Suzanne quickly kicked him in the ribs with the hiking boots she'd purchased in town after meeting up with the rest of the crew.

Everyone froze for an instant as a gun went off. Vince's voice followed, "The next one of you dumb fucks who try to help your boy is getting the next shot in the head. You got that? They're both adults they don't need no one holding their hands."

As Vince's voice echoed off the walls a few of Vukan's henchmen moved back away from the fight. Around the same moment, Chris and Jake noticed they were suddenly unhanded. While that hadn't been part of Vince's demands, the guys holding them must have taken that as a given. Not ones to look a gift wolf in the canine, Chris and Jake used the respite to quickly scurry over to Vince and his men.

Both combatants had separated after the gunshot. Vukan was up and he was beyond pissed. His face had managed to turn bright red and a vein was visible in his temple and not from exertion. Nothing had gone even close to the easy victory he'd foreseen and he was not a man who took getting hurt and just brushed it off, as Chris could attest to. He'd honestly been only thinking about what he'd do to Suzanne after he had her on the ground and now it had already gone south. Not only had his fantasy fight not happened, he'd lost face in front of people. In light of his current anger issues, he could probably be excused for not having a learning curve and trying to charge Suzanne again. This time he ran directly into an uppercut to his jaw. He stumbled back almost falling in the process, waving his arms to maintain his balance.

"Oh, but I am going to enjoy you," he snarled, his bravado not noticing what was happening to his suddenly swollen facial features.

Suzanne ignored his bullshit and started peppering his face with jabs, a few of which he actually managed to block, but not very many. Let him flap his jaw, she'd keep hitting it. She was fighting to get her boyfriend and his friend out of here, she was fighting to get herself out of here, he just wanted to be a tough guy and get his way. But there was more to it now that the fight had actually started. Vukan's comments had added something more to the proceedings for her, something more deep-seated. Vukan represented every sexist piece of shit she'd ever dealt with. From her own father trying to talk her out of the army, to the shit-heels in that army that caused her to leave when her last hitch had been up. It had been a constant stream of variations on the theme of, "You're just a girl." It didn't matter how well she performed, she was always second class to them, even the ones she outperformed. Always "just" a girl. Well now, this girl wanted to make a point about the word "just" and what it meant. As in more than just enough to kick his ass.

"You are such a dumb fuck, you know that?" Suzanne demanded as she hit him with a cross this time just to mix things up a bit.

Vukan tried to laugh, which made him make a face, causing the blood that had begun to trickle out of his nose to splatter on the cobbles, "I am a very rich man, how can that happen if I am so stupid."

"You inherited a castle! Coming out of the right vagina however long ago doesn't make you smart, it makes you lucky," Suzanne snarled as she snapped a kick towards Vukan.

She must have let her annoyance throw off her kick because Vukan was able to knock her foot away from his chest while grabbing her leg. He used her being off balance to jerk her into a punch of his own. The force of the blow sent Suzanne to the ground and rolling backward until she came to rest a few feet from Vukan.

Vukan turned to his men and pointed at her prone form, "See, even when they are strong, they are no match for a real man!" This got the approving laughter he'd been looking for.

Vukan didn't look particularly steady on his feet, but he looked extremely confident as he walked over to Suzanne. His legs straddled her as he stood there for a moment to enjoy his triumph. It had probably been meant to show dominance, like he'd pull her now obedient form up by her hair from there and show everyone that she was out cold proving how tough he was.

It was probably meant for that.

So it was a shame Suzanne's leg shot straight up at that instant to land a really good one in a really bad spot. Even if he won now, Vukan wouldn't be up for any breeding any champion purebred puppies for a couple of weeks at the earliest. Not that Suzanne intended to give him a chance. She scrambled away and was on her feet as Vukan dropped to his knees with a groan. Taking advantage of the fact that both of Vukan's hands were clutching at a pressing pain, she swung a roundhouse kick that caught him in the side of the head slamming him to the ground.

Suzanne straddled the definitely not playing possum Vukan and started pummeling him while yelling at him the entire time, "And do you know what else makes you a moron? Do you? I mean one of the big ones, instead of your normal stupid? Your wives aren't barren you idiot! They just got sick of you 19th-century dimwits treating them like brood mares! If maybe you talked to them and discussed children instead of treating them like all they exist for is social engagements and pregnancy they'd consider it! But until then they've taken steps! Not one kid here is younger than thirteen and in all this time you didn't figure it the fuck out?"

At this point, Vukan had stopped moving more or less and Suzanne was getting sick of hitting him, so she pushed off his chest and climbed to her feet. This time she addressed all of the werewolves, "The world is changing you dumb fucks. If you want to survive in these times you're going to at least learn a little." She kicked Vukan again eliciting a soft groan and causing blood to come out of his mouth, "You need to figure out that in a world where you need brains, you're going to think more, especially if this guy's the one to lead you. Considering he traveled all the way to America because he was too stupid to consider contraception, I have my doubts about how good a job he'll do even with your help. If you want my advice I'd go with Adja, she's the brains of the operation anyway, he just uses her ideas and tells you he thought of it."

She thought about that for a moment, and how unfair all of this had been to Adja and kicked Vukan even harder.

Suzanne turned to Vince, "Well, he said he could beat one of us dogs in a fair fight or we could go, and he couldn't. So, I guess that means it's time to go."

The Slovenian werewolves made no move to stop them as they walked out. If anything they looked like they were considering a world that was shaped differently than it was yesterday. A few of the men from Vince's troop of hired guns took off with Suzanne in the Mercedes to go and get the vehicles they'd stashed down the road. Jake fell into step next to Chris.

"So everything good at home?" he asked.

"Sure, why wouldn't it be?" Chris asked surprised.

Jake chuckled, "Dude, I'm pretty sure your girlfriend can kick your ass!"

Chris shook his head, "Yeah, but I can kick your ass, and it doesn't mean I do it. And think about how much you deserve it more than I do most of the time."

Long before nightfall, they were over the border in Austria, staying at a manor that Vince was borrowing from a friend of a friend for the night. It was a massive place. There were walls out there somewhere keeping anything that might find small dogs appetizing out. They had seen the big stone things driving in but you couldn't see them from the great big rolling lawns that stretched out from the manor house itself,

Chris was enthusiastic to get out and run. Maybe it was because for the first night ever, there was nothing planning to or actively trying to eat them once for starters. They could just run around the grounds and be free dogs. There was also a feeling of accomplishment, he hadn't done it by himself, but that only seemed to sweeten things. They'd come together as a pack, even with the late addition of Jerry. They had faced insurmountable odds, and yet none of them were dead. They were in wide open fields, they were mostly whole, except for Sal and Chris's butts, and there had been steak left out. How could you not be proud of everyone after all of this? And the most important part of all, Suzanne was safe. Of course, after watching her performance against Vukan, he wondered how much danger she was ever really in. He, for one, had been impressed.

Also, they had vaca days they hadn't used yet because nobody knew how long this would take and they certainly couldn't fly back during the full moon. To sweeten the pot Vince was picking up the tab by his own offer. In Europe. Dude, free European vacation.

He called over to Jake as he saw the sun setting over the nearby Alps, "You better get inside quick, the moon will be up soon."

"Umm, yeah... about that," Jake replied coming over.

Before Chris could respond Jake took off his shirt and showed Chris a rapidly fading scar on his ribs. It was barely a scar; it was more of a faint line that was lighter than his other skin.

"When did you get that?" Chris asked with concern.

"Yeah, about that. I thought it was glass that cut me when the werewolf came in through the window. But then I checked it in the car coming to save Suzanne when I had a moment. Since I figured it was pretty deep and all... and... well, nothing heals quite that quick, now does it?" Jake shrugged.

There was a long silence while they considered a world that

contained a were-Jake.

"Well, you still have the moon to enjoy as a human this month, we'll figure it out next month. I mean hey, I got a doggie door and everything, you can crash at my place I guess. Now that you're not banned for those three nights, " Chris sighed.

"Good thing I pestered you with all those questions, huh?"

"Yeah, but I get the couch, if anyone is going to be a bad dog in my house it's going to be me," Chris said emphatically.

At least he hadn't done it to Jake, so maybe it should be looked at as just one less worry.

Later that night the dogs roamed the grounds with abandon. This was even better than the farm they'd enjoyed so much, knowing that at this moment they were not prey gave their freedom added flavor. They weren't hiding from a damned thing, and they could enjoy the knowledge that they might not be ever again. Jerry even fit in with the pack, he would just run wide loops around the group and then come up to chat happily with his tongue lolling out. The other dogs were happily chasing after him yapping at his heels as soon as he'd gallop away. Chris was happy when they all took off since that meant he could hang back and be with Suzanne.

And no, they didn't try for doggy sex. Sal was hanging about and that would just be nasty.

Dear Suzanne, et al.

I wish to thank you for visiting us in our beloved homeland of Slovenia. Vukan sends his love, at least that's what I believe he is trying to say, it's hard to understand with his jaw wired shut.

Things have changed here considerably in a little bit of time. Would you believe I have been named the new leader of the pack? At first, I wanted to refuse, but I understand how wolves work, they wish for someone to be in charge. But one of the first things I did is make it more of a constitutional monarchy if you would. I wish to hear the ideas of all the pack, we are stronger this way.

It may be some time before new pups are born, but unlike before, negotiations are underway.

Thank you again for coming to stay with us.

We would love for you to visit our beloved homeland again, but we would certainly understand if you wished to stay somewhere other than the castle. But rest assured, Vukan will be no trouble, frankly I think he's a bit afraid of you. Again, it's hard to tell with his jaw.

With Fondness:

Adja

BIO

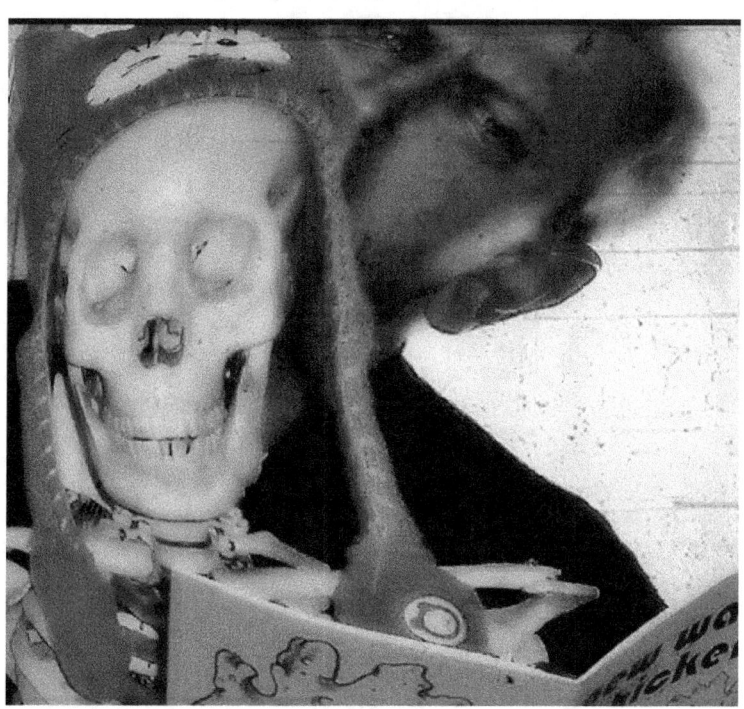

Paul has lived all over the country before settling in Appalachia over fifteen years ago with his wife Leslie and their son. He also has two adult children living in his native Pennsylvania. He is the author of numerous novels, two collections, and more on the way. Paul is a member of the Horror Writers Association, appearing on the panel for horror comedy at the 2021 and 2023 Stoker Cons. He has a dark and serious horror side, but he has also never answered the question, "Is everything a joke with you?" correctly once in his entire life.

ABOUT THE
PUBLISHER / EDITOR

————————|————————

Dawn Shea is an author and half of the publishing team over at D&T Publishing. She lives with her family in Mississippi. Always an avid horror lover, she has moved forward with her dreams of writing and publishing those things she loves so much.

Follow her author page on Amazon for all publications she is featured in.

Follow D&T Publishing at their website, **www.dt-publishing.com**, or search for their Facebook Group

Or email here: dandtpublishing20@gmail.com

Curse of the WerePoodle by Paul Lubaczewski

Edited by Tasha Schiedel

Cover Art by Art Fuentes

Formatting by Ash Ericmore

www.ingramcontent.com/pod-product-compliance
Lightning Source LLC
Chambersburg PA
CBHW070918180626
46817CB00003B/1116